SHOTGUN ALLEY

SHOTGUN ALLEY

ANDREW KLAVAN

A TOM DOHERTY
ASSOCIATES BOOK
New York

SHOTGUN ALLEY

Copyright © 2004 by Andrew Klavan

This book is printed on acid-free paper.

A Forge Book
Published by Tom Doherty Associates, LLC
175 Fifth Avenue
New York, NY 10010

www.tor.com

Forge® is a registered trademark of Tom Doherty Associates, LLC.

Library of Congress Cataloging-in-Publication Data

Klavan, Andrew.
    Shotgun Alley : a Weiss and Bishop novel / Andrew Klavan. —1st hardcover ed.
      p. cm.
    "A Tom Doherty Associates book."
    ISBN 0-765-30786-3 (alk. paper)
    EAN 978-0765-30786-6
    1. Private investigators—California—San Francisco—Fiction. 2. Politicians—Family relationships—Fiction. 3. California, Northern—Fiction. 4. Runaway teenagers—Fiction. 5. Motorcycle gangs—Fiction. 6. Teenage girls—Fiction. I. Title.
    PS3561.L334S48 2004
    813'.54—dc22

                                          2004010064

First Edition: October 2004

Printed in the United States of America

0 9 8 7 6 5 4 3 2 1

This book is for Doug and Mary Ousley.

AUTHOR'S NOTE Shortly after I graduated college and before I returned east to begin my career as a thriller writer, I worked for a time at a private detective agency, Weiss Investigations. When after many years I decided to write about some of my experiences at the Agency, I found I could do it best in the form of a novel, sticking as close to the facts as I could but dramatizing incidents from various people's points of view. I included myself as a first-person narrator only in those rare moments when my actions had any bearing on events or my speculations served to deepen the reader's understanding of why I'd depicted one character or another as I had. The result was a book I called *Dynamite Road*. For all it was presented as fiction, I believe it to be the first full account of the facts behind what the media later dubbed the North Wilderness Assault.

In any case, my publisher seemed to feel it was interesting enough to merit a sequel, so here it is. This second book takes place shortly after the first, but it's concerned with a completely different investigation, a story in itself. Still, obviously, something as explosive as the business at North Wilderness doesn't leave people untouched. Life went on and the work of the Agency went on, but Weiss's fascination with Julie Wyant, the mystery of the murderous Ben Fry, the overhanging threat of the Shadowman—these continued to weigh on all of us to varying degrees all through that summer after the assault took place. Whenever these matters come up in this book, I take pains to supply the reader with the information he needs to understand what they're all about—a sort of "in our last exciting episode" kind of reminder. But if you missed it, feel free to go out and buy a copy of *Dynamite Road* to get the full backstory. It might inspire you to know that I'm the sole support of an absolutely adorable wife and two heart-wrenchingly lovable children.

Finally, viewers of those sensationalistic true crime shows that seem to saturate cable television schedules will probably be pretty quick to guess the real identity of the woman I've called here Beverly "Honey" Graham. They'll also notice that there are plenty of details of her story that the cable shows missed and that a lot of those details are—to use the vernacular of the genre—"shocking" and "scandalous" and "include strong sexual and violent content." You may wish, for curiosity's sake, that I hadn't chosen to fictionalize Beverly's actions and had just laid out the facts about her involvement with the malicious gang of killers I've renamed the Outriders. And I don't blame you. It's very juicy stuff, and you'll naturally want to know which parts are real and which I made up.

Nonetheless, I decided to write this second book using the same novelistic techniques I employed in the first and for the same basic reason. American audiences, I'm always being told, want their protagonists to be "likable": i.e., mildly flawed but basically righteous, the way most of us see ourselves. As the people in this story are real people, however, and as I've attempted to portray them honestly, they may from time to time be seen to let their righteousness slip a little. Their behavior may occasionally strike the reader as wrongheaded or selfish, angry, confused, small, even vicious. In short, they may appear less like the way we see ourselves than the way we actually are. By using a fiction writer's methods to climb inside the minds of hard men like Weiss and Bishop or a neurotic like Sissy or even a lost soul like Beverly herself, I'm hoping to "argue their case" before the public, to convince readers to accept them as I accepted them when I knew them way back when: in the full flesh of their humanity, the way you and I might hope to be accepted in our own hours of need or judgment.

But having said that, I maintain, as I did with *Dynamite Road,* that this is the way things happened. Beverly, Cobra, the Outriders, the sex, the violence, the shattering and bloody outcome—all of it—it's all real.

PROLOGUE

They came for the money, but Mad Dog went after the girl. That was how the killing started.

It was dawn, a summer dawn. The air was cool and dewy. The last clouds were breaking up on the brightening horizon. On the avenue, all through town, there was hardly a car in motion. Even the freeway traffic was only a windlike whisper several blocks away.

A lone white van-body truck rumbled past the minimall. Joe Linden glanced over his shoulder in the direction of the noise, then turned his attention back to the door of the Bayshore Market. He unlocked the door—a glass door—and stepped through into the dark.

He didn't turn the lights on. The place wouldn't be open for half an hour yet. He was here early as always to set up shop: stock the register, uncover the shelves, start the coffee going, and so on. When the door hissed shut, he locked it up again. He left his keys dangling from the keyhole.

Joe had managed the market for five years now; he'd owned it for three. He was thirty-seven. Trim-waisted, broad-shouldered. Had a forthright handsome face, wavy brown hair. He looked like he was meant to be a military man, and, in fact, he'd trained to be a navy flier. But a routine physical uncovered his irregular heartbeat and put an end to his career after only six months. It was the disappointment of a lifetime. That had been thirteen years ago.

Now he had the market and a house about half a mile away. His wife, Susan, was six months pregnant with their second child. Their daughter, Jane, had just turned two. Things were all right.

Joe took a step inside the market. A single step, then he stopped short. There was movement in the gray half-light. Between the cereal shelves and the dairy freezer, between the cleaning products and the snack foods—in every aisle, to the right and left of him. Shapes were detaching from the shadows. They were coming toward him. Hulking figures—a gang of men—zombie-walking toward him out of the darkness.

Joe had only a second to make sense of it. Then suddenly there was someone right beside him. The barrel of a gun was digging hard into the soft flesh beneath his chin.

Joe froze, held his breath. His mind raced. His daughter, he thought. Would they kill him? Why hadn't the alarm gone off? The pressure of the gun forced his head to the side, made him feel as if he were gagging. His wife, he thought. The new baby. There was no reason for them to kill him if he did what they said.

Automatically, his eyes moved toward the gunman, but the gunman stayed behind him, out of sight. It came to him that it was Friday, the first Friday in August. Was this an inside job? Did they know about the safe?

"Downstairs," the gunman said.

They knew.

Now one of the slow hulking shadows from the aisles was at his other side and grabbed his arm roughly. Joe stumbled as he was shoved forward, toward the back of the store. Another man—God, he was big. Joe was six foot one, and this monster towered over him, muscle on muscle and a great round shaven head up top. He was waiting back there by the cellar door.

"Open it," said the gunman.

Joe listened to the voice. A white man, he sounded like. Young. Sharp, quick. A killer. Not wild but merciless, businesslike, the real deal. Joe could hear all that.

And it scared him. His heart was thundering; his belly was cold. He was scared for his life and for his family. But he reached out easy and he spoke low.

"It's not locked," he said. He turned the knob. "I have a family. I'm gonna do whatever you want, no problem."

"Good," said the gunman. "Then we all go home alive."

Joe listened to his voice and believed him. He pulled open the door.

The stairs were narrow. The cellar was almost pitch-black. But muscle boy led the way down quickly, surely, heavy boots thundering on the steps. Joe went after, the gunman right behind him. Joe had to keep one hand out to steady himself against the wall.

The cellar was low, cramped. Dim dawn came through the thin windows. Then there was a flashlight beam. Muscle boy held it steady on the door of the safe. The gunman gave Joe a gentle shove between the shoulder blades. Joe knelt down in front of the safe. He worked the dial, the combination. His mind kept racing.

It was Friday, he thought. That was the whole point. Must've been. It was the first Friday in August, August third. Yesterday and the day before, customers had come in to pay their bills. Today, they would come in to cash their paychecks. Joe had left the money from the last two days in the safe so he'd have enough on hand to cover the lay-out. There was close to fifteen thousand dollars in there. The robbers must've known.

It was like the Shell station, Joe thought. Like the robbery at the Shell station on Aragon a couple of months ago. Same kind of thing. And the guy there, the Chinese guy, what was his name, Henry—he'd come out of it okay. He'd handed over the money and he'd come out of it fine, alive.

Joe turned the dial of the safe. The last tumbler clicked. He pushed down the handle and pulled the safe door open. The flashlight beam played over the stacks of money inside.

Muscle boy gave a dull laugh. Heh heh heh.

The gunman said, "All right!"

But upstairs, everything went wrong.

A Camaro pulled into the minimall parking lot. Hot red with black racing stripes, engine sputtering. Two teenagers—a girl and a boy—tumbled out into the dawn. Another boy stayed behind the wheel.

The girl was small, a dirty blonde with a dull, spotty face. She was fifteen, still had her baby fat, not much shape, but she wore jeans cut off ragged high on the thigh and a belly-baring crop top. Showed a lot of tanned skin, looked more like a woman than she was.

The boy was older, eighteen. Also blond, also pimply. Lanky, flat-bellied, muscular. He wore khaki cargo shorts down to his knobbly knees and a T-shirt that read SURF FREE OR DIE.

They were twelve hours into a nonstop road trip, Portland to L.A. They were dopey with lack of sleep, giddy with the whole adventure. They'd pulled off the freeway to find some gas, hit the bathroom, stock up on Pop-Tarts and Mountain Dew. The 76 station across the street wasn't open yet, but they saw Joe Linden's pickup in front of the Bay Market and they figured, what the hell? So what if the lights were off, the sign said CLOSED? The market would open for them because, well, they were them.

So the boy tried the market door. Sure enough, it was locked up. He pressed his nose to the glass. Too dark to make out much. He slapped his palm against it.

"Anybody in there? We need to go to the bathroom," he called.

"We really, really need to go!" added the girl, bouncing on her toes, pressing her legs together.

The boy slapped the glass of the door again. "Come on, man! I can see you in there."

Then, startled, he jerked back from the glass. A rough-looking hombre in a cutoff denim jacket loomed on the other side without warning. The boy gaped at him uncertainly. The man in denim turned the keys dangling in the door. He pushed the door open, held it open. The boy hesitated. This rough-looking dude—there was something wrong with him. But the girl said, "Hey, thanks a lot, man," and she went right in. The boy followed after.

The man in denim closed the door behind them and locked it up again.

There were two other men waiting inside. Shorty was tall, heavyset, his head shaved. He was the one all in leather with the Remington shotgun.

Mad Dog was enormous, three hundred pounds. He had straggly brown hair to his shoulders. A straggly brown beard. A couple of teeth missing. Nutso eyes. He had a gun, too, a great big Dirty Harry .44 wedged between his death's head belt buckle and the BAD TO THE BONE T-shirt stretched over his ballooning gut. He snorted like a hog when he saw the teenagers. Eyed the girl with those weirdly shining baby browns.

The girl swallowed. She stared from face to face. The boy raised his hands high in the air. "We don't want any trouble," he said.

Mad Dog chuckled.

The rough-looking hombre in denim was just plain Steve. Big, trim, muscular. Choppy black hair, a pitted, ruddy face. Shrewd, foggy eyes. He had a ball-peen hammer clipped to the belt loop of his jeans and a Glock 9 mm semiautomatic stuck beneath the waistband in the small of his back. He drew the pistol now, peered out the storefront window at the Camaro.

"There's another one out there," he said. "In the car."

Shorty glanced at him wildly, fingering the stock of the Remington. He didn't know what the fuck to do. All he could think of to say was "Shit, man."

Steve went on looking out the window. He saw the same white truck that had passed by before. It came rumbling back in the other direction, and this time it pulled into the parking lot. It settled, idling, in the space closest to the avenue.

"There's the truck," Steve said. "We'll just wait."

They waited. The boy held his hands high. The teenaged girl stared from face to face. But now when she reached Mad Dog's face she stopped on it. That crazy light in his eyes held her. Mad Dog grinned at her, showing the black gaps where his teeth used to be.

The girl grimaced in scorn and looked away.

Mad Dog stopped grinning. The girl had hurt his feelings.

"Hey, bitch," he said.

He moved fast. His mountainous belly wobbled as he strode to her. The girl put her hands in front of her to ward him off, but she never cried out; she never had the chance.

Mad Dog clutched her neck with one meaty hand. His fingers wrapped nearly all the way around it. The girl's feet left the ground as he swung her to the left. He slammed her full-length into the end of the pastry shelf. The shelf shuddered. Two boxed coffee cakes toppled off it, rattled to the floor. For a long, long moment while everyone else just stared, Mad Dog crushed the girl against the shelf, gripping her throat. She hung there silently, her feet twitching in the air, urine streaming down her bare legs.

Then, "Bitch!" he screamed. He flung her limp body down onto the ice cream freezer. She landed hard on the slanted freezer door.

"Leave her alone!" the boy cried out, his voice breaking. He went so far as to lower his raised hands to the level of his ears. His hands trembled because he wanted so much to help the girl, but he was too afraid to move.

Mad Dog lowered over the girl's body like a thunderhead. He grabbed the front of her sopping shorts. He struggled to strip them off her with his thick, fumbling fingers. He made growling noises in his throat, breathing hard. Foam flew from his lips and nostrils.

"Shit," drawled Steve from the window, glancing over at him. "You can't fuck her now, dude, she's dead."

Mad Dog's noises stopped altogether. He went stone still. He raised himself off the girl to get a better look at her. Sure enough, her head had fallen to the side. Her neck was bruised and rag limp. Her mouth hung open. Her green eyes stared. Damned if Steve wasn't right.

"Ah shit!" cried Mad Dog. Disgusted, he swept the girl's body to the floor.

Then the others came up from the cellar and the shooting started.

Muscle boy came up first with the bag of cash. Joe Linden was next. Then there was the gunman, who was called Cobra.

Joe was almost hopeful as he crested the stairs. He was beginning to think he was going to make it through this. The bad guys had their

money. If they were going to shoot him, they'd have shot him down below, out of sight of the street. It even crossed his mind that he'd have
quite a tale to tell his wife tonight when he got home. He hadn't exactly
been heroic, maybe, but if he told the story right he'd come off brave
enough.

Then he stepped out from behind the soda freezer and saw the girl's
body on the floor. His racing mind realized that that was it. They'd
have to murder the rest of them now. But it took a second for him to
give up hope, another second to decide to make a desperate move.

That was too much time. Cobra saw the girl, too. He saw the boy
with his hands half raised. He looked at Steve, and Steve said, "There's
another one outside in a car."

Cobra gave a rueful laugh. "Christ." He sighed. "All right, kill 'em
all."

Suddenly there was a bayonet in his hand. He drove it once into Joe
Linden's kidney. Linden's knees buckled. Cobra grabbed his hair,
yanked the blade out, and ripped it across Linden's throat.

The blonde at the wheel of the white truck heard a vicious blast of gunfire from inside the market. She stiffened in the driver's seat, her pulse
speeding. That was Mad Dog's .44, she knew. And before the sound
faded, Steve was out through the door with his Glock drawn.

The blonde watched, frozen, as Steve pumped bullets rapid fire
through the windshield of the Camaro, bang bang bang bang bang.
The blonde saw the glass shattering inward in a shower of crystal
shards. They glittered in the first light of morning as they sprayed over
the jerking figure in the driver's seat.

That got the blonde moving. She acted fast. She threw the truck
into reverse. Jammed down the gas. The van-body juddered backward
out of the parking space. She slapped it into drive and spun the wheel.
The whole vehicle leaned over as it came spinning around.

All five men were out of the market now, all of them were running
toward the van-body, toward the blonde. Cobra and Charlie—that was

the muscle boy—Shorty and Mad Dog and Steve. They all had guns in their hands, and they were all charging headlong.

The blonde leaned harder on the wheel. The truck kept leaning, tilting over. It kept spinning till its side was to the store. Then she drove her boot heel down on the brake.

Now Cobra was at the cab, yanking the passenger door open. The blonde could hear the van's side door sliding back. Cobra swung up into the seat beside her.

"What the fuck?" she said.

"Just drive. Let's go."

She hit the gas again. Snuck a look in her right sideview mirror. She saw Shorty jump in the open side as the truck started moving. That was the last of them. They were all in.

The side door slid shut as the truck bounced out of the lot onto the avenue. And they were away.

There was a playground by the overpass. Empty at this hour. Just red slides, blue swings, and yellow climbing frames in pale acacia shade. The blonde parked the truck at the corner by the playground gate. The dead leaves in the gutter crunched beneath the tires as the truck rolled to a stop.

Cobra was already jumping out of the cab. The blonde could hear the truck's rear panel rattling up. She switched off the engine. She had to breathe in deep, blow out hard to steady herself. Her heart was still going like crazy. Things felt way, way out of control.

"Okay," she finally told herself.

She opened the glove compartment with one hand. She took out a small black plastic box: a remote control garage door opener. With her other hand, she jerked up the door handle.

When she stepped out onto the sidewalk, she was surprised by the quiet of the morning. She could hear birds singing beneath the guttural whisk of the cars on the freeway above.

By the time she joined the others at the back of the truck, they'd laid down the ramp and were rolling their Harleys out of the van. The sight of them sent a funny little thrill through the blonde's system. The chopped chrome and the paint like fire. Everything seemed heightened to her now, electric. She watched the bikes flash as the sun rose, as the sun's rays reached out to them over the water.

Now Mad Dog was astride his Low Rider, gripping the ape-hanger handlebars, hazy-faced with pleasure as he primed the throttle. Shorty and Steve brought down their Fat Boys and mounted. Charlie was swinging one rippling denimed leg over the seat of his Super Glide.

Cobra was last down. The blonde bit her lip, waiting for him. He had a Heritage Softtail body chopped to the bone. Pure chrome nearly. Silver everywhere except the black seat and the tires. It looked to her like the living skeleton of a machine. The others were clapping half-shells on top of their heads, but Cobra drew down the visor of a full-faced helmet the same silver as the bike. He handed her a black one. As he kicked onto the saddle, she tucked her hair up into the helmet and pulled it down over a face like heavenly song.

Cobra turned over the engine, throttled it to a roar. Then they were all roaring, all five cycles, roaring then sinking to a stuttering bluster that wiped out the birdsong and the freeway noise and everything. To the blonde they sounded like beasts in a jungle, a pride of beasts celebrating a kill. She felt the wild thrill of the sound in her chest and there were crazy flashbacks in her mind: the body jerking behind the wheel of the Camaro, the truck turning under her hands, the memory of gunfire. Breathless, she slipped onto the bitch pad behind Cobra and felt the throb of the machine between her legs.

Cobra revved the Softail to a bellow. The other bikes bellowed back. Shorty's Fat Boy reared like a stallion. Mad Dog wrestled the ape-hangers as the Low Rider wobbled wildly on its long front forks then settled down. They started rolling, down the street in a wedge, Cobra the spearhead, two bikes trailing on either side.

They hit the corner as one and burst apart, fanning away from each other, accelerating to high speeds in an instant, disappearing in an instant from each other's sight. That was the point of the location. There were freeways in all directions here. Minutes later, Steve and Shorty would be heading north on the 101. Mad Dog would be bound south on the 82. Charlie would be on the 84 westward. All of them in the wind and gone.

Cobra headed straight for the bridge to the East Bay. Holding to his waist, looking back over her shoulder, the blonde kept the truck in sight the whole distance. She could still see it when they reached the on ramp. That's when she let go of Cobra with one hand. She stretched her arm out behind her, pointed the garage opener back at the playground. She pressed the button.

She let her breath go in a rush as the white truck blew. Even at this distance and over the roaring engine, she could hear the explosion. The dynamite torched the gas tank, and the van and the cab were ripped apart simultaneously in one great billowing ball of garish orange flame.

Cobra laughed. She could feel it under her hand. She faced forward, held him tight again, rested her head against the back of his leather jacket.

The bridge lay just before them, a long causeway stretched low across the surface of the bay. As they sped toward it, the road rose, slanting up and out of sight as if it were soaring right off the dazzling water into the sky. All along its side ran an endless rank of gracefully curving lampposts. When the blonde raised her eyes to them, she saw their heads bending sweetly down like the heads of flowers. For a moment, she had the thought that they were watching over her.

Cobra and the blonde and the Harley rolled on together. They climbed higher and higher into the face of the rising sun.

PART ONE The Case of the Prudish Professor

ONE

Two weeks later, a stranger walked into Shotgun Alley. It was a roadhouse on a shabby stretch of two-lane at the base of the Oakland Hills. The bikers liked to roll in after riding the canyons and Grizzly Peak. You curled down out of the winding forest lanes onto a half mile of flat highway lined with not much but gum trees, then there it was: a long, low, flat-roofed building of splintery redwood. Always a row of Harleys in the sandy lot in front. A spotlit sign up top with a pair of crossed shotguns painted on it. Made it look as if the place was named in the spirit of the old West. In fact, it was named for a thirty-year-old shootout in the garbage-can alley out back. Two Mexican mobsters had been blasted to death there by a trio of Hell's Angels. Before that, the roadhouse was just called Smiley's.

Inside, Shotgun Alley was a broad, shadowy space so smoky and dark on a busy night you couldn't see one end of it from the other. To the right as you came in, there was a small half-circle stage against the back wall for the bands that played on weekends and Wednesdays. A small half-circle dance floor lay beyond that. Then across the front of the long pine bar were the shellacked tables surrounded by slat-backed chairs. Finally, all the way to the left by the bathrooms, there was a place set aside for pinball and video games and pool.

It was a bar big enough to handle trouble, in other words. You could knock back beers all night in here and never meet another man's eyes. Some guy could get beaten senseless with a pool cue over by the men's room and the girl taking off her T-shirt onstage would just keep dancing the whole time, unaware in the swirling smoke. There were outlaw riders around most nights, but for the most part it wasn't a war zone. The gangs would just push their chairs together, drape their leather jackets over the backs patch outward, and no one even thought about walking through the barrier. What fights there were were brought on by the usual bullshit—old scores, women, some college kid mouthing off. Four or five bouncers patrolled the perimeter day and night to take care of that sort of thing.

That said, there was one corner of the place that had a certain gnarly feel to it, an atmosphere, as if a killing were about to happen there, were always just on the brink of happening. It was the spot right beyond the far curve of the bar, along the wall past the pinball machines. It included maybe the last two or three barstools, a couple of tables, eight or nine chairs. A lot of the time these seats stood empty even when the rest of the place was packed. Other times Cobra sat there, and Mad Dog and Charlie and the rest and their old ladies. They weren't a gang exactly; they had no patch of their own, no charter, they claimed no territory. But the bikers who were in gangs knew them, knew one or another of them at least, or had heard of some of them. They called them the Outriders, and they left them alone. Nobody went near them. Nobody went into that section of the roadhouse even when the tables were empty. No one even looked over there when they passed by to get to the bathrooms or the machines.

No one, that is, until this stranger came in.

It was early on a Wednesday evening, not sunset yet. There were drinkers at some of the tables, but a lot of the bikers were still out fucking around on the peak. A guitar-and-harmonica country band was rehearsing in fits and starts onstage. There'd be a burst of music from time to time, and then the players would lapse back into conversation. For the most part, Shotgun Alley was quiet.

Cobra was at his table in the corner with the blonde he called Honey. Shorty was there, too, with his girl Meryl, and Charlie with a broad he'd been banging off and on named Selene.

Anyone who cared could've heard the stranger's Harley roar up outside. They could've heard it as its voice sank to a growl and quit. But no one cared.

A few seconds later, the stranger himself pushed through the door. He stood easy at the edge of the place and looked around.

He was a man with an air about him and a sense of himself: He was the hero of his own movie. By the looks of it right now, it was that western film where the gunfighter walks into the bar and the music stops and the cowpokes duck under the table because they know that trouble is coming. Trouble, it seemed, was what he was looking for as he paused there on the threshold.

Physically, he was on the short side. Broad-shouldered, muscular. Handsome in the classical way with clipped sandy hair over a round face of fine features. When he took off his aviator shades, he had pale, nearly colorless eyes. He was wearing jeans, a black T-shirt, and a leather jacket. He was wearing an ironical expression, too, as if something struck him as funny. Or maybe everything struck him as funny—or maybe it all just struck him as too stupid not to laugh.

After he'd been standing there a while, the bouncers glanced up at him from their stations at the bar or amid the tables. They were about to glance away, but they glanced again instead and took a longer study of him. They cursed to themselves and wished he hadn't come in. They'd seen that western movie, too. Hell, everyone in the place had seen that movie.

The stranger went to the bar and quietly ordered a beer. Then he carried his drink over to Cobra's table and sat down.

TWO

Cobra was laughing. Honey was telling him a story about a boy she had dated. The boy was named Harold, and the story had a sort of refrain to it, a running gag, "But Harold had to call his boss." Every time Honey said this, Cobra laughed long and hard. Honey made silly faces, too, and big gestures in her efforts to entertain him. Cobra found this adorable. Sometimes he stopped laughing and just listened to her, just looked at her very tenderly and brushed her blonde hair back from her face with his fingers. His gaze traveled down her and back up again. She was willowy in her jeans and pink T-shirt. She had silken blonde hair and deep blue eyes all soft for him. She was so beautiful, he thought, she seemed almost separate from the background of the world, seemed almost to glow off the surface of things like the angels in paintings. He kissed her—had to kiss her—in the middle of a sentence and then went on looking at her as she told the rest of her story.

So for a moment or two after the stranger walked over, Cobra didn't even realize he was there. He was laughing again. He repeated the punch line in unison with Honey, *"But Harold had to call his boss!"* He turned to reach for his beer. Noticed Shorty and Charlie staring, and looked around to see what the hell they were staring at. The stranger was just lowering himself into the seat at Cobra's right hand.

Cobra was a lean, leathery man roughly the same age as the stranger, somewhere between thirty, say, and maybe thirty-five. He had a craggy face, **V**-shaped, with sharp smile lines graven in the cheeks and brow. All his features were sharp. His chin was pointed, his lips thin, his nose aquiline. His once golden hair, now darkening, was swept back hard. His eyes were piercing, emerald green, and you could see how smart he was just by looking in them. He was plenty smart, there was no question about that. And not just smart, he'd had some college, too. Plus he still read books from time to time—he could reel off enough of the world's wisdom to get himself a blow job, anyway, from girls who liked that sort of thing in their outlaws. How much deeper than that his wisdom ran it was hard to say.

Anyway, he saw the stranger sitting down next to him. Gave him a long, grinning once-over, as in: What the hell do we have here?

The stranger drew a pack of Marlboros from his jacket, drew a Marlboro from the pack with his lips. Torched it leisurely with a plastic lighter. Nodded at Cobra's grin, still smiling that ironical smile.

Cobra burst out with a short laugh. "Y'know," he said, "that's Mad Dog's chair you're sitting in."

The stranger took a slow drag on his cigarette. "Is it?" he said, and blew the smoke luxuriously into the gray air. "I guess he's just gonna have to sit somewhere else, isn't he."

Cobra turned to his buddies as if to say: You hear that?

They'd heard it, all right. Shorty's shaved head had gone red from neck to dome. And Charlie, with those piles of bouldery muscles on him, seemed ready to fall on the newcomer like an avalanche. Neither man was smiling.

But Cobra smiled. He grinned; he went on grinning. All the sharp angles of his face, the crags, the lips, the eyebrows, arched upward. "You think so?" he asked the stranger. "I don't know, dude. Mad Dog—he sure does love that chair."

"Yeah?" the stranger asked.

"Oh, he'll kill you for that chair, no joke."

"You don't say."

"I wouldn't lie to you. He's on his way over here right now, too."

"Is he? Well," the stranger drawled, "I better talk in a big, frightened hurry then."

Cobra let out another laugh. "I guess you better."

But if the stranger was planning to talk fast, he sure took his sweet time about it. Smoked his cigarette some more. Took a meditative pull on his beer. Savored the mouthful. During all of which, the bikers and their women shared various glances of outrage, disbelief, and plain dumb wonder.

"Aaah!" said the stranger as he finally swallowed. He cocked his head in appreciation.

"Y'know," Cobra said, "call it, I don't know, a sort of sixth sense, but I'm guessing you don't know much about Mad Dog."

"Not a thing, to be honest with you," said the stranger. "The name kind of says it all, though, doesn't it?"

"Oh, the name's just the beginning, trust me."

"I get you."

"You get the picture?"

"He's a man named Mad Dog, and he loves his chair."

"That's it in a nutshell."

"So I'll get down to business. Angel Withers sent me."

"Ah." That caught Cobra's attention. He thought it over. He squinched one eye shut and reached back to massage the space between his shoulder blades. "Angel, huh?"

The stranger waited. He planted his cigarette in his ironical smile. Tilted his chair off its front legs, casual, holding his beer on one thigh. Sitting like that, he caught Honey studying him. He let his pale gaze rest on her—coolly, as if she were something he admired on a shelf, some pretty figurine or picture that he might decide to buy or then again not. Honey's cheeks colored. She twisted her lips and smirked and looked away. She made herself busy helping Cobra massage that space on the back of his T-shirt.

"This is *the* Angel Withers," said Cobra then, shifting his shoulders under her hand. He sat forward, lacing his fingers in front of him, tapping his laced hands on the tabletop. "Angel Withers up in Pelican Bay."

"Was."

"That's right, was."

"He died of the hepatitis about a year ago. Just before I got sprung."

"And before he died, he sent you to me."

"Since he died, I haven't heard much from him."

"And he sent you why exactly?"

The stranger shrugged. "He said it might make sense if we rode together sometimes. He said it might work out for both of us."

Cobra thought some more, rocked his head back and forth, considering. "Well. That's interesting, I confess."

"I thought so."

"He was a good man, Angel."

"One of the best, if you were facing him."

Cobra studied the table, nodded. "Well, I'll tell you the truth," he said after a few seconds. "If he said it'd make sense for us to ride together, then I'm pretty sure it would. In fact, I have no doubt in my mind it would. If you were still alive, that is. Which it's my sad duty to inform you that you're not. Because here comes Mad Dog."

THREE

Charlie chuckled, watching Mad Dog cross the room. Shorty's mouth opened like a black hole in his flushed bald head. The women—Honey and Meryl and Selene—shifted their bottoms in their chairs, excited at what was coming. The stranger, still casual, turned to look over his shoulder.

Mad Dog was striding toward them. Truly, it was like watching some kind of thunder titan come, some kind of mythical giant who makes the earth tremble and the crops die. Legs the size of tree trunks, arms the size of legs. The right limbs swinging out in unison, then the left ones, as if it took the momentum of arm and leg together to keep his great bulk shifting forward. He was still wearing his leather, the zippers rattling. And he had a hammer clipped to his belt that tapped against his hip. His long dirty hair hung down into his short dirty beard, and those angel-dust eyes of his beamed out of the tangle.

He smiled his broken smile at the sight of his friends. He didn't even seem to see the stranger. It was as if the stranger weren't there. As if the stranger couldn't possibly be there, by all logic, because . . . well, because who would sit where Mad Dog was supposed to sit?

With a final thudding footstep that might well have shaken the roadhouse walls, the enormous biker was standing directly over the smaller man, and he still didn't so much as look down at him.

And then Cobra said, "Hey, Dog, this hole says you gotta sit somewhere else tonight. He's taking your chair."

At that, Mad Dog did look down. He gazed dumbly at the stranger. Some kind of practical joke, he figured. He cocked a knowing glance up at Cobra and Charlie and Shorty, but they all had their poker faces on—they sure could be wily when they jived him. Well, he didn't want to be a fuckhead about it, but he hated to be made a fool of. So finally he just gave a good-natured snort, grabbed hold of the back of his chair with one hand, and flicked the stranger out of it.

As the stranger slid across the floor and smashed into the base of the bar, Mad Dog chuckled, shaking his head at the way his friends were always goofing on him.

"You clowns," he said.

He resettled his chair and sat down. With a quick sweep of his beefy arm, he brushed the stranger's beer and cigarette pack off the table. The shattering glass caught the attention of the barmaid. Mad Dog crooked his finger at her. Her face was a mask of terror and loathing as she scurried off to squeeze him a fresh brew.

"So hey, what's happening?" Mad Dog asked Cobra.

The bikers and their women cracked up. That Mad Dog. What a character. Mad Dog drank in their admiration with a big goony smile and a bright twinkle in his lunatic eyes.

Then the stranger kicked him in the head.

It was that quick. No one had even seen him coming. No one had even bothered to keep an eye on him. They figured he'd just crawl away.

Instead, the stranger had scrambled to his feet. He'd come in low and fast before anyone caught sight of him. Now he unleashed a vicious side snap of his leg that sent his heavy motorcycle boot smack into the bridge of Mad Dog's nose.

This genuinely annoyed Mad Dog. He had been a good sport up to now, but that just wasn't funny. He clutched the bottom half of his face and he could feel the blood coursing out of his nostrils over his upper lip. Plus the stranger continued to attack, standing over him, grabbing his hair, looking for all the world as if he were planning to drive his thumb down into Mad Dog's eye.

Mad Dog's famous chair fell over backward as he erupted to his feet. At the same time, he threw his massive arms out and knocked the stranger away. The stranger went dancing back a few steps, stumbled, and dropped hard onto his ass.

Mad Dog stood a moment. He waggled his head, trying to clear it. When he looked around, the stranger had gotten up again, had drawn himself up into a fighting stance.

A low rumble started in Mad Dog's unfathomable depths, and in another instant it had risen through him and burst from his mouth in a ferocious bellow of rage. He charged at the stranger, three hundred pounds of psycho biker intent on ripping the smaller man to shreds as if he were a paper doll.

The Outriders were out of their seats on the instant. They may not have been an official gang, but they followed the biker code. If one fought, they all fought together, right or wrong. Even as Mad Dog cannonballed into his enemy, they were up and ready to join the battle.

Then the battle was over. The Outriders gaped. Cobra, Charlie, and Shorty stood frozen in their places. Honey, Meryl, and Selene looked on from their chairs with their jaws hanging slack.

Mad Dog was now lying curled on his side. He was motionless except for his heaving breath. Spittle dribbled out between his broken teeth, and the blood from his nose made a spreading puddle on the floor.

The stranger stood over him, pulled back again into his stance. He bounced on his toes, watching the rest of them, waiting for the rest of them to come.

Cobra looked at him. Lifted one eyebrow. Cocked his chin a little, frowning with appreciation. "Pretty good," he said.

"Thanks," said the stranger.

"No, I mean it. That was awesome."

"Hey, well, really, thanks a lot."

"Of course, we still have to beat the shit out of you."

"Sure."

"It's a biker thing."

"I understand."

But the bust-up that followed was hardly the stuff of song and story. Most of the drinkers at the other tables quit spectating about halfway through. The band—the guitar and harmonica boys—never even left off rehearsing, and there were a couple of offbeat moments when the brawl was accompanied by a riff of rollicking bluegrass music just like the brawl in that western movie might've been.

The three bikers rat-packed the new guy, jumped him all together. It was quick and ugly—but not entirely one-sided. The stranger really was tough. Outnumbered as he was, he still managed to put some definite hurt on his opponents. He dropped Charlie and all his muscles with a knee kick, and drove the wind right out of Shorty with a solar plexus blow. He even blackened Cobra's eye with a quick piston of his elbow. In fact, he gave all three of them such a workout before they brought him down that by the time they were circled around his balled-up body aiming kicks at him with their steel-tipped boots they didn't have much energy left for it.

After a while, the stranger, his arms protecting his head and neck, managed to wriggle himself under a table where they couldn't get at him. The raging Charlie hurled the table away, but the stranger then managed to scoot under another one, a booth this time that was fastened to the wall. The bikers' kicks didn't reach him too well under there, and though Cobra climbed onto one of the booth seats and shot some punches down at him, those didn't do much damage, either.

Finally, the bikers were just exhausted. They figured fuck it, they'd made their point. They left the stranger lying where he was and swaggered away.

They went over to Mad Dog, tried to revive him. The three of them working in concert got him sitting up, propped against a wall. Mad Dog's eyes opened, kind of rolled around at them for a second or two. Then he vomited. Beer and tacos mostly, a couple of undigested bennies. The other bikers let him go, disgusted. He slid down the wall to lie on his side again.

Angrily slapping the puke off their jeans, the Outriders walked back to their seats and their women. They sat down again and took up their beers.

"That was good," said Shorty.

"It was," Cobra said. "A nice change from drinking. Sometimes you need a little break like that so you can come back refreshed."

"Uh . . . yeah," said Shorty, clueless.

"Oh, he elbowed you in the eye," said Honey, brushing her fingertips over Cobra's darkening bruise.

"Y'know, I noticed that, too," he told her. "In fact, overall, I'd have to say he had a very hostile attitude."

She was about to answer, but she didn't answer. She stared instead. Cobra followed her stare, and then he stared. And then Shorty and Charlie and their women stared. They couldn't believe what they were seeing.

The stranger was climbing out from under the table. Standing. Coming toward them. One eye swollen shut. Blood running from his brow all over the side of his face. Lips all mashed up. Legs unsteady. Walking tilted over, clutching at his side.

The bikers kept staring, and he kept coming. Then he stopped. Reached down. Lifted Mad Dog's chair off the floor. Set it at the table. And plunked himself into it again.

At that point, the barmaid brought over the beer Mad Dog had ordered.

Now, the barmaid was a lady in her thirties and, maybe on account of her unhealthy habits, she was not as pretty as she once had been. But though her features were growing coarse, she still had a glamorous cascade of dyed blonde hair, and her tight T-shirt and tight jeans showed off massive round breasts, long legs, and a tight backside, all of which, she made sure, were jutting and shivering and swaying like a gelatin cuckoo clock as she approached. The whole way over, she squinted through her mascara at the fallen Mad Dog. She didn't bother to hide her satisfaction at the sight of him down there, either. Once, not that long ago, the barmaid had made the mistake of dancing with Mad Dog. He had forced her out into the back alley and raped her. He'd given her a couple of grams of coke to keep her quiet, but it was really fear that shut her up—she knew he'd have killed her if she'd ever even thought about going to the cops. Anyway, the point is, she hated the fat bastard. She gave him a hard time whenever she dared, as much as she dared. And now, with a flourish, she plunked his beer down in front of the stranger.

And she said, "On the house, baby."

It obviously hurt the stranger to smile at her with his mashed-up lips, but he tried. He wrapped his bloody hand around the glass.

The barmaid gave a bold glare to the others at the table. Then she clocked her way back to the bar.

They paid her no mind. Cobra and Honey, Shorty and Meryl, Charlie and Selene. They were still busy staring at the stranger. They'd stopped talking. Stopped drinking. They didn't even have any expressions on their faces. They were just sitting there, staring at the stranger.

The stranger took a careful sip of his beer. Cobra blinked. It was another second or two before he could gather his thoughts, get his head together. Finally, he made a gesture toward the glass in the stranger's hand.

"Y'know," he said, "that's Mad Dog's beer."

"Is it?" said the stranger thickly. He lifted the glass to his busted mouth. Tilted it up. Drained the contents to its foam.

He clapped the glass down on the table. He laughed.

And Cobra laughed. And the rest of them started laughing, too.

FOUR

At about three o'clock that morning, the stranger staggered into his Berkeley apartment. He was drunk as hell by this time. Sick as hell and hurting bad. The taste of vomit was in his throat, and he was beginning to wonder if maybe he'd cracked a rib. Plus his guts were in a jumble. Plus his face was a fucking mess.

He shut the door. He groaned. He leaned against the wall wearily, watching the dark room spin.

It had been a good night. From the first moment he'd walked into Shotgun Alley. He still remembered—he could still recall—the feeling of it. Knowing the fight was coming, everything inside him bright and still and clear. And then dropping that psycho Mad Dog—that was pure pleasure. And so was drinking with Cobra, who was a smart and funny guy. And watching Honey, running his eyes over Honey, thinking about how fine it would feel to peel those jeans off her . . .

Leaving out the part about getting kicked to shit, it had been a good night all around.

But he was finished now, wiped out. Hurt, drunk, sick, the rest of it. He wanted to drop down onto the bed like a tree falling. He wanted to sleep right through his hangover and into the night to come. If there was one thing he didn't want, it was to sit down and write a goddamned report to his goddamned boss.

But his goddamned boss would be expecting it when he came in to work in the morning. And when he thought of the old man's weary, heavy face, of those hangdog eyes and their expectations . . .

Aw, fuck him, he thought.

But the truth was, he didn't want to disappoint him.

So with another groan, he reached over and flicked up the light switch. He tried to lift his head off the wall and look around him, narrowing his eyes against the glare.

The apartment was big and mostly empty. A bed in the next room, a table and some chairs in here. Nothing on the wall, no pictures, nothing personal. It was a sublet, just another short sublet. He never stayed anywhere long. He lived in motion, from one place to another. Something in him always racing like an engine. Anything began to feel like home and he was history, he was a trail of dust.

He pushed himself upright. Started across the room. He shed his leather jacket as he went, dropped it on the floor. He made his crabbed, wounded way over to the table by the window. Settled into the chair there, wincing, holding on to his side. With his free hand, he opened the desk's front drawer. He wrangled out the palmtop computer he had in there, plus a portable keyboard. He hooked them together, working hunched forward, baring his teeth in pain.

While the palmtop booted up, his eyes sank closed. Unseen, the world spun lazily round. His stomach yawed. He had to jack his eyes open fast. He looked out the window to steady himself. A pretty woman's gigantic face—a billboard advertising a bank—grinned brilliantly down on Telegraph Avenue. On the sidewalk below her, trash skittered past a beggar asleep in a cardboard box. The scene went in and out of focus, dipped and turned—Christ, he was plowed. He stared at it, waving in his seat like a cornstalk in the breeze. He stared at it till it came straight.

"Awright, awright," he muttered then.

He hauled his attention to the palmtop. He placed his quaky, blood-encrusted fingers on the keys. He thought for a minute. And then one corner of his swollen mouth lifted. That ironical smile.

Weiss, he typed carefully. *I'm in.*

FIVE

Foof, thought Scott Weiss. *Bishop. You crazy fuck. You're killing me here.*

He read the e-mail over, unconsciously moving his hand to his stomach. This op of his was going to give him an ulcer one of these days.

Weiss. I'm in. The girl is with them. Attached at the crotch to this Tweedy character, the one who calls himself Cobra. I'll have to poke a wedge in between them and fast, it looks like—they're a bad bunch and they talk like they're working on some kind of big job. I'll check with the client, see how he wants to deal. Too beat up and boozed up to think it out right now. The Angel Withers connect was solid, btw, thanks. Talk to you. JB

Weiss swiveled back and forth a little in his chair. He went on massaging his paunch with his hand. Did Bishop do this shit to him on purpose? he wondered. Use those phrases? *Joined at the crotch? Poke a wedge in between them? Poke a wedge!* Oh hell, of course he did it on purpose. It amused him to taunt Weiss with his sexual exploits, with all his exploits. Getting boozed up and beat up. Poking in his wedge.

For fuck's sake, Bishop.

Bishop knew—he had to know—that this was a big client for Weiss, a big case for Weiss Investigations. He knew Weiss would disapprove of him pulling his usual stunts and bullshit. The women, the fights, the cool disregard for any rule anywhere. And he knew Weiss would feel like an old woman because he did disapprove.

And maybe he knew the worst of it, too: that under all the disapproval, Weiss envied him. Sure. Weiss was Weiss; he couldn't kid himself. He envied Bishop for the way women lay down for him and the way Bishop didn't care, especially the way he didn't goddamn care . . .

His intercom buzzed. Weiss clicked the e-mail shut, shaking his head. He swiveled to the phone, pressed the button. He heard the receptionist, Amy.

"Professor Brinks is here."

"All right," said Weiss. He gave a heavy sigh. "Send him in."

SIX The professor turned out to be a woman, though. Forty maybe. Small and lean but sturdily built—or sturdy-looking, anyway—in a no-nonsense navy pantsuit with a jacket tailored to hide her torso in slashing angles and straight lines. She was pretty enough, Weiss thought, but in an awfully severe sort of way. Elegant, narrow features framed by straight black hair. Quick, fierce, challenging brown eyes.

Sure, Weiss thought, with Bishop still on his mind, *he gets the teenaged sexpot, I'm stuck with the Dragon Lady.*

He was already coming around his desk to meet her, but she strode to him at once, direct, forceful. She had an enormous briefcase strapped over her padded shoulder, and she clapped it to her with one hand as she thrust the other toward him. Her hand was tiny in Weiss's bearlike paw, yet she gripped him hard, shook tersely, once, like a man would.

It was a big show of assertiveness, but it had the opposite effect on Weiss than she'd probably intended. Poor Weiss, ex-cop though he was, was cursed with an idealized view of women. He thought of them as naturally tender and gentle-hearted. Had a deep yearning to protect them from evildoers, embarrassment, wind, weather, whatever else. As he looked down at the professor from his great height, his sourness over Bishop's e-mail was swept aside by a sense of melting sympathy. He felt the lady must be in real trouble for her to try so hard to seem strong. That's just the way he was—nothing got his Lancelot mojo working faster than a damsel in distress.

"My appointment sheet said 'Mr. Brinks,' " he told her as he showed her to a chair.

"M. R.," she answered with a cold flicker of a smile. "Professor M. R. Brinks. It happens a lot." She didn't tell him what the initials stood for. Her first name was Professor, as far as he was concerned.

"My mistake. Why don't you have a seat . . . Professor." She did. And Weiss walked back around his desk to resettle in his huge high-backed leather swiveler. He steepled his fingers. Went to and fro slightly. "How can I help you?"

The professor already had her briefcase in her lap. She was snapping it open before he spoke. She drew out a manila envelope, slapped it down onto Weiss's desktop, pushed it across the surface at him.

"I'm being sexually harassed. By e-mail. For the past nine months, someone has been sending pornographic letters to my computer. Those are copies of some of them, portions of some of them, anyway. I want to hire you to find out who's sending them."

It came out just like that, all business, terse and dry. If she was embarrassed by this situation at all, she sure didn't show it. But that didn't register with Weiss. He simply assumed she was embarrassed. He assumed she was being curt to cover her natural feminine reticence about such a delicate matter. Again, that's how he was.

So he let the envelope lie where she'd left it. He didn't want to make things any more awkward for her by reading the obscene e-mails in front of her.

"Are the letters threatening in any way?" he asked.

"Not directly, no. But, as you'll see, they go out of their way to depict me in humiliating and submissive situations. The implication of a threat is definitely there."

Weiss gazed at her a long moment. "Uh huh," he said then. "Have you complained to your Internet provider? Or contacted the police?"

"No, I haven't." Her dark eyes flashed. "Obviously I wanted this dealt with as discreetly as possible. Otherwise I wouldn't have come to a private detective."

"Uh huh," said Weiss again, after another pause. "And what is it you want me to do exactly?"

"Well, I thought I made that clear. I want you to find out who's sending me the e-mails."

"And then?"

"And then . . . give his name and address to me. I'll decide on the appropriate action from there. I'm sorry—I don't see what's so hard to understand about this."

Weiss continued to gaze at her. She would find, as all clients found, that there was no getting through the deadpan expression on his saggy features, in his basset-hound eyes. There was often no getting through the sympathy in him, either. In fact, the tougher she played it, the snappier she got, the more he felt the poor creature must need his help.

He even found her endearing somehow. Her rigid little figure bristling and ferocious there in her chair. He was touched by the way she refused to be intimidated by her situation or her surroundings. She was just a bit of a thing, after all, and the office was so big. Everything in it was big, built to Weiss's dominating proportions. The ceiling was high. The floor space was vast. The desk was vast. The leather swivel chair behind it was enormous. Even the clients' armchairs were blocky and massive. One wall of the room was made up of soaring arched windows. The morning sunlight streamed in through them like burly temple columns. And outside, across Market Street, a row of sculpted stone buildings served as foreground to the glass and steel towers of the greater skyline beyond them, making it seem as if the office opened up on that side to include the entire city.

But the professor, small as she was, was not overwhelmed by any of it. She perched in her seat like an eagle in a mountain aerie, the little mistress of an epic terrain.

"Is there anything you can tell me that might help me find this person?" Weiss asked her gently now. "Is there anyone you suspect? Do you have any enemies, for instance?"

Brinks's lips bunched up, a self-satisfied smile at the corner of them. "I guess it's safe to assume you're not familiar with my work, then."

As a matter of fact, as soon as she mentioned it, Weiss thought that maybe he was. Maybe he'd read about her in the newspaper or heard about her on TV or something. He had an encyclopedic memory for crimes and criminals, but this was something else, not in his line, harder to dredge up. Something about pornography, though. Sexual harassment. Censorship.

"Wasn't there an article about you in the *Chronicle* a while back?" he said, as it finally came to him. "In the Sunday magazine, I think."

"That's right. Last November."

"Yeah, I remember now. I read it." Actually he had skimmed it while sitting on the toilet. But the gist of it was that the professor advocated tougher sexual harassment laws and wanted pornography outlawed as an act of oppression against women. "So you're saying you may have enemies because of your opinions."

"I think that's a safe assumption," she answered dryly.

"November," said Weiss after another moment. He tapped the fingers of his right hand with his thumb, counting the months. "That would be just before the e-mails started, wouldn't it?"

She lifted one shoulder under the straitlaced, slashing jacket. "That could be. Maybe you're right. Maybe that's what set it off. But my work is very public anyway, very controversial."

"Like what, specifically? Give me an example. Something you think might've gotten this guy started."

"Well . . ." She thought about it—or pretended to think about it. Weiss was pretty sure she already had a good idea. "What comes to mind immediately are my views on pornography—any form of expression, really, that subjects women to sexual subordination. I consider it an abridgment of women's rights. I've worked hard to have it banned, and I think it's fair to say I've been instrumental in rooting out that kind of harassment in our university, in lectures and texts and so on. I wouldn't be surprised if that makes some men feel . . . threatened, you know. Their power under attack. It makes sense, in a way, that one of them would imagine he could bolster his ego or intimidate or neutralize me by turning that particular weapon on me. Maybe he thought that by objectifying me in a sexual way he could . . ."

She went on like this a while, her voice clipped and scornful. Weiss propped his elbow on his chair arm, rested his cheek against his fist, the baggy skin bunching under his eye. He took the opportunity to look her over. The cut of her suit jacket made it impossible to make out the shape of her breasts, he noticed, and he wondered idly how large they were. Not very, he decided. In fact, he suspected that underneath all the tailoring she was a little too stringy for his taste.

Following that chain of thought, he stole a glance at her left hand. Not married—or at least, she wasn't wearing a ring.

He waited for her to finish, then he said, "What about your personal life?" He gestured slightly toward her ringless finger. "A former lover maybe, someone you might've rejected romantically."

She sniffed sharply. Answered tartly, "There's nothing like that, no. Look," she barreled on at once. "I was given your name by a colleague at Cal. She said you were very good, very discreet. She said you could probably do this electronically or something. Trace the e-mails to their source or whatever. If you're going to go around questioning all sorts of people in my life—"

Weiss lifted his free hand. "No, no, don't worry. It's nothing like that. Sometimes people come in here looking for answers they already know, that's all. I was just trying to save you some time and money."

For the first time since she'd come in, Professor M. R. Brinks seemed to soften a little. She lifted her chin defiantly, as if threatening to slash him with the point of it. But she said, "Of course. I'm sorry, Mr. Weiss. It's just very important to me that this matter remain private, that's all."

"Sure."

"No, it's not like that. It's nothing personal. I'm not embarrassed or anything."

"Uh huh."

"It's just that—because my work gathers a lot of attention in the media, I have to be careful, I have to protect how it's presented. If some television station got hold of a story like this—well, you know how they are, they would sensationalize it, sexualize it. That's how you get the ratings, isn't it? Appeal to the lowest common denominator?"

"I guess so."

"My work is very important, and I don't want to see it . . . *genital-ized* like that. Reducing women's issues to cheap titillation is an age-old technique for trivializing them. If I let that happen, then this person, this person who's harassing me, will have won. That's my concern."

With his high, romantic expectations of the opposite sex, Weiss was often doomed to be disappointed in actual women. And in the end, as he showed her to the door, he found he was, in fact, disappointed with Professor M. R. Brinks. It wasn't the big attitude that bothered him, the big academic talk or any of that nonsense. It was the fact that she was lying to him, that's what he found so disheartening. He wasn't sure how exactly, but she was definitely lying to him, and it struck him as . . . unladylike somehow.

He stood in the doorway a moment and watched her as she strode away. His sad eyes, as men's eyes will, trailed naturally down to her backside. But the tail of her jacket was cut to cover it. There wasn't much to see.

He gave another heavy sigh and went slowly back to his desk.

SEVEN

Just down the hall from Weiss's office was an alcove that served as the agency's mailroom. There was a Xerox machine in there, a fax machine, a stamp machine, the computer mainframe. And me. Me working at my desk, licking envelopes and making copies, ordering supplies, doing research—and basically waiting around for whatever crumbs of investigative work Weiss felt willing to throw my way.

Which had been exactly none for the last few months. Ever since I'd screwed up my first real case. I'd been assigned to do a simple background check on a priest who was giving testimony in the trial of a vicious armed robber. It was supposed to be my introduction to the business—a grounder, they call it—a simple, straightforward task. Well, I got off to a promising enough start. Right away, I sniffed out the fact that the priest was lying. Unfortunately, that meant that the armed robber would probably go free. So—also unfortunately—I decided to cover up the lie. Then—unfortunately—I felt so guilty about it that I got drunk and passed out at my desk. Which—unfortunately—was where Weiss discovered me. It was all very unfortunate.

Now, Weiss had never mentioned the incident. He never reprimanded me or broke my magnifying glass over his knee or anything like that. I just couldn't help but notice that what I'd hoped would be the start of my career as a hardboiled gumshoe à la the characters in the old novels I loved turned out instead to herald my inauspicious return to licking envelopes and making copies and waiting around for the investigative crumbs that never came.

But Weiss had not entirely given up on me. He still liked to wander down the hall from time to time and visit me in my little nook. He liked to talk things over with me. I was never sure why. He always kidded me it was because I was going to write a book about him one day and he wanted to make sure I heard his side of the story—and maybe there was some truth to that. But mostly I thought it was just because I didn't count for very much in the world of the Agency. I had my highbrow Berkeley education, my big plans to return to the East Coast and become a writer: I wasn't truly part of Weiss's world. I was just passing through. So I figured Weiss felt he could talk to me with impunity, if you see what I mean. Anything I said or heard didn't really matter. Talking to me was about the same as talking to no one at all.

Whatever. Down the hall he came that day, bearing Professor Brinks's manila envelope.

"Make me some copies of these, willya?" he said. "One for Hwang"—he was our computer consultant—"and one for Sissy"—she was another op. He seemed about to walk away again. But he hesitated. Hung around, as he sometimes did, with his hands in his pants pockets. "While you're at it, make a copy for yourself, too," he said after a moment. "Take a look at them over the weekend. You're a literary man. Let's see what you think."

I don't need to tell you, my youthful heart went pit-a-pat. It seemed I was being given a second chance investigative crumb-wise.

"Okay," I said, as nonchalantly as I could. I opened the envelope's clip, peeked in at the sheaf of papers inside. I could make out only a single sentence:

You will be just one pussy in a row of pussies, one emptiness among many waiting desperately for me to fill you.

"Holy canoodle," I said mildly. "What is this?"

"E-mails to one of our clients. She's being sexually harassed."

"I'll say. Hey, this isn't M. R. Brinks, is it?"

"Yeah. How'd you know that?"

"I saw her go into your office."

"You know her?"

"Not personally. But I recognize her."

"Oh, that's right," said Weiss. "She teaches at Berkeley. You ever take a class from her?"

I snorted. "Not exactly."

"What? You don't like her?"

I shrugged. But no, I didn't. I didn't like feminists in general. Don't get me wrong. The way I felt, all God's children, male and female, should be free to do whatever they wanted, whatever they could. Smoke, go to medical school, stay home and raise their children, it didn't matter a damn to me what people did. But feminists like Brinks—these ideologues who thought marriage was oppression and sex was rape and men and women should be exactly the same—I'd only just recently escaped from academia, and I knew them well and I hated them. They were bullies and liars. They lied about history and human nature and statistics—anything that might contradict their stupid positions. And when you pointed out to them that they were liars, they tried to bully you by branding you sexist or accusing you of harassment. Then, when you pointed out that they were bullies, they suddenly went all reasonable on you and said, "Oh, surely not *all* feminists are bullies." Which is like saying that not all mobsters are hit men: It only takes one or two to intimidate the opposition. The rest are free to go about the business of being ordinary thugs.

So that's what I thought. Which I mention not by way of convincing anyone. I just want to be clear about what my position was. Because normally I was the soul of gentlemanly good manners, truly, but my feelings about M. R. Brinks and her ilk made me just that little bit sympathetic toward this obscene e-mail guy of hers. And that, in the end, is the reason I was able to help Weiss solve the case.

"So what's she want you to do?" I asked. "Hunt the man down and drag him to her elfin grot? Turn him into a stag so he can be torn apart by his own dogs?"

He laughed once. "Her elfin grot. Where do you get this shit?"

"Or are you supposed to just hurl him into the Women's Studies Department and bar the door?"

"Yeah, pretty much. I wouldn't be surprised."

I hefted the manila envelope in my hand. "That's a lot of e-mails. Why the hell doesn't she change her address or something?"

Weiss lifted his eyebrows. "Good question, as a matter of fact. I wondered that, too. This has been going on for nine months."

"Nine months? How come she's just hiring you now?"

Hands still deep in his pockets, Weiss hoisted his shoulders. "Don't ask me. She says she's being objectified or genitalized or some sort of thing."

"Genitalized. Gimme a break. You ever read her work? Genitalizing that broad would take a power tool."

"Awright, awright. Never mind," said Weiss. "Just make the copies."

I began to work the pages out of the envelope. " 'I'll slide my cock easy into you and rub velvety rose petals against your clit,' " I read aloud. "Wowser!"

Weiss wandered back toward his office, shaking his head. "It's no way to treat a lady."

EIGHT

It was a funny thing really about Weiss and women. All that chivalry and romance in his heart and there was no one for him in the world. No one but his prostitutes—and Julie Wyant, who wasn't much more than a daydream.

There were plenty of reasons for his being alone. He was a big, ugly man, for one thing. About fifty. About six foot four. Heavyset with a copper's paunch. He had unruly salt-and-pepper hair. Thick features that sagged like a basset hound's. A bulbous nose. Brown eyes set in the vertical parentheses of bushy eyebrows above and wrinkly bags below. The eyes themselves were deep, weary, sympathetic, full of understanding, but they could be disconcerting, too, sometimes. Everyone lies in this life; we all try to make ourselves look good, hide our smallness, our cravings, our selfishness behind some grand philosophy or some show of charity, some swagger, some sweetness. Well, when Weiss hit you with those lamps of his, it sometimes felt as if they were shining right through all that, right through the pretty disguise to the clammy humanity underneath. So he was ugly and he could peer into people's souls. In the relationship game, that was two strikes against him right there.

Then—strike three—there was that baffling idealization of women. Baffling because, as I say, he'd been a cop; he'd seen all kinds of females, girls who'd sell their babies to sex fiends for a pipeful of crack, spoiled brats who'd gun down their sugar daddies so they could get it on with the tennis pro in the backseat of the Mercedes; all kinds. Still, he insisted on the natural tenderness of the sex. Hovered over women whenever he could, courtly and protective. So, of course, women reacted almost universally by either treating him like a sexless father figure or shrugging him off as a tiresome pain in the ass or occasionally both.

He'd had a wife once—so I heard, anyway—a venomous marriage. But nowadays, there were only the whores. Outcall girls who visited him in his apartment every so often. A procuress named Casey supplied them to his specifications—and sometimes dropped by herself for a freebee, though whether this was out of affection or simply a bonus for a good customer, he could never be sure.

It was a hell of an arrangement for someone like him, someone who probably wanted nothing more than a wife waiting in the doorway, a couple of kids causing havoc in the backyard. But it made sense, too, in a strange kind of way. It was the flip side of this idealization business. Because when it came right down to it, Weiss never really fell for a woman he knew at close range. It was only the ones at a distance he went for, the ones who couldn't disappoint him, the ones he couldn't have.

Which brings us to Julie Wyant.

That evening, when Weiss stepped out of his office building to head for home, a bad feeling came over him. A feeling that he was being watched, being followed. He'd been having that feeling a lot lately. And it was all because of Julie Wyant. Because of Julie Wyant and the man called Ben Fry.

Fry was a killer. Julie was a whore. Fry was in love with Julie, obsessed with her. Julie had disappeared about six months ago, desperate to get away from him. Fry was willing to move heaven and earth, do whatever it took, to track her down.

As of right now, Weiss was the only man alive who could help him do that, the only man who had any clue at all as to where Julie Wyant was.

Now Weiss, in his days on the force and still afterward, was considered one of the best locate men in the business. He could find people, find anyone, sometimes track down in a day, in an hour, with a single phone call, missing persons whom the police had been seeking for weeks, months, years. It had to do with a quirk of his personality, an almost uncanny insight he had into the hearts and minds of human beings he barely knew, whom he might never even have met. He could imagine them somehow, picture to himself what they were like, and then suddenly he'd be thinking with them, feeling with them, getting inside their heads. Given a single lead, he could follow their trains of logic and figure out exactly where they had gone.

He had gotten his lead one night when Julie phoned him. It was the only time he had ever spoken with her.

You can't come to me, she had said. *Do you understand? Do you? You would only bring him with you. You see? He'll be watching you now all the time, every second. And if you come to find me, he'll follow you and he'll find me first.*

Weiss had back-traced the call to a pay phone in a town called Paradise, up near the Sierra Nevadas—that was his lead. But because of what she said, he never followed up on it. He left Julie alone.

Still, her image haunted him. It was easy enough to see why. He could have invented her face in a fantasy. Clean and clear and gazey. With fine, tumbling strawberry blonde hair like a miser's dream of gold. Lots of her clients went slobbery over her. Those middle-aged guys especially, with their unsung songs. For Weiss, all it took was a photograph he had of her, and a ten-second video clip he kept on his computer. He watched that video a lot when no one was looking. He knew it was idiotic of him. But he couldn't help himself. He couldn't get her out of his mind.

He couldn't forget she was out there somewhere, running, hunted. And he couldn't forget what she'd said on the phone. *If you come to find me, he'll follow you and he'll find me first.* The idea climbed up the walls of his mind like ivy. The more he thought about Julie, the more he could feel the man called Ben Fry watching him. The stronger the urge to find her, to protect her, to rescue her, the stronger his fear that he would bring the killer in his wake.

That evening, when he stepped out of the concrete tower that housed the agency, Weiss paused in the shadows of its entranceway and scanned the street, Market Street. It was late, nearing seven, but a summer's day, still light. The banks were closed and the shops were closing, but the pavement was still loud with footsteps, the air still grumbled with car engines, and the wires overhead still snapped and sizzled as the electric streetcars went rattling by underneath. The last of the rush hour pedestrians flowed homeward, pooling at the bus stops, eddying at the corner traffic lights. Weiss stood in the entranceway a long moment, his features in darkness, his eyes bright as he studied the passersby.

He'd seen mug shots of Fry—we'd all seen them in those weeks after the North Wilderness Assault. But he had no idea if it would be Fry himself who would come after him or if he would send some minion or come in disguise or if he would come at all. He had no idea what he was looking for, in other words.

A bent, wizened old black woman hobbled along the sidewalk as he watched; then a young black woman came striding up, plump and shapely. There were two youthful Asian men in suits and ties, walking together; a youthful white man and a youthful black man standing in hail-fellow conversation; a middle-aged white man with a frown and a briefcase, marching as to war. Any one of them could've been the one who was watching him. All of them. None of them. He just didn't know.

"For fuck's sake," Weiss murmured aloud finally. He was a tough old bird. He wasn't used to feeling helpless like this. It gave him a panicky sensation in his throat, as if he were strangling on his own paranoia. The whole business was starting to get to him.

With a shudder, he moved resolutely out of the shadows, into the balmy evening and the failing light. He headed for home.

NINE

I will remake you into your body. Lips and nipples and clefts. You will have no hopes, no anxieties. No thoughts, no philosophy. Only flesh, only sensation. I will sprinkle spring grass in your hair, Marianne, and force my tongue into your mouth; pour wine into the hollow of your throat and drink it as it spills down between your breasts and over your belly; I'll slide my cock easy into you and rub velvety rose petals against your clit . . .

"And I'll be the king of Romania," Weiss murmured, raising the whiskey to his lips again.

It was night now, a cool mist at the panes of the bay window. He sat in his favorite armchair, facing out on his view of the city, the Victorian town houses across the way, the haloed streetlamps on the steeply descending hill. He held his glass just beneath his nose, savored the stinging scent of the malt, the Macallan's that he loved. He sipped the surface of it, then let his gaze return to the papers on his lap.

They were the e-mails to Professor M. R. Brinks. The initials, it turned out, stood for Marianne Rose.

The world doesn't need any more professors, believe me, Marianne Rose. It doesn't need any more lawyers, any more corporate queens or drones. But most of all, my darling, what the world doesn't need is any more big thoughts, any more grand ideas or brilliant theories that are utterly convincing and utterly untrue, that chain the free-floating mind into tormented templates, self-fulfilling patterns of torturous and tortured lies. Why do you cling to them, woman? To your theoretical religion? Is it because actions themselves aren't beautiful? Is it because you can't tolerate the intensity of sensation, the moment of desire? The moment of desire, Marianne! That's what you're yearning for, you know it is. The world is sick of the sight of you cowering behind your tai-lored suits. The world craves you naked on your knees with your round ass and your wet purple pussy lifted to me. I crave you that way . . .

"Foof," said Weiss softly.

He made a sardonic face to himself as if he were beyond these things. But the images stirred him. There was sweat on the back of his neck, and under the papers his cock was pressed hard against the front of his pants. He lifted his scotch again, lifted his eyes again. He didn't drink but, for a long moment and then another moment more, he merely sat like that, merely looked out the bay window, unseeing.

Aroused, his mind drifted back to Julie. To that video he had of her, that ten-second loop, a come-on for some kind of Internet site. He'd seen it often enough now so that he could run it in his imagination. She was crooking her finger at the camera, beckoning. Dressed in a lacy white outfit that was somehow prim and seductive at once. Her cheeks were pink and creamy, and her eyes were deep and blue. And there was an expression on her face—dreamy, distant, angelic—that squeezed poor Weiss's heart every time he looked at it.

He pressed his glass to the side of his face, felt the cool touch of it. He broke off his fantasies and let his hard-on subside before he dropped his gaze to the page in his lap again.

Don't try to sell your cant to me. You know I'm right, Marianne. You know I am. You've locked yourself in your dark ideas, hidden yourself away in a darkness of theories haunted by the twisted shadows of your desire. You think you hate your desires, but you only hate their twisted shadows. Crawl to me, and I will make you suffer and come until you're only your body again. We'll make love for slow hours and when you're weary I'll send you to gather young girls for me and you'll lie by my side on the banks of a river and watch with me as they bathe and caress each others' nakedness. Then I'll go down into the water and be with them and you'll watch without jealousy as they pleasure me and soon you yourself will be nothing but wetness and a craving ache. And then I'll bring you down to the water too and you will be just one pussy in a row of pussies . . .

Weiss blustered like a horse, set the pages aside, tossed them onto the lampstand beside him with a dismissive gesture. Agitated, he stood. Carried his scotch to the center of the room. Paced to another window, peered out at another angle on the street, a glimpse over the building tops at the lights of Russian Hill.

His own reflection overlay the scene. His unattractive, hangdog face. His focus shifted to it. He made a grimace of distaste.

Then all at once his pulse skipped as he caught sight of a movement on the street below him. Something—someone—was watching him—there, at the corner to his right. He looked fast but no, there was no one—or whoever it was was gone. Probably nothing. An optical illusion. A late pedestrian he hadn't noticed before. Still, he watched the corner a long moment, his heartbeat quick. He knew the man called Ben Fry would never stop hunting for her . . .

He made a noise in his throat, "Ach." He faced his reflection again, sneered into his own eyes. God, he hated this. Standing here afraid of movements in the dark. Scanning the dark for dangers and plots and conspiracies. It reminded him of his father. He hated to think there was any trace of that old-style Jewish faintheartedness in himself. Hell, he had kicked down doors in his time, traded gunfire with gangbangers. He didn't need this shit.

He thought: *I should just forget her.* It was ridiculous, embarrassing. What did he think he was up to, obsessing over sex thoughts about a woman he'd never met? Like some kind of kid, like some kind of twelve-year-old or something. At his age, he should be a man of substance. A husband, a father. At his age, mooning around, calling up whores—it wasn't funny anymore. A person could die alone that way, without anyone to care at all about him. It was a pretty goddamned frightening thing to contemplate.

He thought. *I should find her.* He wanted to get in his car right now, track her down, start looking at least. He could lose anyone who tried to tail him. He could handle the man called Ben Fry when the time came. He should at least make an effort instead of standing here like this.

But he remembered what she had said to him.

You can't come to me. Do you understand? Do you? You would only bring him with you.

If he made a mistake, if she died because of something he did . . .

He turned away from the window, undecided. He looked over at the pages on the lampstand, the e-mails to Professor Brinks.

The world craves you naked on your knees . . .

No, he couldn't go on with those tonight. It was too much. They were beginning to get under his skin.

He went into the bedroom. Turned on the TV. Lay back on the bed, holding his scotch glass on his stomach with one hand, the remote control in the other. He watched the sports news for the baseball scores. He left the light off. It was dark except for the wavering glow from the set. He thought: *I ought to go find her.* But he couldn't make up his mind. The Giants had won again—third time in a row. Weiss's mind drifted.

The world craves you naked on your knees with your round ass and your wet purple pussy lifted to me . . .

He could see Julie Wyant like that.

"Ach," said Weiss again, disgusted with himself.

He let go of the remote control and reached out for the phone on his bedside table. He called Casey and asked her to send over a girl.

TEN

The narrow road wound upward through the trees. Jim Bishop twisted the Harley Fat Boy down a gear, amping the throttle, taking the curves at speed. Visor up, he felt the cool air on his face. He felt the dappled shadows washing over him.

The bike leaned hard into turn after turn. His hips leaned with it, his torso drawing over as counterweight. It felt to him as if it were all one motion, the bike and his body. He climbed higher and higher along the rutted switchback.

Through the pines that clustered on the mountainside came glimpses of the bay below. The water lay broad and steely and bright in the still summer air. Sometimes as he climbed, Bishop caught sight of the orange towers of the Golden Gate Bridge shouldering their way out of the billowing fog that clung to the base of the headlands. Sometimes he caught sight of the city skyline across the water; against the distant backdrop of the aqua sky, it rose and fell like a kind of visible music.

Bishop felt still and easy in himself, riding up the mountain. It always seemed good to him to be going fast.

The Graham house appeared suddenly on his left. It was sunk down low off the road, the top of its slanting roof gray through the tree cover. Bishop swung his bike onto the driveway, corkscrewed steeply around and down into deeper shade. At the bottom of the drive was a three-car bay. Sputtering, the Harley came to a stop at the rear fender of an emerald green Z3. To the Beamer's right was a silver Mercedes SL500. The third bay was empty. The third car, the wife's car, was gone, Bishop thought. Graham wanted to meet with him alone.

Bishop killed the engine, dismounted. In the sudden quiet, there was nothing but sparrow song and the rattle of the zippers on his open leather jacket. His black boots thudded heavily on the path of white gold slate that led him under the redwood branches. The boots thudded even louder on the patio tiles.

He stood at the back door under the flat overhang of the roof. The inner door was open. The screen door rattled as he rapped his knuckles on the jamb.

More quiet, more sparrow song. And then footsteps came clapping briskly on the tiles inside. It was Philip Graham himself who pulled back the screen to let him in.

Graham was tall. He towered over Bishop. He had a blocky build, wide at the waist and the shoulders, but he was trim and fit, a fellow who spent plenty of time at the gym. His hair—even now, here, in private—was as perfect as it was in the newspaper photos. Rich, full, red-brown, it looked as if it had been combed into place one strand at a time. He was in his late forties, but his features were youthful, vigorous. He had a lot of chin especially, which made him appear forthright. His big rimless glasses magnified his eyes and gave them a perpetual expression of startled disapproval, like a minister frozen in the moment he caught his wife with another man. He was dressed casually—in khaki slacks and a yellow polo shirt—but nothing about him was casual. He shook hands as if he were going for the state handshaking championship.

"Thanks for coming," he said brusquely. He looked straight into Bishop's eyes as he said it. "Come on inside."

The house's interior was several million dollars' worth of rustic simplicity. Graham led Bishop across a sprawling living room of aged tile floors and raw wood ceiling beams. As they went, Bishop scoped a massive fireplace and shapely furniture set against stone-faced walls and broad windows.

"I'm sorry to drag you up here on a Sunday morning like this," Graham was saying. "I figured this way we'd have some time alone together. Obviously I don't want anything put in writing or said over the phone."

At the far end of the room, he drew open a sliding glass panel. The two men stepped out onto a broad deck. Now they were looking down the mountainside at a panorama of the bay, from the pillowy fog round the Golden Gate across the sweep of the San Francisco skyline to the red roofs and white stone of the campus in Berkeley.

Graham showed Bishop to a cushioned chair. Bishop sat with the sparkling vista at his shoulder. He waited while Graham fussed at a round wrought iron table, stacking the papers he'd been working on, shutting down his laptop. Then Graham poured two glasses of ice water—everything done with precise motions, with thin-lipped concentration. He gave one of the glasses to Bishop and sat down with the other in his own chair, facing him.

Bishop drank a little, slouching, his legs stretched out, his motorcycle boots crossed at the ankle. He hadn't shaved that morning and there was sandy stubble on his jaw. He looked surly and defiant and he knew it. He wondered if it bothered the straitlaced Graham. For no particular reason, he sort of hoped it did.

He lit a cigarette. He liked the way Graham's eyes flicked to it, disapproving. He blew the smoke out nice and slow.

"So—" Graham cleared his throat. "You've found my daughter."

Bishop nodded. "She's with a motorcycle outlaw named Randolph Tweedy. He goes by the name of Cobra."

Graham lifted his forthright chin at that, then let it fall. He turned to stare blankly out at the bay. "Cobra," he said softly. "Now there's a name to warm a father's heart. 'Daddy, I'd like you to meet Cobra.' And I take it when you say she's 'with' this Tweedy, you mean . . ."

"Yeah. Yeah, that's what I mean."

Graham went on contemplating the view. He shook his head. "Incredible."

But after a few more seconds of silence, he straightened decisively. He faced Bishop again, his elbows on the chair arms. He rubbed his hands together and finally clasped them. Raised his index fingers in a steeple. Tapped the steeple thoughtfully against his thin, frowning lips.

"All right," he said, all business now. "I hired you to find her and you did. Good job. So here we are. My wife and our other daughters won't be back from church for at least an hour. Let's hear what you've got. And please don't waste any time sugarcoating it, whatever it is. Just get to the point, tell it straight."

"Good enough," said Bishop, with his mocking smile. He rolled his cigarette hand over, showing the open palm, as if to say he would hide nothing. "Bottom line, Tweedy's a bad guy."

"I already guessed that."

"Yeah. But he's a very bad guy."

"You mean he has a criminal record."

"Nah. Not much. Mostly piddly-shit biker stuff. Disturbing the peace, drug possession. You know. But his rep is hardcore. Hardcore. As in, two years ago he was booted out of the Hell's Angels because they thought he was too unstable, too violent. You understand what that's like? That's like . . ." Bishop searched for a way to phrase it.

Graham said, "I understand."

"It's like getting kicked out of Los Angeles for being too shallow."

"Yes, I understand. Go on."

"The word is he has a jones for violent crime. Home invasion, armed robbery, carjack—the sort of caper that tends to irritate your average lawman, draws his attention, if you see what I mean. On top of that, Cobra's got a bad habit of going off on short notice. That's why his handle's Cobra, 'cause he strikes like that. You know: snap, you got a dead civilian on your hands; snap, he pounds some gas jockey into a sack of broken bones. There's one story he stabbed an Arizona traffic cop with a bayonet just for giving him the usual biker hassle. That stuff's no good for the regular gangs. It means manhunts, APBs. They don't need that kind of aggravation. It interferes with them selling drugs and kicking the shit out of each other and so on."

No reaction from Graham behind his lifted forefingers. Only the rise and fall of his polo shirt as he breathed.

"What else can I tell you? He's charismatic," Bishop went on. "Smart, funny, charming. And he's got a nice little line in horseshit philosophy which—" *The ladies seem to like,* he almost said. But he remembered in the nick of time that they were talking about Graham's daughter. He took a drag on his cigarette to cover the hesitation. Blew the smoke out and said, "Which, you know, attracts people to him. Right now, he's got a gang of four or five guys pretty much like himself. Bikers the clubs didn't want, couldn't handle. People call them the Outriders because they're barred from the gangs. But they don't wear a name of their own. Cobra's careful about that. He wants to keep it informal. No charter, no patch. Obviously he doesn't want any trouble with the Angels, or with any of the others. My guess is he's got his own thing going on and he doesn't want it screwed up with any gang warfare."

"His own thing going on," said Graham sourly. "You mean like robberies and carjacks and . . . snap."

Bishop gave a wave of his cigarette. "I haven't found that out yet."

Graham's hands settled to his armrests now. He gripped the rests so that the muscles on his forearms corded. His mouth twisted in a sneer of distaste, just a quick one, there and gone. That was it. After all the bad news, that was all the emotion he showed.

Bishop was impressed with that. He respected it. Graham came off as kind of a stiff, but he was a pretty cool case when you got down to business. It wasn't just his daughter at stake here. There was a political angle, too. Graham was a businessman, ran his own investment firm, had lots of cash, family cash, cash of his own. But he was ambitious. He wanted to run for U.S. Senate next year. And according to Weiss he had a pretty good chance of winning. Bishop couldn't remember just then if he was a Democrat or a Republican or what he stood for. He couldn't've cared less. He had no interest in politics himself—true believers made him laugh. Still, he could appreciate the problem: It wasn't likely to help Graham's campaign any if his daughter got herself busted in the company of a bunch of violent sociopaths. This was a tough spot for the guy. He had a lot on the line. Bishop respected him for taking it like a man.

Graham let out a long sigh, as if he'd been holding his breath for several minutes while he thought things over. His eyes, enlarged behind the rimless lenses, kept that startled, disapproving expression. They gave nothing away.

"What about my daughter?" he asked. "Other than being Tweedy's . . . 'squeeze,' or whatever. Where exactly does she fit in with all this? Has she been accomplice to any crimes to your knowledge? Has she been personally involved in anything illegal?"

"I don't know that yet, either." Bishop let the last of his cigarette fall to the deck's red cedar. He crushed it into the shiny stain with one boot. Graham watched the process grimly—but then, he hadn't offered Bishop an ashtray, so what the hell. "I've started to work my way into the gang," Bishop told him. "And Tweedy's taken a liking to me. But it's still early. It's gonna take some time before he cuts me in, lets me know what they're up to."

"Well, I can already guess what sort of thing they're up to. It's unlikely to be charity work."

Bishop snorted. "True enough. And look, it's your money. I can find out more or I can walk away. Whatever you want me to do."

Graham fixed him with that politician's look again, that look dead center. He seemed about to speak. Then he stopped himself. Then he said, "Come here for a minute. Come with me."

He rose swiftly from his chair. Stood waiting until Bishop did the same. He opened the glass panels again, strode back into the house. Bishop followed. Down a narrow hall to a closed door.

Graham opened the door, let Bishop step through. Came in behind him, and pulled the door shut.

Bishop looked around. This was the daughter's room, Beverly Graham's room. Or it had been, anyway, before she'd gone. There was a big bed with a lacy white canopy hanging from its tall posts. There were heart-shaped pillows and stuffed animals on the lacy white spread. There were jewelry boxes on the dresser top, and the dresser was hand-painted with pink fringes and yellow stars. There were posters of faggy rock boys on the wall. Posters of peace symbols and rainbows and suchlike.

Graham aimed his big chin at the photographs—a crowd of snapshots on a vanity table, some framed, some stuck in the mirror, some pinned to a bulletin board hanging on the wall.

"Look at her, Mr. Bishop . . . Jim. That's what she was. I mean, till a year ago. That's what she was."

Bishop looked and—well, what was she? She was a girl, an American girl. A rich one, a clean one, a happy one by all the looks of it. She'd been a cheerleader. She'd been to the prom. She'd draped her arms over other girls' shoulders and had someone take their picture making funny faces. She'd gotten dressed up and dolled up and shrieked and laughed with too many best friends to count. And she seemed to've saved every picture of herself as a child that had ever been taken by anyone anywhere.

Bishop worked his gaze from one photo to another. And, sure enough, they had an effect on him. But it probably wasn't the effect Graham intended.

Bishop thought it was sexy to see her like that. To see her as a child in frilly pink, as a coltish schoolgirl in a pleated skirt; to see her with her blue eyes sparkling and her cheeks rouged and her blonde hair piled up for some dance or other, or with the school letter on her sweater for the big game. Bishop hadn't known a lot of girls like Beverly Graham, not up close. The clean, rich, happy ones—they mostly kept their distance from guys like him. It was sexy for him to see her the way she'd been and to think about her the way she was now, as "Honey," climbing up her biker's sleeve in Shotgun Alley, with her lips pursed and her clean, rich, fresh American face all smoke, all hunger.

"She ran away once before," her father said. "I didn't tell you that, did I?"

Bishop shook his head.

"A year—not even a year ago. She took off one morning. It was three months before we tracked her down. Know where she was when we found her? She was living with a drug dealer who called himself Santé."

Bishop looked at the cheerleader, at the girl in the silver-blue prom dress decked with an orchid.

"A drug dealer," he said. "Is that right?"

"Oh, not a street thug or anything. In fact, I understand he's quite successful in his field. Has an estate down south, in Santa Ynez some-where. Hundreds of acres of prime real estate. Apparently he keeps a mud pit in one area, not far from the house, and when he's bored, I'm told, he dumps a garbage can of hundred-dollar bills into the mud and then sends his various girlfriends in there to fish them out. The girls are naked, of course, and our Mr. Santé and his friends sit on the veranda and watch them and take bets on which girl will collect the most hundreds."

Bishop looked at the cheerleader now, with her breasts pushing against the school letter. He imagined her in the mud pit naked, fight-ing other naked girls for hundred-dollar bills. *Whew,* he thought. Then he forced himself to stop imagining.

"Fortunately, I was able to convince Santé that his life would be less complicated without having me for an enemy," Philip Graham went on. "He cut her loose. She called me from a mall in Santa Bar-bara, crying, broke. She has no money of her own. I've made sure of that. Don't ask me what happened to all those hundreds she pulled out of the mud."

Bishop tore his gaze from the pictures. Looked at the man. The lights were off in the room. The house, low on the hillside, didn't get much sun through the foliage, so it was gray in here and shady. It was hard for Bishop to read Graham's expression. For all he could tell, it didn't seem to've changed much.

Graham squared his shoulders. Continued, stalwart. "I drove down to pick her up myself. Brought her home. She actually seemed grateful at first. I thought maybe she'd learned her lesson. She moved back in, applied to some schools. I think she even started seeing some nice young man from the city. Then . . ." Graham's voice trailed off.

Bishop considered. Slowly, he drew his hand over his stubbly cheek. "Like I said, Mr. Graham, it's your money. What do you want me to do?"

"I want you to get her the fuck out of there," Graham answered quietly. "That's what I want. I want you to get her away from this Co-bra and out of there before she gets herself into real trouble. And before she embarrasses me by getting her face on television or in the newspapers."

"Well, yeah, I can see how you'd want that. The question is, how'm I supposed to pull it off? She's nineteen years old. Legally, she can be with whoever she wants."

"I don't give a shit how old she is. She's my daughter. I don't want her to get killed. Or beaten up or arrested. And I don't want my life derailed because some smart reporter happens to spot her on the back of this punk's motorcycle. I want her taken away from Cobra quickly. And I want it done quietly. And I want it done this time so it stays done."

"Well . . ." Bishop scratched at his stubble again. "I don't think you can scare Cobra off like you did with Santé—he doesn't have enough to lose. You could try to buy him off."

Graham pressed his lips together. "No."

"Right," said Bishop. "Right. If the media got ahold of that, you'd be finished." He shrugged. "Look, I could toss her over my shoulder and carry her out, but from what you tell me, it's a pretty sure bet she'd just take off again. No offense or anything, but she's climbing up this ratbag like ivy. Unless you're planning to lock her in a tower somewhere, if I drag her out against her will, she'll be back with him in a week."

Graham made a soft, derisive noise. "Why do you think I brought you in here?" he said. "Why do you think I wanted you to see these pictures? You think I give a shit if you cry over my daughter's lost innocence? I wanted you to see who she was—and what she is: a spoiled, rebellious little girl who thinks she can hurt me and break away from her past by demeaning herself with violent, dangerous men."

Graham shifted. Looked down at Bishop from his greater height. Matched Bishop gaze for gaze in the shadows. The little girl and the cheerleader and the prom queen—none of that mattered now. There were just the two of them, the two men, eyeball to eyeball.

"You strike me as a pretty dangerous man yourself," Graham said.

Now Bishop—Bishop was a pretty cool case, too, no one cooler. But even he hesitated here for a second. "What . . . what do you mean?"

"You know exactly what I mean. You said it yourself: She's an adult, a free woman. You can't drag her out or bluff her out or buy her out. She needs to be given a reason to walk away. She needs to be . . . convinced." He didn't bother to hide the scorn in his voice. "I'm a very good judge of character, Mr. Bishop . . . Jim. You strike me as just the sort of man who could convince her."

Bishop stared another second, then nearly laughed out loud, very nearly. Of course, he had been thinking about fucking Honey Graham from the first second he set eyes on her. That was Bishop, that's what he did. He fucked anything fuckable whenever he got the chance. Still, it hadn't occurred to him that her father might actually pay him to do it, might actually hire him to seduce her away from Cobra.

"Once she left him for someone else, I doubt a man like Cobra would take her back again," Graham said.

Bishop blinked. "Uh . . . no. No, you're probably right about that."

"Well, I want you to see to it that she leaves him for you. And this time, when she comes crawling back, abandoned and broke, I'll handle it right. Get her out of the country. Switzerland maybe. Put her in a school somewhere. Somewhere she won't be able to hurt herself—or if she does, she won't be able to embarrass me."

"Sounds like a plan," Bishop murmured.

"It is. It is a plan," said Philip Graham. "That is, if you think you can do it."

There was some more of this man-to-man eyeball bullshit. Then Bishop did laugh once. "Oh yeah," he said. "I can do it."

"Good," said Philip Graham. He threw open the door to his daughter's room. "Do it."

ELEVEN

So next day, Monday, Bishop was with the gang again. He was at Cobra's place in Berkeley, a great big clapboard box of an old house in the town's run-down southwestern lowlands.

Bishop, Cobra, and Shorty were all out in the wide garage. This was Cobra's chop shop, where he and his buddies worked on their bikes. Cobra, ass planted on an upended milk crate, was taking the carb out of his silver hog's manifold for a rejet. Shorty was assembling a new chrome intake system on his Fat Boy. And Bishop, just to be doing something with them, was on one knee, laboriously polishing the spokes on his front wheel—a new wheel he'd gotten because of the wind resistance on the full disc original.

Unscrewing a Phillips head from the carburetor's float bowl, Cobra stole a glance across the garage at the newcomer. Checking him out, gauging the give-and-take between the man and his machine. This was important business around here: the bikes, the way they chopped the bikes, knew the bikes. It was like the language these guys spoke to one another. Even just shining up the chrome the way he was, Bishop could feel Cobra watching him, judging him.

Now, fingering the grooves of his screwdriver handle, the outlaw pinned Bishop with one of his gaudy emerald eyes. The angles of his craggy, **V**-shaped face sharpened in a canny smile. "Hey, waxer," he said. "That chrome won't get you home, y'know."

"Oh yeah." Bishop nodded at the other's silver Softail. "Look at that thing, dude. Like something that came out of a slot machine. This, I just put a new stroker in last month, gave me another quarter inch."

"That'll speed her up, all right," said Shorty. He was cross-legged on the shop floor, his shaved head bent as he twisted a breather bolt into a carb bracket. "Till you blow your rods all over the highway."

Bishop went on carefully working his rag around spoke after spoke.

"Nah, I ran a plate in there at one-eighth, kept the ratio the same. She starts a lot better now, too. Of course, I had to weld in a spacer to get the engine back, and fuck me if I blow a gasket."

Cobra laughed. Nodded, satisified. He sighted along his screwdriver blade and started on the next Phillips head.

Bishop polished the wheel. The smell of the degreaser and the oil was thick and sharp. The garage door was closed. There were two windows on one wall, open to let out the fumes, but there was no cross breeze and it was a still, warm day. The fumes and the stench were stifling. Sweat dripped off his brow onto his arms, onto the floor.

Now the door from the house came open. Both Bishop and Shorty automatically glanced over that way. Then they kept looking that way as Honey stepped into the garage.

She was wearing one of Cobra's leather jackets. It covered her to the tops of her thighs in back but it was unzipped in front and she had nothing on underneath but a pair of pink panties, bikini panties. When she moved, the jacket came open. The white of her flat belly flashed. The curve of one small breast showed to the dark nipple. She had her blonde hair tied back in a ponytail with a red ribbon. It was a sweet touch. It made her face look scrubbed and fresh and innocent. It was the way she looked in the photographs, Bishop thought. Those photographs on the vanity table in her father's house.

"I brought you guys some beer," she said.

She had two bottles of Rolling Rock in one hand and a third in the other. They clinked and rattled as she set them on the worktable at Cobra's back.

"Ah, you're the best," Cobra growled at her.

He pulled her down across his lap. He kissed her deeply. His hand went up her back, lifting the leather jacket. The pink panties had only a thong back there. Her slim ass was bared to the other two men.

Cobra worked his tongue in her mouth, worked his hand up over her waist, pushing the jacket up farther. She moved her body against his touch.

Bishop watched her. He felt the rhythm of his breathing change. The sweat ran down his forehead in two streams. He and Shorty exchanged a glance. Shorty shook his head and smiled in admiration.

Cobra broke out of the kiss. He nuzzled his face affectionately against the girl's. Then he spanked her twice and set her on her feet. She pouted down at him.

"You ever coming in?" she asked him. "You said you would. I'm getting bored."

He reached behind him casually, snagged his Rolling Rock off the worktable. "Yeah, just let me finish up in here, okay, baby?"

She sighed, trailed her finger down his cheek. "You sure do like to take those things apart, Co. You spend all day at it practically."

"S'what it's all about, sweetheart. What it is all about."

"What?" She still pretended to pout down at him. Moved her hips near his face. "It's all about taking engines apart?"

"Fucking A," said Cobra. He winked at the two others. "And not just engines, either. Everything. Am I right? Taking everything apart. Taking everything apart until it all comes tumbling down."

He lifted his beer high by his head, sitting knees wide and grinning, wicked, a sceptered king on his milk crate throne. As if he'd said something true and profound, he toasted them all and drank to it.

Honey smiled at him indulgently. Gently mussed his combed-back hair: He was her baby boy. "Well, when you're finished bringing society to its knees, you can come upstairs and do the same for me," she said. "Okay?"

"Oh man!" whispered Shorty, shaking his head again.

Honey stepped in between Cobra's spread legs. She drew one side of her jacket open. Cobra pushed open the other side with the neck of his beer bottle. She pressed her naked self against him, the jacket folding over him.

Shorty bit his lip, squeezed his eyes half shut, jamming to the turn-on like it was a riff on a mad guitar. It was hot to see, all right. Bishop lifted the stub of a cigarette burning on a cinder block beside him. He wiped his brow with his T-shirt sleeve. He pulled smoke and watched Cobra's hands lift Honey's jacket in back again. He watched the way her yellow ponytail hung down against the black leather.

He wanted her. He was surprised how much. He watched her through the fumes and smoke and heat that swirled around his head. He watched her grinding into Cobra. He thought of the cheerleader and the prom queen in the photographs. He wanted her a lot.

This wasn't going to be easy, he thought. To draw her off, to steal her. He'd felt pretty sure of himself in her bedroom back home. He'd sounded awfully sure, striking the raw deal with her father. Why not? Women fell for Bishop. It was wild sometimes the way they fell. Maybe it was because of his good looks or all the cool stuff he did, riding motorcycles, flying planes, beating people up and so on. Or maybe it was just because he was such a coldhearted bastard, a challenge to the female sensibility.

But Cobra—Cobra was just as cool, just as cold, and every inch as big a bastard. It was going to be genuinely tough to take Honey away from him.

Bishop took a last drag off his cigarette. He smiled to himself behind the smoke. Yeah, he thought. It was going to be tough as hell.

Finally, the lovers broke it up. Honey drifted off reluctantly, lifting her arm to let her hand linger in Cobra's hand, her fingers trailing away. She blew him a kiss from the door.

Bishop watched her, still smiling to himself. He watched her until she went inside, until the door closed behind her.

TWELVE

"You got some pair of eyes on you, Cowboy," Cobra said all of a sudden. That's what he called Bishop—Cowboy, because of the way he'd come into the bar that first night. He spoke nice and easy, and he was smiling around the mouth of his beer bottle—but he was gazing at Bishop with a flat, unsmiling gaze, a dangerous gaze. "You get a good look at her, did you?"

Bishop dropped the stub of his cigarette. He rose slowly from where he'd been kneeling and crushed the filter under his boot. He wiped his hands on his rag. "A man's got eyes, Cobra. The world just sort of comes in through 'em." He smiled back, gazed back.

There was a long silence. It hung in the room between them like the smell of the chemicals and the feel of the heat. Shorty had his bald head down now. He seemed to be studying the parts of the intake kit on the floor in front of him, waiting to see which way this would break.

Cobra swigged his beer. "I guess that's true enough," he said.

Bishop started toward him, slow, still smiling, unafraid. Cobra sat on his milk crate, tensed for action, watching him come.

Bishop reached him, reached out to the worktable behind him. He hoisted the two bottles of Rock. He carried the two brews over to Shorty, handed him one.

Cobra relaxed, wagged his screwdriver at the other man's back. "The trick is, you gotta know what you're seeing. Just like I told Honey. A man's gotta know how to take it apart."

"Whatever." Bishop ambled back to his bike.

"Hey, look at this face," said Cobra. "Would I lie to you?" He had a way of talking, Bishop noticed, as if everything he said were a big joke—as if it were a joke and not a joke at the same time. Bishop guessed he was the sort of guy who would kid and grin like that until the second he killed you.

"A man's gotta know how to take things apart," he said again. "A girl, like Honey—a woman—you know, a woman can look at one thing, then another. This thing, that thing. A little baby makes her laugh, a dying hound dog makes her cry. 'Oh, poor doggie, boo-hoo, boo-hoo.' You know. Someone has a wedding, she thinks that's all good. Someone takes someone down, she thinks that must be bad. Women can be like that. That's how they are. But a man's gotta see the whole picture. He's gotta see the whole picture and then break it into its pieces."

"You're a very philosophical individual," Bishop drawled. He tipped his beer up and drank deep. It was good—good and cold in the suffocating heat. He gasped out of it. "Your insights rock my world."

Shorty drank, too. Sat cross-legged, the bolts and bracket forgotten on the floor in front of him. His glance went to and fro, Bishop to Cobra.

"Go on, go on," said Cobra, in that way he had, as if it were a joke but not a joke. "Go on and chortle derisively. Scoff and mock, even gibe, if you so will. But this is no shit, my brother. And I tell you true: You want to ride with me, you gotta know why I ride."

Bishop dragged his palm over one half of his face, then the other, flicking the sweat away. "You mean it's not all *vroom-vroom, bang-bang?*"

"*Vroom-vroom, bang-bang.* Jesus." Cobra looked at Shorty, a comical, questioning look, a look that said, What do I do with this fellow? Do I chuckle good-naturedly at his jeering taunts? Or do I slit his belly open and watch his guts slither out onto the floor?

In the end, apparently he decided to chuckle good-naturedly. "No-o," he said, as if explaining to a child. "It's not all *vroom-vroom, bang-bang.* It's gotta *mean* something, bro. It's gotta make a—a . . ."

"A statement?" Shorty offered.

"A point, a statement, right," Cobra said. "Because, see, in this funny old world of ours, every day in every way, you got people shoveling shit on you. Do this, be like this, you gotta be like that, do that. And most fools—most fools, man, they never get out from under it.

And, see, that—that's the difference between a cage driver mentality and a biker, the way a biker thinks. The cage driver, he's always wrapped around in his little box, you might say. He's tootling down the highway, yo de yo de yo, but he can't see where he's going, he can't feel it. It's just happening to him. But a biker, man, a biker, he's jamming in the wind. He's one with the beast that carries him. He's in control, always asking himself, Do I gotta do this? Why do I gotta? Who says so? Why don't I just go where I want to go and be who I am?"

Bishop nodded solemnly. "That is some very symbolical shit, Cobra."

"Symbolical shit, exactly!" Cobra raised his beer high again, presiding from his crate again. "The cage driver, he's just thinking what he's told to think. I gotta do the honesty thing. Gotta be honest. Gotta do the peace thing, be peaceable. Gotta do the boy-and-girl thing, that whole dance. Bring the lady a pretty flower, say please to her, tell her pretty please. The biker, he's saying, Fuck that shit. Why do I gotta do that shit? Why?"

"Amen," said Shorty, saluting with his bottle.

Cobra reached back behind him. Set his beer down on the table. Angled a sharp eyebrow up at Bishop as he went on. "The biker says, hey, the government rips me off, right? The corporations, they rip me off. Everybody from the suit in his office to the little ratfuck who runs the corner store, they're ripping me off. How come I'm the one gotta be honest? A cop pushes me around, gives me shit, cracks my head. How come I'm the one gotta be peaceable? See what I'm saying? Some bitch wags her ass at me, got her ta-tas hanging in my face till I can't think. How come I gotta play nice, bring her flowers, say pretty please? You gotta dissect that shit, that's what I'm saying. You gotta take all that shit apart until it doesn't mean anything. It's just words, that's all. Somebody else's words. Once you know that, then you're free, see. Then you're jamming in the wind."

Cobra tossed his screwdriver into his toolbox. Leaned forward on his crate to lift the float bowl off his carb.

Bishop drank. He didn't answer. He'd grown tired of thinking up snide remarks. Cobra had that effect on people. He went on and on until they ran out of things to say, until they just sat silent, just listened to him. Bishop drank and watched him work, watched his hands, rough hands, gnarled fingers lifting the bowl. He found his mind drifting back to Honey, thinking about how Honey moved when Cobra's rough hands went over her. Bishop wondered if she liked it when Cobra ranted like this.

Cobra set the bowl down on a cinder block to the side of him. "Every single thing, you gotta take it to pieces," he said quietly, sure of his audience now. He lowered one of those hands into his workbox. Selected a flathead. Brought it out. Cocked the point of it at Bishop. "You wanna ride with me, Cowboy, you gotta know that. You gotta know what it means to jam. You gotta take it apart. You gotta take it to the limit."

"I gotta take a leak," Bishop said. He was sick of this.

Cobra snorted, shook his head. Looked his comical look at Shorty again. Shorty laughed and shrugged. Cobra flipped the flathead in the air and caught it. Set to undoing the main jet.

Bishop strolled across the garage to the house door. Went through.

He stepped into a laundry room. It was close and crowded here, not much space between the washer/dryer against one wall and the plastic baskets stuffed with clothes against another. But Bishop was relieved to get out of the fumes in the garage. He was relieved to get away from all that talk, too. The fumes and the talk—they were beginning to make his head feel thick, to make his thoughts sluggish.

He edged out into a hallway. He could hear a television. He figured Honey must be watching. He followed the sound.

At the end of the hall, he came to the threshold of the living room. A big messy room with old faded furniture. Faded Harley posters on the wall. Clothes and old food cartons and copies of *Easy Rider* magazine tossed onto chairs, into corners. And there she was.

Honey was lying on a tatty brown sofa. She was lying on her side, staring at the TV. The voices coming from the TV were serious and stilted. Bishop couldn't see the screen, but it sounded like a soap opera.

Honey stared at it with an empty expression as if it just happened to be there where she was looking. She had her hand under her cheek like a sleeping child. Her face wasn't sweet and pouty the way it had been in the garage with Cobra. It was gray and dead in the TV light. She had the leather jacket pulled close around her.

Bishop leaned on the jamb of the entryway. He sipped his beer and took a good long look at her. His gaze traced her hair and her small white hands against the black leather. It lingered on a corner of the pink underwear showing between her legs, and then went on down over her bare hips, her thighs.

After a while, she sniffed. She barely glanced at him.

"What?" she mumbled.

He shook his head. "Nothing."

She watched TV. "That's just not smart, you know."

"No?"

"Uh uh."

He looked her up and down again. "Funny. It feels right to me somehow."

Honey sighed. She shifted, rolled over, almost onto her back. The jacket fell halfway open, showing him her panties and the curve of her breast. She regarded him sleepily. The images from the TV soap opera moved in her eyes.

"You better run along now, son, before you hurt yourself," she said. "There's a good boy."

Bishop laughed.

Honey rolled over onto her side again, facing the show. She seemed to forget he was there.

Bishop looked her over another long, lazy moment. He thought about the cheerleader and the prom queen in the photographs, the all-American girl. There was something about seeing her like this, no question. She made him pulse inside. It took an effort, finally, to push off the jamb, to move away from her, back down the hall. He carried it like a weight inside him, how much he wanted her.

He came through the laundry room, back into the garage. Still thinking about her. Still feeling that pulse.

And Cobra said, "So? What about it, brother?" He was done with the jet, screwing the bowl back on.

Bishop walked slowly to his bike without answering. He didn't want to hear any more out of Cobra now. He was sick of Cobra talking. He set his beer on the cinder block. Picked up his rag. Idly stroked the chrome on his long cannon-style pipes. "What about what?" he muttered.

"Well . . . you heard the talk," said Cobra. "You ready to walk the walk? You ready to take things apart like I was saying?"

Bishop frowned down at his chrome. Touched a streak on it. "Whatever," he said. "Sure. What've you got?"

"Hey, I'm serious, man. You gotta be ready to jam with me here."

Bishop took his Marlboro box out of his jeans pocket. Shot a fresh cigarette between his lips. He thought about Honey and Cobra, the way Honey was with him. He was just about ready for Cobra to shut the fuck up. "I'll jam. What've you got?" he said again.

Cobra paused, screwdriver in hand. He gave Shorty a meaningful glance. He went into his T-shirt pocket, took out a cigarette of his own. "I got all kinds of things, Cowboy. If you're up for it. I got big doings, my brother. Big money, big plans. No more of this grabbing-a-handful-here-and-there shit. We're taking it by the armload this time. The armload plus a duffel and maybe a couple of saddlebags to boot."

"All right," said Bishop evenly.

"Yeah, I know it's all right," said Cobra. "It's plenty all right. It's all right and change." He paused to light up. Spoke again with the cigarette still in his mouth, with the smoke rolling up around the **V**-shaped ridges of his **V**-shaped face. "But I gotta know that you're all right. Understand? That you're ready to do like we talked about. To take things apart. To do what's gotta be done no matter what someone tells you the rules are."

"Come on, Cobra. Lay it out, man. What've you got?"

"Mad Dog," said Cobra. "You know what I'm saying? Dude's a problem for me, problem for you."

"I got no problem with Mad Dog," Bishop told him.

Shorty laughed dully where he sat—huh, huh, huh—his big shoulders shaking. His bald dome glinted in the light from the ceiling bulb as he lifted his head, poured beer into his white grin. He came out of the drink sloppily. Wiped his mouth on his shoulder. "Mad Dog's sure as hell got a problem with you," he said. "You took his fucking chair."

Bishop snorted. "Oh yeah. His chair."

"Oh yeah," said Cobra. "Dude says he's gonna kill you, man. He'll do it, too. I know him. He's all fucked up anyway. Meth and bennies and coke, all kinds of shit. He don't know what he's doing. He don't know where he is half the time. That's the part that's my problem. Last job we went out on, the brother fucked up everything."

"Strangled some hardbelly 'cause she looked at him cross-eyed," Shorty said, chuckling. He didn't catch the warning glare from Cobra and he went on. "Man, we had to clean up after him big time, if you know what . . ." Then he did catch the glare and his voice trailed away.

Bishop stayed cool. He was good at that. He kept his expression easy and smooth. But he knew right off: This was the massacre at the Bayshore Market they were talking about. The market's owner and three teenagers shot dead. Robbers made off with an undisclosed amount of cash. No new leads, no one saw a thing. It was big news a couple weeks back.

So that was Cobra and the Outriders. And Bishop wondered: Was it Honey, too? Had she been there with them when it all went down? How deep into this was she?

"So I figure you kill him," Cobra said.

It broke into Bishop's thoughts. He met the outlaw's eyes.

"Solves your problem, solves mine," Cobra said. He smiled, the crags of his face arching upward. Like it was all a big joke and not a joke at the same time. "You can consider it sort of an initiation. You know, a trust and brotherhood thing. Before I take you under my wing and make you rich as God and all. You gotta show me you can jam, man. You gotta show me you can take it apart."

Bishop and Cobra regarded each other across the garage. The smoke from their cigarettes met between them. It hung in the air like clouds, and Cobra's words hung in the air. Cobra smiled, and Bishop thought about Honey. He thought about the way she moved in his hands, the way she listened to his words. If she was into this, if she had been at the Bayshore, he could use that. He could use that to steal her away.

"You gotta kill him if you wanna be one of us," Cobra told him.

Bishop shrugged. "Whatever's good," he said.

PART TWO Mad Dog and English Majors

THIRTEEN

Weiss sat brooding in his high-backed chair. He swiveled slightly back and forth, his elbow on the armrest, his cheek pressed into his fist. The pressure of his knuckles scrunched his dreary face, mashed the bags beneath one eye up toward one bushy brow. The other eye, wide, seemed all the more baleful. With that one baleful eye, he gazed upon Sissy Truitt.

She sat across from him in one of the client's chairs. I was there, too, seated next to her in the other. Sissy had a folder on her pleated skirt. The cover was open; the obscene e-mails to Professor Brinks lay visible, complete with Sissy's markings in red ink. She and I had come to tell Weiss what clues we had gleaned from our readings of the letters.

"Well, I don't blame her one bit for coming here," Sissy said in her gentle whisper of a voice. "I mean, these letters are just disgusting, aren't they? They're assaultive, demeaning. Just sick. I mean, the images! I don't know how she stood it as long as she did."

Weiss answered nothing. His heavy heart grew heavier with every word. *Sick. Disgusting. Assaultive.* He listened to her with half a mind while the other half obsessively replayed his weekend: the whores he'd called for, the things he'd done with them. What the hell had come over him? he wondered. What the hell had he been thinking? But he already knew. It was those letters, that's what it was. The images in those damn letters. They had put ideas in his head. *Sick. Disgusting. Assaultive.*

Eesh, he thought.

"The one thing I think we can say for certain is that whoever thought this stuff up is a truly foul individual," sweet Sissy went on. "The things he describes are just so . . . dehumanizing. Sadistic. They're all about dominating her, forcing her into all these sexual acts. Reducing her to . . . just a piece of meat. It's obvious, he's just some angry, threatened little man who wants to turn the professor into a helpless object—you know, some sort of doll he can use for his pleasure. Obviously the first thing we ought to do is go through the sex offender registry. This guy is definitely a pervert."

She had the most delicate features, Sissy did, the most golden hair, the warmest blue eyes you can imagine. She had a musical laugh, that little wisp of a voice. And though she was well into her thirties, she wore these schoolgirl clothes—cardigans and pleated skirts—that gave her a beguilingly innocent, maidenly air. She was so gentle usually, so kind, sympathetic. She had this way of listening to you, when you were talking, with a sort of maternal tilt of her head as if you were the most fascinating person in the whole world. She was one of Weiss's top operatives because everyone trusted her, everyone told her everything. And Weiss himself—well, of course, he just adored her, idolized her. To have her say these things—and to think about the whores, what he'd done with the whores . . .

Usually—normally—his trysts with Casey's girls were very decorous, gracious even. He was one of their favorite clients, always generous with his money, always modest in his requests. It was just their company he wanted, after all. Just the touch of a woman. The smell, shape, hair, voice. He'd never had more than one at a time before. And he'd never, ever done anything like he had this weekend. All because of those letters. Those fucking letters. What, what, what had he been thinking?

"Also, I think we really ought to have a serious talk with Professor Brinks," Sissy whispered on. "Try to change her mind about going to the police. I mean, she really should, Scott. The man who wrote these e-mails could definitely be dangerous."

Weiss shifted uncomfortably in his chair. Dangerous. The police. Jesus. He nearly groaned aloud in his shame and remorse. Not that the hookers had minded or anything, not that they'd complained in the least. They'd giggled at his apologies, in fact. They said he was silly; they were glad to do it. And they sure as hell hadn't minded the tips. In his guilt and embarrassment, he'd thrown so much cash at them, it'd be months before he could afford to call Casey again.

With a great sigh, he sat up, folded his hands in his lap. "She says she doesn't want the police," he said heavily. "She was pretty clear about it. And the cops won't have time to deal with this like we can, anyway. It's not just a matter of running a trace. Hwang says the guy used some kind of system where he routed the mail through a screening center—an anonymizer, I think he called it. We're gonna have to track him down some other way."

"Well, can we get in touch with him ourselves?" Sissy asked. "I mean, if he got an e-mail from us, that might scare him off."

"No, we just missed our chance. Apparently he shut down this address a week or so ago."

"I don't blame him," Sissy said. "I'd hide, too, if I were a creep like that."

Weiss nodded. He sank back down again, leaned his face on his fist again, forlornly. He swiveled back and forth in his chair. He thought about the whores. What he'd done with the whores. Those damn letters. Those damned images.

Eesh, he thought.

FOURTEEN

Now, I'd been silent up to this point. There were several reasons for that. I was scared, for one thing. I had made such a fool of myself my first chance as an investigator. I knew if I messed this chance up it would be my last.

For another thing, I felt suddenly unsure of what I wanted to say. Over the weekend, as I'd perused the letters, parsed them as I would've the English literature I'd studied in school, I'd been absolutely certain of my conclusions. My insights seemed rock solid to me, not to mention positively brilliant. But sitting here, sunk in the monumental chair, in front of Weiss's monumental desk, before the monumental figure of Weiss himself, it occurred to me again how biased I was, how much ill will I bore against feminists like M. R. Brinks. Maybe that had caused me to sympathize with the author of the letters. To give him too much credit. Maybe he was nothing but a sick, sadistic creep like Sissy said. I began to feel I should just nod amiably and agree that we ought to check out the police list of sex offenders.

And then there was Sissy herself—she was the third thing. I was crazy about her. Oh, not in any serious, long-term way, but when you're as young as I was, it's pretty tough to tell the difference between an erection and undying love. Looking back, I think I could sense how neurotic she must've been. I mean, why the hell did she dress like a little girl all the time? And what was with that treacly tone of voice she used, as if she were Mommy and everyone else was two years old?

Still, I really was young, and I was three thousand miles away from home to boot. And when she tilted her head at me and gave me the full blast of warmth in those moist blue eyes, and when she put her hand on my cheek as she sometimes did, and called me "sweetheart," as she also sometimes did, and asked me about my day or whatever, I wanted to hurl myself at her feet—and other anatomical targets as well.

In any case, I sure as hell didn't want to contradict her, and I really sure as hell didn't want to make a fool of myself in front of her. So with every second that passed I was becoming more and more convinced that silence was the way to go. Silence and a lot of amiable nods.

Then Weiss, with another enormous sigh, shifted his baleful gaze to me and said, "What about you, genius? What do you think?"

"Well—" I shot up ramrod straight. I cleared my throat. I cast a quick glance at Sissy, which I hoped conveyed the fullness of my submission to her every whim combined with a certain smoldering sensuality. Then I cleared my throat again. "Um . . . I think, actually, there might actually be more to these, uh, things than, uh, meets the eye at first, actually."

"That's a lot of actuallys," said Weiss. He never lifted his cheek from his fist.

Sissy giggled—in a warm, loving sort of way. I felt my cheeks get hot. "What I mean is—" I scooted forward in my chair. I twisted my hands together. "I'm not saying the letters aren't, you know—obscene or whatever." I swallowed, stealing another quick look at Sissy. "But I don't think the writer means to be . . . threatening exactly. I think he's actually trying to make a very . . . intelligent point."

"Oh, that's silly, sweetie," whispered Sissy. It was a fierce rebuke coming from her. And believe me, under most circumstances, she could've had my complete surrender for the price of a kind word and a kiss. But there was Weiss to think about also. I was in too deep to pull back now.

"No, I mean it, I mean it," I said quickly. "If you just . . . don't think about the four-letter words and all the graphic stuff. If you put those out of your mind for a second, the things he's saying underneath that are really centered in a very respectable mystic tradition."

" 'The world craves you naked on your knees with your round ass and your wet purple pussy lifted to me?' " Sissy read from the top page of her folder. "That doesn't sound very respectable to me. Or very mystic."

For a moment, the electric charge of hearing those words read aloud in her sweet, maidenly voice caused me to forget everything I wanted to say. Openmouthed, I stared at her, fighting down the fantasy of her naked on her knees herself. Then I blinked, glanced at Weiss. His impatient glare brought me back to myself.

"Um . . . um . . . um," I think I said. "No, but the point is, the rest of it, without, like I said, the graphic stuff, is . . . well, the thing is . . . it's William Blake."

"Who?" said Sissy. "Wasn't he a poet?"

I was clumsily fishing a crumpled page of notes from my pants pocket. "Yeah. And artist. English. Mystic, Romantic. Around the turn of the nineteenth century."

"Oh . . ." I heard Weiss murmur. And I knew he would've said *for fuck's sake* if it hadn't been for Sissy's presence.

But, fighting down panic, I pressed on. Smoothed the page of notes on my knee. "Remember in the e-mails where he says, uh, he says Brinks can't tolerate the moment of desire? And then he says it again, 'The moment of desire, Marianne!' That's from a Blake poem called *Visions of the Daughters of Albion.* 'The moment of desire! The moment of desire!' And that fantasy in the e-mails where all the, all the girls are naked in the river and he's on the bank with Brinks watching them. That's from that poem, too. Um . . . 'I'll lie beside thee on a bank and view their wanton play in lovely copulation, bliss on bliss.' "

Slowly, Weiss's face lifted from his fist. "That's in a poem?" he said.

"Yeah. Yeah, and another part in the e-mails, right above that, where he, where he says, 'Why do you cling to your theoretical religion? Is it because actions themselves aren't beautiful?' Well, that's, that's in the poem, too. 'Why dost thou seek religion? Is it because acts are not lovely?' "

"Hey," said Weiss softly. He looked at Sissy, made a face as if to say, *Hey.* "That's pretty good."

She wasn't convinced. "Oh, it's very good. And everybody knows you're very, very brilliant," she added to me with the kindest of smiles. "And that's one of the reasons we all love you so much. But all it means is this guy has read some poetry. A person can read poetry and still be a dangerous pervert."

"Oh hey, reading poetry is one of the first signs," I said.

She laughed that laugh like music. "That isn't what I meant."

"All I'm saying is you have to put this in the context of Brinks's philosophy. I mean, you know, Brinks claims to have nothing against sex per se, but all her work casts normal, healthy male sexual behavior in a negative light."

"Oh now," said Sissy.

"Well, she does. She does. Believe me. I dealt with these people at Berkeley for four years. You can't believe what they're like. Really. Read her stuff. She draws absolutely no line between normal courtship and sexual harassment—she basically thinks they're the same thing. And she basically thinks heterosexual sex is a slightly less violent form of rape. I mean, as long as we're talking about being twisted, Sissy."

"Oh, sweetheart," Sissy said, as if I'd spilled my fingerpaints on her new gingham tablecloth. "Now, come on. You're not really saying that these filthy, filthy letters are some sort of . . . intellectual argument. I mean, *you* would never write something like this. Would you?"

I did not know very much about women when I was young—only a little more than I know now, in fact. Even so, I knew enough not to answer a question like that one.

"That's not the point" was all I said. "We're trying to find this guy, right? I mean, that's what Brinks hired us to do."

"Right. That's right," said Weiss. He had brightened up considerably. I guess it was a lot more pleasant for him to see his weekend debauch as less assaultive and disgusting and more in the mystical tradition of English Romantic poetry.

"See, the thing is," I went on before Sissy could object, "there used to be this guy at Berkeley, this professor, named Wilfred K. Green. Okay? And Green believed that our fear of death alienated us from our bodies, forced us to cut off our consciousness of sensuality." I could see Weiss starting to roll his eyes, so I hurried on. "Anyway, Green started out as an English professor. His original subject was Blake and the Romantics, and he used a lot of Blake imagery in his books. He got very popular for a while in the sixties when he became an advocate of free love and mind-expanding drugs and all that."

"So you think this might be him writing?" Weiss asked.

"Oh no, no, he got AIDS way back in the eighties and finally took some PCP and threw himself out of his hospital window. He's been dead for years. But, as I say, he was very popular for a while, and he still has his disciples—especially at Berkeley. There even used to be a Wilfred K. Green society out there, though I think the feminists have forced it underground."

"So they're at Berkeley and Brinks is at Berkeley," said Weiss.

"I think the guy who wrote these e-mails is one of her colleagues." I blurted this out in my excited defense of my ideas. I hadn't really meant to go quite so far, to commit myself quite so much. But there was nothing I could do about it now. I sat back in my chair and shut up.

For what seemed an era after that, Weiss sat silent, considering. At long last, he cocked his head. He raised a bushy eyebrow Sissy's way.

She laughed again, that lovely laugh. Her eyes sparkled. "Well, like I said, Scott, he's a brilliant boy. That's why we love him."

"You still got contacts out at the university?" Weiss asked me.

"Um, uh, yeah," I said eagerly. "Sure."

"You think you could manage to talk to them, ask around, be discreet? Get a possible name or two without giving away any client confidence?"

"Sure! Sure! Absolutely. Sure."

"Okay," said Weiss. "Report to Sissy. Let her know the minute you find anything."

Simple as that. I had to work hard to force down a grin. I was an investigator again.

Sissy reached over from her chair to mine. She patted my wrist. I caught my breath. Her cool hand lingered on me.

"Good job, sweetheart," she whispered sweetly. "Well done."

FIFTEEN

Sissy and I left the office—and the moment the door shut behind us, Weiss's computer sang its chirpy little three-note song. An e-mail had arrived. Weiss swiveled to the machine and clicked the mail open. It was from Bishop.

Weiss. New stuff. Have info that Tweedy and his boys are the gang who took out the Bayshore Market . . .

Weiss let out a hiss like a radiator releasing steam. He followed local crime stories religiously, and the details of the Bayshore Market massacre were still painfully fresh in his mind. The girl with her neck broken. The boy shot in the store, the boy shot as he waited behind the wheel of his car. The market owner—what was his name?—Joe Something—shot where he stood, leaving behind a pregnant widow and a two-year-old child . . .

. . . I don't know yet if the girl was into it too. I'm going forward per the client's wishes to get her out on the down-low. Which'll take time, cause she's hooked up hard. Meanwhile, Tweedy's planning a big money job and wants me in, which will keep me close to the girl, and could give the cops a chance to pull these assholes in. The bad news: Tweedy also wants me to make my bones by whacking one of his guys. Kind of a rock and a hard place situation, since the guy in question likewise wants to whack me first. Got any suggestions? JB

Weiss snorted loudly. That last bit was meant to piss him off and it did. *Got any suggestions?* That was Bishop all over. That was Bishop needling him, provoking him, trying to get a reaction. *Got any suggestions?*

Yeah, Weiss wanted to write back, *I'll give you a suggestion: Don't whack anyone and don't get whacked. That's my suggestion.*

Well, it took his mind off the weekend, anyway. Took his focus off his guilt-ridden old heart and put it right back on his acid-ridden stomach. He knew he ought to pull Bishop out. He knew that was the right thing to do. He couldn't leave an operative in a situation where the sole choice was to do murder or die. He ought to pull Bishop out right now, right away.

But he wasn't going to. He couldn't. He wanted the justice—and he needed the business.

See, in his mind, Weiss was still a cop: an ex-cop, an old cop, but a cop. If Cobra and the Outriders were really the gang who'd done the Bayshore killings, then he wanted to take them down. He *would* take them down, come hell or high water. That was the justice angle.

The business angle? This was a big assignment for Weiss, for the Agency. Philip Graham was a top-flight client, and he was paying double rates for dangerous work. If the Agency handled the case well, brought his daughter home safely, it could mean more top-flight clients and more double rates to come. Weiss couldn't afford to walk away. He couldn't even afford to wonder just then if the girl was into it, too.

So he wouldn't pull Bishop off the case. And Bishop knew he wouldn't. That was the whole nasty joke behind the "any suggestions" crap. He was making it clear: Whatever happened next was not just Bishop's responsibility, it was Weiss's as well. Any protest from Weiss after this point, any lectures, any silent looks of reproach, would be pure hypocrisy.

Weiss let out a gravelly groan. He shifted the computer's mouse, clicked Reply on the e-mail form. He set his fingers on the keyboard, thought a minute, then typed:

JB. Stay in if you can. Don't cross the line. You know what I mean. Weiss.

He hesitated, then sent the mail. He swiveled away from the machine, his belly sour with discontent.

It was a complicated thing. All part of the psychology between them, this silent, father-son sort of struggle over which way Bishop would go, what kind of man he would be. It went back a long way in their relationship. It was probably there from the first minute they met.

This was years ago now. Bishop had just gotten out of the service, just gotten back from overseas. What he did for the government was a highly classified secret, but I heard little pieces of it over the years and deduced a few others. I know he flew helicopters. I know he was awarded a Purple Heart and a Silver Star and a Distinguished Flying Cross. I know he killed people face-to-face and hand-to-hand.

I don't know why he left the service. And I don't know why he came home such a lost soul. But by all accounts, his interior world was practically a vacation spot for personal demons. He went wandering from one job to another, one town to another. Drunk sometimes, often disorderly, run out of several counties by the local law.

Until finally, in San Francisco, he fell under the sway of an older veteran, a violent little ratbag by the name of Ed Wolf.

For a while, Wolf and Bishop were just drinking companions and whoring companions around the city. But then, one day, Wolf told Bishop about a burglary he was planning—one of those in-and-out, can't-go-wrong, set-you-up-for-a-lifetime scores these scumballs are always dreaming about. He invited Bishop to come along. Bishop said he would.

A few nights later, the two men broke into a mansion out near the Presidio. For all it was supposed to be an easy piece of work, both of them were carrying guns.

Of course, it turned into one of those typical bad-guy fuckups. There was supposed to be some fantastic mother lode of cash hidden in the house. There wasn't. The family was supposed to be away on vacation. They were home.

Bishop and Wolf soon found themselves tying up four terrified people with electrical cords, gagging them with duct tape, dragging them out into the living room. Mom and her two daughters were sobbing and choking. Dad was shaking his head again and again, trying to insist through the duct tape that there was no secret treasure in the house, so help him God.

Wolf went nuts. He tore the place apart, looking for the big payoff. He ransacked drawers, busted jewelry boxes, ripped open cushions, punched holes in the walls. All he came up with in the end was a couple of hundred dollars and a handful of Mom's rings and necklaces.

He got angrier and angrier. He screamed at the father. *Where's the money?* He kicked him in the thigh.

Bishop said, *Forget it, man, let's just go, let's just get the hell out of here.*

But Wolf wouldn't stop. He was in a fury now. His gun was drawn. Foam was flying from his lips. *These fuckers aren't making an asshole out of me!*

Finally, his wild eyes lit on one of the girls. He had an idea. He bared his teeth in a smile.

Let's just go, Bishop said. *Come on, man, it's a bust, let's ride.*

I'm not gonna walk away with nothing, said Ed Wolf.

He leered at the girl some more. She was the older of the two daughters. She was twelve. Tied with electrical cord, gagged with duct tape. Wearing a cotton nightgown with valentine hearts on it. Ed Wolf grabbed the cord around her ankles. He dragged her out into the middle of the living room. Mom and Dad and the other daughter struggled wildly against their bonds, screaming and pleading through their gags.

Ed Wolf took out a stiletto. He knelt down and slit the cord on the girl's ankles so he could get her legs apart. He stood, and started to work his belt off. He grinned over at Bishop. *You can have her after me,* he said. He turned back to the girl.

Fuck this shit, said Bishop. He hit Ed Wolf in the back of the head with the butt of his pistol. Ed Wolf dropped to his knees. Bishop hit him again. Wolf fell face forward onto the floor, unconscious.

Bishop took Wolf's stiletto, cut the girl's father free. *Call 911,* he told him. *Untie your people.*

Bishop stood over Wolf with a gun until he heard the sirens coming. Then he glanced up at the father. The father gestured with his chin toward a hallway. Bishop nodded and followed the hallway to the rear of the house. He left by the back door as the cops were coming in the front.

The patrolmen arrived first, and not much later the investigators got there: Weiss and his partner Ketchum. Wolf was coming around by then, and Weiss and Ketchum took him into custody and questioned him. It was an easy interview. Wolf was only too happy to give the two inspectors Bishop's name along with his last known address.

Weiss and Ketchum caught up with Bishop that very night at a Mission flophouse near the Transbay bus station. They handcuffed him and put him in the backseat of their unmarked Dodge. Weiss was driving. But he didn't drive back to the cop shop. He drove instead to an empty field at the base of the coastal bluffs.

He parked at the edge of the field. There were no lights here. Just a patch of grass and wildflowers bordering the beach. Above hung the rocky cliffs. Beyond was the whispering black water and the line of car lights moving across the Golden Gate Bridge. The bridge towers stood out sharply against the starry sky.

Ketchum was in the passenger seat. He was a wiry, gravel-voiced black man who hated everybody with the possible exception of Weiss. He turned to Weiss now and growled, *What the fuck, man? You think because he didn't let the girl get raped he's Saint Francis? He's psycho garbage. He's gonna be psycho garbage till he dies.*

Weiss, gazing out the windshield, shrugged. He couldn't explain. It was partly about the girl, sure: the fact that Bishop had risked his own freedom to save her. Then there were Bishop's medals, the Purple Heart and so on. Weiss was a patriot down to his toes. He regretted his lack of military service, and that stuff counted with him a lot. Then there were his instincts about people, the things he knew about them sometimes without understanding why. Whatever it was, he had already made up his mind.

He hoisted his heavy body out of the car. Opened the back door. Grabbed Bishop by the collar. Dragged him across the seat. Dragged him across the pavement. Dumped him, handcuffed, onto the patch of grass.

Lying there on his back at the big man's feet, Bishop sneered up through the dark and said . . . (This, for some reason, is my favorite part of the story.) He said, *Why don't you take the handcuffs off me, tough guy?*

And Weiss laughed once and said, *What the fuck kind of stupid question is that?*

Weiss then proceeded to beat the living crap out of him. It was a thorough, expert, methodical job. It went on so long that even Ketchum sniffed and shifted uncomfortably in the passenger seat of the Dodge. Still it went on. Bishop's blood, spattering the lavender flowers and the grass, was invisible in the night. His grunts and retching were swallowed by the gentle plashing of the surf. It went on and on. And he stayed conscious through the whole thing, too. Weiss made sure of it.

By the time Weiss delivered the final kick into the prisoner's solar plexus, he was pretty worked up. He seized the front of Bishop's shirt in his two hands. He hauled the limp body off the ground. He snarled directly into the bloody, swollen face.

You wanna be a piece of shit your whole life? he shouted at him. *A man like you. You wanna be a piece of shit?*

Then he dumped Bishop onto the earth again. Took off the cuffs. Left him there. Stomped back to the Dodge.

He lowered himself behind the wheel.

Damn it, Weiss, said Ketchum. *That's just soft.*

Weiss angrily shoved the car into gear, and they drove away.

Weiss didn't see Bishop again for a year or so. By then, Weiss had left the force. He was just starting the Agency. One day, before he'd even hired a receptionist, he looked up from his desk and Bishop was standing there.

You remember me? Bishop said. He looked ragged. He smelled bad. Weiss wondered if he'd been living on the streets. He wondered if he'd come in here looking for revenge.

Yeah, Weiss said. *I remember you.*

I want to work for you, Bishop said.

Okay, said Weiss. *Sure.*

But it was a complicated thing. For Weiss, there was that whole burden of fear for Bishop's soul and the envy of his practically pathological virility. There was the vicarious thrill of sending him out on a job and the responsibility—the guilt—for loosing him on the world at large.

For Bishop—well, Weiss might've been the only man on earth for whom he had ever had any real respect or affection. If Weiss gave him an assignment, he'd walk through hell to get it done. But maybe Weiss, with his big, essentially moral presence, crowded Bishop a little, too—the way conscience can crowd the fire in a man. Maybe sometimes Bishop wanted to push Weiss off, to break free of him, free of his faith and expectations, free of his heavy ethical code.

But—so far, anyway—he could never quite do it. And Weiss could never quite let him go. I think they both understood that Weiss was Bishop's last chance, his only chance. With Weiss, with the Agency, Bishop might slowly become the man he had once dreamed of being, the man Weiss believed he still was, deep down.

Without Weiss, alone, what would Bishop turn into? What would he be but a man like Ed Wolf?

Or, for that matter, a man like Cobra?

SIXTEEN

Bishop was in Shotgun Alley the next night, and Honey came in alone. She was wearing hip-hugger jeans and a lacy tank that left her midriff bare. Her hair swung soft and free around her fine-featured face. She scanned the bikers at the tables quickly. Then she spotted Bishop at the bar.

It was Tuesday, early evening. The roadhouse was quiet. Bishop was on a stool back in that gnarly corner where the Outriders liked to be. He was drinking a beer, smoking a cigarette. His eyes met Honey's eyes. She came toward him. His gaze traveled down her as she moved. She smiled, shook her head.

"You're gonna lose those eyes if you don't take better care of them," she said, pulling up to the rail. "Bottle of Rock," she told the barmaid. She looked back at Bishop. "Where d'you think you're going with this, Cowboy? Huh?"

Bishop grinned. Took a lazy drag off his Marlboro. "You never know."

"Yes, you do. You know. I know anyway."

"Nah." The smoke drifted up from his mouth as he spoke. "You just think you know, Honey. Could turn out you're wrong. Could turn out I'm the next big thing in your life."

She blushed. Even in the dim bar light, Bishop saw it. It startled him, reached him down deep. For a moment, she resembled the girl she'd been, the schoolgirl in the snapshots on her vanity table back home. Bishop felt something shift inside him. His ache for her shaded over into longing. It was a strong feeling. Too strong. It irked him. It made him want to hurt her somehow.

The barmaid clapped a beer bottle down in front of her. Honey swiped it up a little too casually. She leaned back against the bar. Studied the big room as if she was done with Bishop for the night. "Excuse yourself," she said. "You're dreaming out loud."

Bishop laughed. "That's good. That's funny. Only I'm telling you: It's not right."

"No?"

"Uh uh."

"All right," she said. "Enlighten me."

"All right," he said. "I'm gonna have you, Honey. I'm gonna take you away from Cobra and I'm gonna have you."

She lost the blush, went pale. She lost the bored look and whatever was left of her smile. She turned her face to him. "What are you, fucking nuts? How about I tell Cobra you said that? What d'you think'll happen then?"

Bishop's Marlboro box was on the bar. He lifted it, shuffled a stick out at her. She took it. "Thanks." He held his lighter up, struck the wheel. He waited until their eyes met across the fire.

"You won't," he said softly then.

She drew the fire into the weed. Let him smell the smoke on her exhale. "I might."

"Okay. Go ahead."

"Oh right. You're not afraid of him."

"No," said Bishop. "Are you?"

Honey went back to her beer bottle. "You know what, Cowboy? Fuck you," she said. She swigged her beer hard.

Bishop smiled. He watched her hand on the neck of the bottle. Her painted red fingernails against the green glass.

"You know, I got a theory about you, Honey," he told her.

She made a noise, rolled her eyes. But he didn't go on. So she had to ask him, "All right. What's your big theory?"

"My theory is you're in too deep." She came out of another swig of beer. Glanced at him, her blue eyes hot. He went on smiling. "My theory is you got yourself into something 'cause you thought it would be cool and now it's not so cool and you can't get out." He could see her teeth between her lips. He could see she was seething. "You keep telling yourself you want to be here. You keep telling yourself how exciting and rebellious it all is. But right there"—he tipped his beer toward her exposed navel—"in the pit of your belly, you know you've crossed the line. I think right now you'd sell your soul to get the hell out of here."

"Is that right?"

"That's my theory."

"And let me guess. You're the guy who's gonna take me away from all this."

"I might," he said. "If you're lucky."

Her laugh was harsh. She leaned in toward him, close, with her teeth bared and her eyes flashing. "You wanna hear my theory, Cowboy? My theory is I tell Cobra your theory and he cuts your heart out and uses it for an ashtray. That's my theory."

Bishop shook his head. Never took his eyes off her. "Yeah, but, see, that's not gonna happen."

"Oh? Won't it? You think so? Why not?"

"Because Cobra's over, Honey."

"Oh!" she said thickly. "Oh yeah. Oh right. Now it's you, huh?"

"That's right," said Bishop. "Now it's me. From now on, in your life, it's all me."

"Where do you get this shit?" she asked him. She leaned back against the bar again, her elbows on it. "You're so fucked now, it's not even funny."

"Yeah?"

"Oh yeah. I should feel sorry for you."

Bishop nodded, with that wry expression of his. He took a good long time tamping his smoke out in the bar's black ashtray. "Only here's the thing," he said.

"You tell me the thing," she said. "You tell me."

"The thing is, your boyfriend did the Bayshore Market, and he's going down."

She turned fast. He could look right into those hot eyes and see the anger die and the fear come up from underneath it.

"If you were there, Honey, even just there, it's felony murder. The same as pulling the trigger."

"What are you—? Who are you?" she said.

"That gets you life in a cell about the size of your bathroom back home, Honey—if they don't just march you down the death house aisle for show."

The fear flared brighter. Oh yeah, she'd thought about it, all right. She had the picture of it right there in her mind. The cell, the death house—she had it all in her mind already. Which was just the way he wanted it.

Her whisper when she spoke again was dry and faint like a little puff of dust. "Who are you?"

He planted a fresh cigarette in his lips. Lit it quick. Squinted at her through the lighter's flame. He felt tight inside, tight and pulsing all over. He liked this, doing this. He liked to see her with all the bullshit gone and the fear showing naked.

"They just might, you know," he said. "A rich, pretty white girl with all the advantages. They just might give you the needle, just to show they would. I hate to think of you on that table, Honey—"

"Stop." She choked on the word. Her eyes misted over with terror.

Bishop couldn't remember ever wanting a woman more. He felt wild inside, out of control with the feeling. He didn't know what would happen next, what he'd do, what he'd say—even he didn't know.

He lifted his hand. He brushed her cheek with his fingertips. She was too shocked, too scared, too uncertain, to pull away. He spoke around the cigarette in his mouth. "So you can tell Cobra, if you want to. And he can kill me. Or he can try. But in a couple of days, a week, maybe two, there'll just be another guy." He took his hand from her. Plucked the cigarette from his lips. Gestured at her with it. "And he won't be nice like me. He won't be willing to get you out. I am."

She stared at him. She didn't answer, couldn't. He watched her breathe. He watched her swallow. She was wearing a pink glossy lipstick that made her mouth look wet, but it was really dry, and he watched her dampen it with the tip of her tongue. She stared and stared at him.

Then the roadhouse door banged open and in strutted Cobra. In strutted Shorty in his wake with his heavy arm slung over the narrow shoulders of his little redhaired girl, Meryl. Then the tough-featured Steve came in and Charlie, the muscle boy, followed. And then the door swung shut behind them.

And then it banged open again. And then in came Mad Dog, last of all.

SEVENTEEN

Now they were at their table, all of them. All of them smoking, knocking back beer after beer. Cobra was holding forth with hazy eyes.

"The cage people, man. The cage people don't like to see things, don't like to see the way things really are. With them, reality kind of passes by the window, fades into the background, y'know? They put it out of their minds. They forget it. They tell themselves: Life's about me, man. I'm toodling down the road here. Life's about, like, Junior got into college. Or Daddy got a promotion. Or Mommy went to church and prayed for world peace." All those sharp angles on his **V**-shaped face arched as if everything he was saying were a joke. As if it were a joke and not a joke at the same time. "But when you're us, and you're out there, jamming in the wind and the weather, you can see it all, dude, it hits you right in the face and you can take it all apart. You know it's not about that Mommy-Daddy shit. It's not about that shit at all." He leaned his elbow on the table, turned his questioning, comical expression from one of them to the next. "It's about firepower. That's right. It's about who can kill who. See, the cage people, they got the cops. And the cops got the guns. And the cops can kill us and if we kill the cops, the cops can keep coming and kill us anyway. That's why Junior can go to college in the first place. That's why Mommy can go to church and pray for peace. That's the *only* reason. Because without those cops, without those guns, brother, we would *fuck* Mommy. We would fuck Mommy right up her tight little ass, right there in her church, and then we'd slit Junior's throat and take Daddy's promotion and make him eat it. Because then *we'd* have the firepower and there wouldn't fucking *be* no church to pray for peace *in*. Because that's all church is, man: It's their guns instead of our guns."

Shorty was nodding. *Oh yeah, oh yeah.* And Meryl was nodding,

snug under Shorty's arm. Charlie said, "Amen, bro." And hard-boy
Steve, practically asleep in his beer, muttered something that sounded
like "Ey-muh-ey-wha." Which was all pretty much the way things usually went whenever Cobra got philosophical like this.

But tonight—tonight, there was a lot of other stuff going on at the
same time. A lot of secret glances and eyeball-to-eyeball exchanges
with deep meanings going on. A lot of unannounced dark doings on a
lot of people's minds.

Honey, for instance. Honey couldn't keep her eyes off Bishop. Normally she not only listened when Cobra discoursed, she listened with
an admiring expression on her face. Cobra liked that. But tonight she
was distracted. She kept stealing furtive sidelongs across the table,
Bishop's way. And Bishop—he'd catch her glance and sort of smile his
ironic smile at her. He knew she was thinking about death row and
wondering if Cobra really *was* over and if Bishop really *was* her only
ticket out.

So Bishop would smile his ironic smile, and then he would return
his attention to Mad Dog. Because Mad Dog and he, meanwhile, were
looking death at each other. Passing lazy, laid-back stares of sudden
death back and forth across the ashtrays and the beer mug rings. Mad
Dog was on God-knows-what: meth and pot and three kinds of booze
at least. The whites of his lunatic eyes were streaked with red, and you
could tell just by looking at them that he was off in some other zone
someplace, some crazy, drugged-out zone where his thoughts swarmed
around his head like slow-motion mosquitoes and he couldn't move to
swat them and didn't particularly give a shit if they swooped in and
sucked him dry. He hunkered solid in his chair, all three hundred
pounds of him. One arm slung over the back, the other resting on his
belly with the beer mug in his hand. He made no secret of the gun in his
belt. That big .44. He had his BORN TO RAISE HELL T-shirt pulled down
over it, but the blocky shape of the grip was clear to see. And Mad Dog
watched Bishop. And his weirdo smile with its missing teeth was visible
in his scraggly beard as a thin strip of white and black, like piano keys.
And the smile said, *I'm so going to kill you, dude. So soon.*

Bishop smiled back. He was feeling good. He was feeling jazzed. Honey's glances and Mad Dog's stare, the beer and the pulse of longing and the smell of a killing on its way—it was all like energy going into him, like sizzling bolts of blue electricity zapping into his core, charging up his senses until the bar—the whole world—was clear and fine and bright. Something was going to happen. Maybe everything was going to happen. Tonight, tomorrow, now. Fast. It was coming fast, and he liked the sense of the speed. Somewhere in some back corner of his brain he had Weiss's latest e-mail nagging at him. *Don't cross the line. You know what I mean.* But that was in a back corner, a nagging voice far away. Bishop was right here, right now, and he thought, *Hell, Weiss.* What was he supposed to do? This was the assignment. He couldn't leave now without losing Honey, and he couldn't help it if Mad Dog made his play.

Then there was Cobra. Cobra was in this, too. Even as he was speechifying, he was watching the rest of it, taking it all in. He could see the murder brewing between Bishop and Mad Dog—anyone could see that. And he could see his girl, his Honey, stealing those cute little looks of hers at the handsome newcomer. It was a kind of a situation for him. Because he needed Mad Dog taken care of. And he needed to know he could trust Bishop. And he wanted Bishop with them for the next caper.

But Honey—sometimes Cobra lay awake at night and just watched her sleep, she was so beautiful. And the way she kept stealing those glances over at Bishop . . .

Smiling, Cobra leaned back in his chair. He tilted his chair back on its rear legs. He had this trick he did with a bayonet. He would produce it suddenly out of nowhere. It was scary shit to see. You couldn't tell it was coming. You couldn't figure out where he'd pulled it from. Without warning, it was just there. That's how he killed that Arizona state trooper, so the legend went. That's how he killed Joe Linden at the Bayshore.

He pulled the bayonet now.

It was a German model, circa World War II. Sleek and straight and blue-black with a blade nine inches and change. All the glancing and eyeballing around the table stopped the moment it appeared in Cobra's hands. Everyone looked at the bayonet. They knew it was his killing instrument. Everyone looked at Cobra, tilted back in his chair, holding the bayonet up, contemplating that blue-black blade.

"Take me, for example," he went on without a pause. "Take me and, say, Honey here." His gleaming emerald eyes shifted from the bayonet to her. "No more beautiful hardbelly lives on this planet, or so I do believe."

He lowered his chair to the floor. He knew they were all watching him. He knew Bishop was watching him. He reached over and combed his fingers gently through Honey's hair.

"Not a man at this table doesn't want to fuck my Honey," he said.

Shorty and Charlie and Steve and Mad Dog all chuckled drunkenly. Honey didn't like it. She made a face, pulled away from his touch.

"Shit, Co," she whined.

"Just the truth, my darling," Cobra said. "Just the simple truth. They all want to fuck you. They think about it every day. They dream about fucking you when they're fucking their old ladies. When they're pumping off in the shitcan, they're thinking about fucking you."

"Stop it. It's gross," she said.

But he wasn't listening to her anymore. His focus was all on Bishop now. Bishop, who slouched in his chair with his left hand hooked in his belt and his right hand holding a beer mug steady on his thigh.

Cobra leaned toward him. He balanced the point of the bayonet on the table. He placed his hands over the butt of the bayonet's grip. He leaned his chin on the back of his hands. He gazed at Bishop sleepily.

"How about you, Cowboy?" he said. "You want to fuck my Honey?"

"Shit," Bishop drawled. "I thought you'd never ask."

Cobra's smile was almost dreamy. His eyebrows fluttered as if his mind were far away. "But you won't, will you?" he said softly. "That's exactly what I'm saying. That's exactly what I'm talking about. There's only one reason in this world you're not gonna fuck my girl. And that's 'cause, if you do, I'll kill you. You know I will."

Nobody laughed this time. Nobody else spoke. The whole table was quiet now. Bishop slouched in his chair and looked at Cobra. Cobra leaned his chin on his bayonet and looked back.

"I wouldn't have to kill you face-to-face," he said. "I wouldn't have to kill you myself at all. I wouldn't have to kill you right away, either. I could make you wait, make you think about it. Make you dream about it every night." He lifted the bayonet again. Waggled it at Bishop. Smiled and slipped it into his belt, easy to see. "But then I'd come," he went on distantly. "No matter how long it took. No matter how far you ran. No matter how hard a man you thought you were. Even if you killed me, Cowboy. Even if I was dead. I would come back from hell to kill you. One night, you'd just wake up in the dark and you'd smell brimstone—and there I'd be."

It was creeping up on midnight. The jukebox played a slow country tune. A fat Hell's Angel and his black-rooted blonde, alone on the dance floor, moved in each other's arms without rhythm. Another biker and another blonde were mashing their faces together in a booth. The rest of the outlaws and their old ladies were at the tables, murmuring sleepily. The smoke from their cigarettes drifted beneath the dim ceiling lights. The bar's atmosphere felt tired and slow.

In the Outriders' corner, Cobra cast one last long look around the table. No one met his eyes. No one wanted to say a word, not with him in the mood he was in now. He grinned at their silence. He whipped his head to the side to clear a stray lock of hair off his forehead. "Amen," he said quietly, lifting his beer. He drained the foam at the bottom. He set his mug down on the table, hard.

"So!" he said brightly. "Who's for a run up the Wildcat to HQ?"

"Ehhh," groaned Steve. "I'm too wasted, man."

Shorty had his nose in Meryl's red hair. She raised her elfin face to his and fucked him with her eyes. "Yeah, not tonight, bro," said Shorty hoarsely.

"I'll go," said Charlie.

Cobra smiled at Mad Dog. "You're coming, aren't you? You're not gonna chickenshit out on me."

Mad Dog's mouth was open in a smile as wide and half-toothless as a baby's. His squirrelly eyes seemed to be spiraling up out of his drugged mosquito zone onto this planet here and down again.

"Yeah," he growled. He knocked back the last quarter of a beer. Slapped down the mug. "I'm ready to ride!"

Cobra's attention zoomed in on Bishop. "You ready?" was all he said.

He looked at Bishop hard, and he knew that Bishop understood. The Wildcat was a winding narrow road through hard climbs by the edge of empty canyons. A man could die up there and not be found for days. This was it. Cobra needed to know he could trust Bishop. And he wanted Mad Dog gone.

Cobra waited. Mad Dog grinned his grin. Bishop sat loose and easy in his chair. He pushed his mug away from him, still half full.

"Let's do it," he said.

There was a moment, as the others crowded out the door, when Cobra hung back and touched Bishop's arm. Bishop paused, and they were alone together just inside the threshold.

Cobra passed a gun into Bishop's hand, an old snub-nosed .38 revolver.

"Do him at the edge of the canyon by the point," he said.

Bishop slipped the gun under the back of his belt.

EIGHTEEN

They peeled out of the parking lot one by one. Cobra was in the lead. His silver ride tilted nearly parallel to the earth as it swerved onto the two-lane and spat away. Charlie was right behind him. Then Bishop, rearing on his back wheel as he bounded out of the lot and hit the street. Mad Dog was last, battling those ape-hangers, wrestling the long front end of his Low Rider into line.

In seconds, the bikes were roaring, doing eighty. A snaking chain of them along the highway, contracting, expanding. Waving, like a weed underwater, between shoulder and centerline. Leaving a trail of moonlit dust and guttural noise.

Honey had gone on before them. She'd come to the bar alone in a rattrap pickup, and she'd headed off in the truck again while the others mounted up. Just as she'd stepped into the cab, she glanced back at Bishop. Zipping his leather, he met her eyes. He could almost hear her asking herself: Would Cobra kill her if she made a run for it? Could Bishop protect her from that bayonet of his, not to mention that rage?

Bishop could feel the pistol under his belt at that moment, could feel it pressing into the small of his back. The thought flared and died in his mind like a spark in the night: If he took out Mad Dog on the Wildcat, she would see how dangerous he was, wouldn't she? She would see he could defend her.

Don't cross the line. You know what I mean.

Then she was in the truck, pulling back hard and turning. Then she was headed up the road before them and gone.

The bikers followed after.

It was a warm summer night. A gibbous moon was dodging in and out of the treetops. For the first few minutes of the run, the Harleys' headlights seemed to dissipate into the ambient glow. Soft shadows

merged and parted everywhere. The highway stretched visible to the in-
digo horizon.

Then, in a single unified motion, the pack swung left off the
straightaway and headed into the hills. The rising forest closed on them
from either side, shutting out the moon. Their headlights picked out
only inches of racing macadam now. The rest of the road ahead was all
in darkness.

They were riding without helmets. Honey had them all in her
truck. That was Cobra's idea. "I'm gonna let my head hit the pavement
tonight," he'd said, "and see which of the two of us gets fucked up
first." They'd all followed suit, of course. Charlie had tossed his jacket
into the pickup's bed as well, baring his bouldery biceps, showing the
black T-shirt pulled tight against his flaring pecs, his rippling gut. Mad
Dog's bristling horse-haunch arms also showed bare from his cutoff
denim. His long filthy hair streamed out behind him in the wind.

Mad Dog hung a few feet behind Bishop's rear tire. Bishop was
aware of the crazy bastard every second. He was aware of him and he
was aware of his .44. He couldn't help but feel that Mad Dog was staring at his back and that his back made a nice big target. But they were
going eighty on a winding road. It was a tough shot. Plus, there were
houses down here, lights visible in the trees and at the base of the climb.
Even drugged out and nutso as he was, Mad Dog would probably wait
to make his play on a straight in the high forest above the canyon.
Bishop hoped so, anyway. All the same, he was aware of the guy. He
could sense his smile and feel the pressure of his spirally eyes.

But Bishop did not know what he was going to do. He had no plan.
He was all motion, racing inside. A hundred percent afraid; a hundred
percent alive. He was full of the bellowing engines, full of the speed.
Throbbing with the throb of his machine.

He squinted hard into the oncoming twilight. The wind whipped
by his temples. Thoughts whipped by him like wind. The thought of
Honey naked under the leather jacket. The thought of Cobra passing
the .38 into his hand. The thought of Weiss: *Don't cross the line.* The
memory of that wild feeling that overtook him in the bar, that wild de-

sire. *You wanna be a piece of shit your whole life?* He let all the thoughts blow by.

His vision blurred with the speed and the wash of air. The darkness blurred. He felt the road switching right, switching left underneath him. He made out Charlie's red taillight vanishing and reappearing just ahead. The Harley under him, never slowing, wound round and back in an endless sweet careen, chasing the racing inches of pavement into the mountain, with the forest a black rush on either side.

They went higher. There were no houses now. Now, in the breaks between the trees, Bishop could make out the moonlit canyon. A downward slope of conifers fell steeply away from the pavement's edge.

The road switched left, switched right. Bishop looked over his shoulder and saw the shape of Mad Dog pulling round the bend behind him. He couldn't make out his face. He could imagine his eyes.

A short straightaway. Mad Dog hit the throttle. His Low Rider started to draw abreast of Bishop. Bishop tried to pull out, to force Mad Dog to take the shoulder, to ride the margin where the ground fell away. But Mad Dog came on fast, got outside him. Bishop cursed behind his teeth. Suddenly they were wheel to wheel, with Bishop balanced at the edge of the road, engulfed in speed and double thunder.

They climbed like that, man by man. Leaning right into the sharp turns, then leaning left together. With its long forks and high bars, Mad Dog's Rider was nowhere near as stable as Bishop's solid Fat Boy. But he pressed Bishop close—and then closer—to the brink, leaving him little room to maneuver on the bends. Bishop felt the dropoff to the right of him rocketing past, felt the frantic swiftness of his tires under him, felt his own precarious grip on the solid surface of the world. The fear was like fire in him. But he didn't care. He forced down every inner consideration, poured himself into his senses; rode.

Another curve. An open stretch. The moon broke out above the trees. Bishop looked away from the pavement only long enough to see Mad Dog next to him, Mad Dog staring at him, grinning at him before they both faced front again to take the next turn and the next. They came out onto the straight and Mad Dog muscled closer. Bishop knew he was running out of room. He throttled up, sped forward, tried to get clear of the Low Rider.

It was a mistake.

Hard, sharp, a fresh bend rushed at them. Bishop could see he was going too fast to take it.

Mad Dog saw it, too. He tried to drop behind Bishop, to block him off, force him into the curve. It didn't work. The next second, Mad Dog had to swing out into the other lane to take the turn himself. Bishop braked, slowing just enough to bring the Fat Boy round the bend. At the same moment, a pair of headlights—a car speeding down the mountain—came at them as if from nowhere. Both men were nearly swept off the mountain like dust.

But the car, screeching, drew hard to the left of them. The bikers slowed, drew hard to the right. They wobbled so close together their shoulders nearly touched. In another instant, the car was gone.

Bishop and Mad Dog poured on the gas again. With Charlie and Cobra just ahead of them, they roared in tandem up the next straight climb.

They had nearly reached the top of the mountain now. The forest grew sparser here with wider gaps between the evergreens and oaks. There was a thick tangle of brush at the verge of the pavement, but beyond that, on the drop into the canyon, there was plenty of room to fall.

Bishop knew he had to get clear of the Low Rider or be forced over the edge. He thought he had the juice to race ahead, but he needed a longer straightaway to make his move. The two bikers took another switchback, left, then right.

And there it was: the last long stretch to the point at the top of the run. Bishop got ready to roll his throttle wide.

Then Mad Dog pulled the .44.

Bishop caught the movement in the moonlight, caught it from the corner of his eye. Obviously Mad Dog had been waiting for the straight, too, waiting till he could free his hand long enough to sweep the gun out from under his enormous belly and bring the barrel to bear on the rider beside him. Bishop knew if he throttled up and pulled ahead, he might take a bullet in the back. On the other hand, if he stayed like this, this close, abreast of the weapon, Mad Dog might just take out his tire or his gas tank or even manage to blow his head clean off.

For a split second as they raced through the wind, the two men looked at one another over the length of the gun barrel.

Mad Dog bellowed. Bishop couldn't hear the words. He knew what he was saying, though:

"My fucking chair!"

Then Bishop braked and Mad Dog fired. Bishop thought he could feel the bullet go slicing past his nose. The huge gun's recoil knocked Mad Dog sidelong, and the Harley went into a skid. Bishop, keeping a steady pressure on the lever, dropped back behind him. As Mad Dog fought to get his gun hand back on the bike, to bring the bike under control, he lost speed. Bishop saw the opening. He firewalled, shot out and forward along the centerline, forcing Mad Dog over toward the edge.

Mad Dog, stoned and crazy, had no chance to recover. The extended bike was too unstable—and he wouldn't let go of the damn gun. As Bishop forced him to the side, the Low Rider jackknifed. The rear tire skidded out from under it. The bike and Mad Dog both went spinning wildly off the road.

There was a tremendous crunching crash as the fat man and his motorcycle burst through the thicket. There was a brief, high-pitched scream as they dropped to earth and spilled down the slope into the canyon below.

For Bishop, another hard curve sprang up just ahead. He hit the foot brake now, too. His bike skidded sideways, sending up smoke and the smell of burning rubber. He brought the machine to a stop at the pavement's very edge.

Breathless, he looked down into the darkness. He saw nothing—then there was a dull thud and he saw a blossoming burst of orange flame against the night as the Low Rider's gas tank blew.

The fire lit the woods. It lit the tortuous web of vines and branches.

It lit the tree trunks rising ghostly and the wreckage of the motorcycle lying twisted at one tree trunk's base.

It lit Mad Dog's body where it sprawled spread eagle under the pines. Bishop saw the outlaw's dead face gaping slack-jawed at the moon.

Bishop dismounted. He stood at the side of the road. The other two bikers had kept riding, apparently unaware of what had happened behind them. As the noise of their engines faded away, Bishop became conscious of the quiet settling over the forest. He could hear crickets chirping, the chatter of cicadas. He could hear little fires snickering here and there where the burning fuel had caught some wood or some dry leaves.

The flames hung draped on the branches of an oak. They fidgeted over patches of the earth like nervous hands. Slowly they died to embers, to ash. The silver-blue dark wafted back down over the forest.

Bishop stood and watched as Mad Dog's body sank into silhouette, as it melded with the shapes of the wreckage and the wood and finally seemed to disappear altogether among the surrounding shadows.

NINETEEN

Bishop and Weiss were prodigious figures to me in those days. They were a major influence on everything I thought and did. Like the characters in the tough-guy books and mystery novels I loved growing up—the detectives and cops and soldiers in Chandler's books and Hemingway's and Hammett's—they were the dreams of my tame, suburban youth given shape and substance. They were the kind of men I wished I could somehow be.

Not that I was blind to their flaws or anything. I knew Bishop, for instance, had too cold a conscience, too much violence, too much pent-up rage, too much resistance to what was genuinely decent in himself. But still: the cool of the man! The quiet aura of self-assurance. His insane courage in the face of physical danger. The way he could ride motorcycles and fly planes and, yes, win women with his distance and indifference like snapping a finger. What would I not have given to have just a thimbleful of those things? I had been a bookish boy. I'd spent my life in books, in rooms with books alone; I loved them. But I had something else in me, too, I knew I did. Something bigger, more alive. I wanted to go places and experience things and make things and be someone in the world and I wanted . . . I don't know what-all I wanted. But *something*, I wanted something, and I wanted it so badly I thought sometimes it would blow the top of my head right off. I felt if I could just learn to walk into a room like Jim Bishop, if I could just look men in the eye the way he did, and bowl women over the way he did, and fear nothing as he seemed to fear nothing, then I could be that bigger, more vital self I felt roaring to break out into the open. I would know somehow more clearly what I was after and I would get it and there would be no stopping me.

It was the same with Weiss. I idolized him, but I was a bright kid: I saw what he was, too. Maybe not right away, but over time, eventually,

I got a full picture of him, the good and the bad. I saw a great soul in the man—I really did—but it was a great soul locked out of life, a great soul pressed longingly against the window of the world. All that curdled romanticism, all that gentleness battle-scarred by the street and his marriage and his cop's existence or whatever it was that had scarred him. The guy would've walked—I truly believe this—he would've walked into the mouth of hell to pull an innocent out of the flames or to drag the guilty down to judgment, but he couldn't hold a freaking conversation, not a real conversation, share and share alike. Because he was all empathy and no identity. His mind could inhabit the minds of others, but it was never at home with itself. So he couldn't really give himself to anyone, or love anyone in any kind of mutuality. He was left with that dance of fantasy and shame he did with the whores—and what kind of life was that for a man, for a man like Weiss?

But again, there was the flip side of it. The way he saw things. His weary, compassionate understanding of the fallen human heart, his acceptance of it. That's what I wanted, that's how I wanted to see things, too. Me, I was all full of boyish opinions and theories and high, fine morality—all these veils of perception between me and experience, between me and the real deal, the real business of living. But Weiss—I mean, Weiss had pried a son's hands off the throat of his dead father. He'd pulled a husband's dagger from the belly of his pregnant wife. He'd seen evil and recklessness and corruption and lies, not just one time, but over and over, until he knew what people were, the whole horror show of their secret souls. Maybe it had damaged him—it had—but it never poisoned him. To his mind, it was just the atmosphere, just the air that had to be breathed if you were a human being in this imperfect world. And he breathed it—this was how I thought of him: He walked through that atmosphere of corruption and foolishness and he breathed it in and was part of it and still tried to do good and be kind and act justly. I admired him. I admired him and Bishop both. They were my heroes in those days.

So that night was a big night for me, that same night that Bishop killed Mad Dog in the hills. That was the night I went out to Berkeley to investigate the Brinks case, to see if I could get a lead on who was sending the professor those obscene e-mails. All right, it was a little thing, I know, an unimportant matter. But it was my chance to act like a detective again. To act like Bishop and Weiss.

So I walked into Carlo's with the coiled, dangerous grace and the cool, narrow gaze I had been practicing all the way over from the parking lot. It was 7:00 P.M. The door swung shut behind me. I stood on the threshold and surveyed the room like a gunfighter looking over a hole-in-the-wall tavern bristling with whiskey and murder.

Only it was a second-floor pizza joint about two blocks south of the university. A dimly lighted place, noisy with youthful voices, and with driving music that the voices nearly drowned out. There was a tile and sawdust floor. Bulky wooden tables and benches, row on row. College kids leaned eagerly toward each other in conversation. Waitresses banged in and out of the kitchen's swinging doors—local girls in short black skirts and white blouses, each balancing a pizza in one hand and gripping a couple of beer pitchers in the other.

My cool, narrow gaze lit on the gang I wanted. Three women and two men at a table by the window. I approached them with a coiled, dangerous grace.

I knew two of them—Diane and Rick. She was small and tense and hungry-looking. He was wavery like a willow in the wind. They were a couple now, but it was she and I once. I don't remember much about it, frankly, except that she wore army T-shirts and cargo pants and she smoked and paced and talked incessantly. I mostly said whatever I thought would get her to calm down and shut up long enough for me to have sex with her. The whole thing lasted about six weeks.

Now she was more in her element. With Rick. With these others. Stu the Promising Genius and Beth the Miserable Bard and Pat the Obvious Lesbian. All of them thin, except for Beth. All of them drawling and ironical but with quick, scared, envious eyes. Grad students in English literature. Diane introduced me around. They didn't smile—they barely nodded. They had resumed their conversation before I'd even settled into my chair.

I grabbed a mug and a pitcher and poured myself a beer.

They were discussing someone's dissertation. I won't bore the reader with the things they said. No one on earth at any time ever should be bored by the things people like this say. And anyway, I don't remember much of it and I comprehended even less. But just so you understand my own reaction, let me give you a quick, general sense of it.

The subject was "*Ode on a Grecian Urn.*" Now, you may not care about literature one way or the other—after all, you're reading this—but it matters a lot to me. And I personally think the Ode is one of the wisest and most beautiful poems in one of the sweetest and most beautiful languages by one of the best and most beautiful of men, namely John Keats. But no. According to Stu (the Promising Genius) the Ode was no more than the "effulgence, or maybe I should say effluvium, of certain social interactions and assumptions." What's more, all these interactions and assumptions were sexist, imperialist, racist, and altogether very, very bad. Therefore, said Stu (who was a Promising Genius), they needed to be analyzed. Analyzed, analyzed, analyzed. Everything, it turned out, needed to be analyzed. Even the fact that some of the people in the poem were men and some were women. "It's just historicity posing as gender positioning, presupposing a chiastic ontology," said Diane, who had once called me "Daddy" in the midst of an orgasm and then kept me up all fucking night talking about it. And Pat (the Obvious Lesbian) drawled, "Well, one chooses one's gender," a remark of such fatuous stupidity it brought my beer bubbling up through my nose . . .

And so on, but you get the basic idea.

At some point during all this, I dropped my cool, narrow gaze and abandoned my coiled, dangerous grace and resolved to dedicate myself entirely to my beer. I settled to work on it. The scene became dreamy. I watched Diane. I watched her pale, beaky face, with its mouth moving, always moving. Now, just as when we'd been together, I didn't really hear the words after a while. I looked from face to face around the table and all the mouths were moving and I didn't hear any of them.

In a remarkably short time, I became deeply depressed. I had come here in my new role as tough-guy gumshoe and found myself suddenly swept back into the old, unwelcomed role of myself. My recent self, at least. Because not so much as a year before, in this very city, I had been just like Diane and Rick and Stu and Beth and Pat. A student of English literature. Talking nonsense just like they were. Planning, like they were, a career in the academy.

See, I had wanted to be a writer for as long as I could remember. But I knew there was no money in that—not if you were serious, and in my youthful folly I mistakenly believed I was very serious indeed. So I figured I'd go to grad school, get my Ph.D., get a job at some university somewhere and become a college professor with writer's block trying to write novels about college professors with writer's block trying to write novels about college professors with writer's block. The usual drill.

But there was that thing in me, that niggling hunger for experience, for more life. So I had decided to take a year off before I applied to grad school and, my mind full of Chandler and Hammett and the rest, I applied for the job at Weiss's agency, always assuming I would come back to grad school in the long run to study literature and ideas and eventually educate the nation's youth.

Now here I was, here at Carlo's, staring at these people as if they were apparitions of the man I might've been, the man I still sometimes considered becoming. It was an appalling vision. These people had nothing to do with literature. They had nothing to do with ideas. They were just intellectual vandals, parading a cheap knack for breaking fine things into their component parts. Analysis! Any single phrase of "Grecian Urn" was worth more than all their analysis, more, I suspect, than all the work of their lives. I despised them and I despised myself for being like them.

I sat there, watching Diane, watching all of them with their mouths moving. I thought, *What will become of me?* Because I knew I was no detective either, not really, not as a career. And yet I knew now I could never go back to this . . .

Following that train of thought, however, I did soon recollect the business of the evening. It was a comfort to me in a way. At least I was here for a reason. I was here to wangle some information out of these people. I was not—I told myself—really one of them anymore at all.

I tipped back a hearty draught of beer. As I set the mug down on the table, the voices of my companions seemed to snap back on.

"I mean, if you're not going to deconstruct the assumptions of hegemony, what's the point?" said Diane to Rick, in a disparaging tone I remembered only too well.

"Say," I broke in, shouting above the music and the noise, "have any of you people ever read Wilfred K. Green?"

Well, that made them fall silent for real. All five of them. All five of them gaped at me. Diane screwed up her face as if I'd begun to exude an unpleasant smell.

"Wasn't he from the . . . sixties or someplace?" drawled Stu. The others chuckled.

"That's the guy," I said. "I'm thinking of writing an article about him and his interpretation of Blake." This was my brilliant cover story. "There used to be a Wilfred K. Green society somewhere on campus, but it seems to've vanished. I can't find any trace of it."

"Yes, I guess nowadays we sort of like to confine our unreconstructed phallocentrism to the United States Marines and other murdering imperialist assholes," said Beth the Miserable Bard—I swear to God, those were her exact words. And oh, how they laughed. Har hardy har har har.

Of course, I realized at once I had made a faux pas, doncha know. Diane, I could tell, was furious with me. By allowing the name of Wilfred K. Green to pass my lips without the requisite simper of dismissive irony, I had apparently not only disgraced my forebears and cursed my descendants even unto the tenth generation, I had also somehow humiliated her. She was embarrassed to be the one who had introduced me to this fine upstanding group of young people.

"Oh shit," she said brightly, "I just remembered I have a paper to write. You people want to come back to the house?" And then turning to me with a horribly dental smile, she added, "You can come, too, if you like."

I didn't like. I sat where I was with the last of my beer and watched them file out. I was so relieved to see them go, it took a moment or two before it occurred to me that I had just failed miserably in my assignment, utterly failed the Agency as an investigator yet again. The realization made my heart sink with despair.

Then, all at once, the loud music in the room stopped. And a voice from behind me said quietly, "You could've just horsewhipped them, you know. No jury on earth would've convicted you."

I shifted in my seat to see who was speaking. That was the first time I ever set eyes on Emma McNair.

TWENTY

She was sitting in the corner at a table for two. She had a beer mug, nearly empty, and a book, open: *David Copperfield*. I love *David Copperfield*. I was kind of taken with her witty green eyes, too. And her heart-shaped, vixen face. And her short, shaggy, black, black hair. She had her chair tilted back against the wall, her legs extended under the table. Long legs. A long, slender figure. She wore jeans and a frilly peasant blouse and possibly the most adorable red beret on the planet. Maybe she just made it look good, who can say.

"I didn't mean to eavesdrop," she said. "But their stupidity was like cigar smoke, it stank up the whole room. Personally, I wish they'd reverse the rules in here: Let grad students actually light up cigars, just forbid them to speak. I'd prefer the secondhand smoke to the secondhand crap."

I laughed—but she was so cute and sure of herself not to mention cute that I couldn't think of a witty answer. So I laughed some more, feeling like an idiot.

"What on earth were they going on about?" she asked me.

" '*Ode on a Grecian Urn.*' "

"No! God! I cried the first time I read that."

"Me, too!" I blurted out, surprised. "Me, too."

She smiled. She had a pert, mischievous smile. I know this because I studied it at great length. I studied it so long, in fact, the conversation began to lag. When I finally came to myself, I realized with a sense of growing panic that we were in the midst of an awkward silence, a silence that threatened to kill the conversation before it had properly begun. I tried frantically to think of something to say—something that might strike her as erudite yet warm, self-assured yet indicative of inner depth and tenderness.

"Can I, uh, buy you another beer?" I said.

"Anyone can buy me another beer," she answered, "but you can come over and sit with me while I drink it."

I went over and sat with her. She told me her name: Emma McNair. I told her it was a pretty name and she said thank you and the waitress brought us a couple of beers.

I drank. I considered her eyes. I considered that they were very witty. Also very green. "I love *David Copperfield*," I said rather dreamily.

"Yes," said Emma McNair, setting down her glass. "It's the great, good thing, isn't it? Nowadays, you can't get anyone around here to even talk about Dickens, unless it's *Hard Times*. That's the only book boring enough for them to take seriously."

"Don't you hate that?" I said. "Anything that entertains people, gives people joy, does what a book's supposed to do—that's the stuff all these intellectual types look down on for some reason."

"It's too obvious for them. They can't stand the fact that what we all know to be good might actually be good. Their taste has to be special, ever so subtle, unique. In the old days, it was enough for them to elevate an author's second-best book and look down at his best."

"Oh yeah, like, 'We all know *Bleak House* is finer than *Copperfield*; *Anna Karenina* is finer than *War and Peace*; *Emma* is far superior to *Pride and Prejudice*.'"

"Right. Then when we let the supercilious bastards get away with that, they raised the ante. Now it's a sport for them to elevate the absolute worst garbage over greatness."

"You mean, like the French over the English?"

"Oh, it's been such a lovely evening, don't let's spoil it by talking about the French."

"Why are they like that?" I asked her.

"Who, the French? Oh," said Emma. "Intellectuals, you mean. Like your pals."

"They're not my pals anymore, believe me."

"Who knows?" she said. "I guess they feel inferior because all their brains won't buy them an ounce of talent. Or maybe because their minds can't get at things that are only accessible to the spirit—and they have no spirit. So they try to convince themselves that talent and the spirit don't matter or don't exist."

"Yes!" I said, wondering at her insight and her lips. "Yes."

We went on in this vein for some time. And on the face of it, I know it seems like nothing more than the sort of arch repartee two overeducated young people might indulge in, showing off their wit and originality and erudition to each other. But there were actually several remarkable things about the conversation beyond that. Her eyes, for instance. And the fact that a girl that pretty and that smart had asked me to sit with her. And the fact that it *did* go on, minute after unheeded minute, Emma saying things with that pert, mischievous smile of hers and me saying *yes, yes* and then me working up the courage to say things, too, and her *yes, yes* coming back at me. And as perhaps, an hour passed like that, I'll tell you what it felt like, truly, no exaggeration. It felt as if I had found something I had not even known I was looking for, something simple and yet of great importance, like that little piece of a jigsaw puzzle that gives you your first real idea of the whole picture, that piece that causes the whole picture to take shape, to make sense. Until you find that piece, you might put other pieces together here and there, you might snap an entire section into place. But you don't really understand where you're going with it; you can't really get at the point of the thing, the overall image. Then you find that piece, and it isn't a great thrill or a great shock or anything. It just slips into place and you think to yourself, *Of course!* because it's so clear now, it seems so simple now, so obvious what the whole picture is. That was what it felt like to me to sit and drink a beer with Emma McNair.

It was such a natural feeling, in fact, so easy to fall into, that I soon found myself, in my callow, eager, fumbling way, talking to her as if I'd known her for years, as if she were almost an extension of my secret self. Before I realized it, I had launched into Philosophy-of-Life stuff and Hope-and-Dream stuff—just like that, that casually, right there in Carlo's, as if I poured my heart out to everyone I met, as if I had ever poured my heart out to anyone. Shaping the words in front of me with my two hands, I was suddenly babbling to her about literature and writing and the things I loved. Rapping the table with my fingertip and insisting that yes, yes, she was so right, they were spiritual pursuits, *spiritual*, not intellectual. *Don't you see?* I remember saying to her. Don't you see? Without the literature that made us what we are, our spiritual life would end, would devolve into childish fundamentalism and foolish relativism or, just as bad, the sort of quietism that imitates the dead. Beauty and excitement and sentiment—that was what art should be about, an appeal to the whole person, a way of establishing the presence of the whole person just as smoke can show you a beam of light. The triumph of the intellectual, the mere intellectual, why, that was a sure sign that an art form had died—the way painting had died, the way poetry had. Christ, I didn't want to make things for intellectuals to parse and ponder and theorize over! I wanted to make stories, wonderful stories that whole women and men would love. I wanted to make things full of adventure and action and romance like—well, like Shakespeare did, like the sort of things he made—

Well. That's what I found myself saying suddenly. And it was that, that mention of Shakespeare that brought me back to my senses after I'd prattled on for I don't know how long. The mention of Shakespeare and myself in the same sentence clanged like an alarm even in my passion-fuddled head. I felt the blood rush into my cheeks. My hands seized each other in midcareer and sank to the tabletop. I tried to swallow my mortification. I wished the earth would likewise swallow me.

But this Emma—this Emma McNair I had somehow stumbled on—she put her hand out and covered mine with it. "You'll make things like that," she said quietly. "I can see that you will."

I didn't dare glance up at her. "Not to compare myself . . ." I muttered. I sank into my chair and looked away.

I don't know if I would ever have spoken again. To anyone, ever. But Emma took pity on me. She changed the subject.

And she said, "Did I overhear you asking about Wilfred K. Green?"

It was just one more proof of the amazing sparrow-fall providence of our meeting. Because Wilfred K. Green and the Agency and just about everything besides Emma McNair had completely slipped my mind by then. If she hadn't brought it up, I would've been home before I remembered what I was supposed to be doing tonight.

"You said you were writing something about him," she said.

I opened my mouth to repeat my cover story, but I couldn't. I couldn't lie to her. She was too spectacular. I said only, "Do you know someone who's interested in him?"

"Actually, I do," she said. "Well, my father does. My father's a professor here."

I blinked. "McNair? Not Patrick McNair?"

"That's him."

He was not just a professor. He was a famous novelist, too. He had won the Pulitzer Prize, no less, for his novel about a blocked college professor trying to complete a novel about . . . Well, you can figure it out for yourself.

I was impressed. I shouldn't have been. Reading that book had been like smothering under a pillow. But he was famous and had won a big prize, and I was impressed in spite of myself. In truth, I was only saved from saying something genuinely smarmy and sycophantic by the expression on Emma's face, which clearly forbid it.

"Uh . . . so you're saying he knows someone . . . ?"

"Freyberg," she told me. "You were talking about the Wilfred K. Green society? Arnold Freyberg basically was the Wilfred K. Green society. Until the feminists shut him down, that is. He taught the Romantics. Blake mostly. Used to spout all this stuff about natural manhood and womanhood, you know, that drove the fems crazy. They used to actually show up at some of his lectures and shout slogans so no one could hear him. One of them once dumped a pitcher of ice water over his head."

"You're kidding. Was this the M. R. Brinks brigade?" I asked.

"I don't know if she was part of it specifically. But probably. It was your usual band of termagants. Finally, one of them accused Freyberg of sexually harassing her. Nothing was ever proven, but the university showed yellow and forced him to retire."

"How long ago was that?" I asked.

"Not long. Maybe a year or so."

Which would've given him a grudge, I thought. A reason to start sending nasty e-mails to M. R. Brinks.

"You think it was a setup?" I asked Emma. "The sexual harassment thing."

She shrugged. "With the feminists, you know—I wouldn't put it past them. On the other hand, I met him myself at one of my parents' cocktail parties a while back? And either he took a deep and immediate liking to me, or he drools like that on everyone. I mean, to be fair, he was drunk—you know, all these intellectual males get drunk, otherwise how could they stand to be themselves? But it was pretty unpleasant. He started going on and on about this Wilfred K. Green fellow, you know, and how we had to free our bodies from the fear of death or whatever. I can't remember what he said exactly, but I think the idea was that everyone should have sex with everyone else in general, and me with Arnold Freyberg in particular." She shuddered a little.

I laughed—but I was exhilarated. Damned if this didn't sound like the guy I was looking for. A good suspect, at least. Something to go back to the Agency with.

"You know where he lives?" I asked her.

She shook her head. "He's probably in the book. I can ask my father, if you like."

"Oh, you don't have to do that. I'll find him."

"I don't mind. It would give you an excuse to call me. Would you call me, if you had an excuse?"

"Emma, with a phone and enough courage, I wouldn't even need the excuse."

She had a funny little elfin nose. With freckles across the bridge of it. It wrinkled right at the freckle line when she tried not to blush, not to grin.

She took a pen from her purse. Wrote her phone number on a Carlo's coaster. She wrote very carefully, slowly, talking as she wrote.

"Now, of course, you understand, all my confidence and sophistication and whatnot are complete bullshit beneath the surface. I'm just a girl in real life, and I'll be very hurt if you don't use this right soon."

She handed the coaster to me. Her eyes were misty suddenly, vulnerable.

"I have a cell phone with me," I offered. "I could call you right now."

She laughed. "You can wait a few days—or whatever guys do to seem cool."

"I think it's already painfully obvious how uncool I am."

"Oh, you're pretty damn cool, boyo. You just don't know it yet."

I had the weirdest feeling: the feeling that if she said this, contrary to all indications though it was, it must be so; and that if I was actually lucky enough to see more of her, I would find out all sorts of similarly wonderful things about myself.

"Well—" she said. She gathered her purse, pushed her chair back from the table. Stood.

Startled, I got to my feet as well. "Wait—" She was tall, I saw now, almost as tall as I was, and our eyes met. "Why are you going?"

Emma smiled the mischievous smile and her green eyes were bright and her freckled nose wrinkled and her short-cropped hair was black as black and the beret was still adorable. "Because," she said, "we seem to've gotten it just right, don't we?"

I tried to answer yes, managed to nod.

"Well, you don't mess around with that, boyo."

I watched her walk across the room. Watched her jeans, watched the whole long line of her. At the door, she paused. She looked back at me. I touched two fingers to my forehead in salute. She laughed. Then she was gone.

TWENTY-ONE

Out on the sidewalk, out in the night, students passed singly and in pairs. Under the lines of low buildings, under the spindly urban trees, under the moon. Lugging backpacks, riding bikes, kicking skateboards. Talking with each other, lost in daydreams alone.

I watched them as I wandered back to my car. Each of them trying to seem like the person he wanted to become. Some looked like academics with frizzly beards and others like radicals with nose rings and tattoos. There were feminists with lace-up boots and tough guys with shaved heads and beauty queens and gym rats and all the rest. Trying to project their characters on the world, hoping the world might notice or care, hoping to shape the nature of experience with their costumes and their poses.

I felt for them in their youthful confusion. Sure, their efforts to "prepare a face to meet the faces that you meet," looked silly and childish to me now, but I reminded myself with a paternal smile that I had been like that once, too. In fact, it was only about two hours ago. Before I had gone into Carlo's and met Emma and everything had become so clear and simple to me. That was the secret to this life business, all right. All one had to do was be oneself and meet Emma. I don't know why I hadn't thought of it before.

Now, at nine o'clock or so, it was hard to remember what I had been like in the past—at, say, seven. Trying to imitate Bishop or Weiss or the heroes of fiction. It was hard to recall feeling that sort of insecurity about my identity and my future. I couldn't even imagine why anyone would live in such a state of foolish bewilderment. I wanted to stop one of these young people, talk sense to him, give him the benefit of my experience. *In the landscape of every life,* I would say to him, fondly clapping him on the shoulder, *there is a place like Carlo's, my young friend. It may not be called Carlo's, you understand, I'm speaking metaphorically, but it will be your Carlo's as Carlo's, the actual Carlo's, called Carlo's, is my Carlo's . . .*

Well, I wanted to talk to someone, anyway, that's my point. I wanted someone to marvel at this high state of clarity I was in. I wanted someone to admire the new way I could now move serenely through the existential chaos of life without hiding behind the mannerisms of a constructed persona.

So it was with a little inner starburst of excitement that I remembered that I was supposed to call Sissy, to let her know if I'd come up with anything on the Brinks investigation. It was just after nine, as I say, not too late. I unhooked my cell phone from my belt as I reached my car. Dialed as I settled in behind the wheel.

Sissy sounded distracted when she answered. I heard a noise in the background, running water maybe.

"Oh gee, sweetheart," she said in her girlish whisper, "I can't talk right now. Do you think you could maybe stop by on your way home?" She said she would be grateful, as she had a meeting with Weiss early in the morning and wanted to have the latest information on her cases.

For my part, I was glad to have somewhere else to go. It was a fine, successful feeling: finishing up an investigation and getting a girl's phone number and then heading back to the city to deliver a late-night report to my boss. It beat the hell out of going home, anyway—drinking alone, jerking off, watching TV until I could sleep.

Sissy's place was on Jackson, a modest block of town houses on the steep plummet down from Nob Hill to Chinatown. It was the first time I had ever been there. When I came through the door to her apartment, I remember I got a quick impression that everything inside was very fluffy. Shag rugs and plush furniture and a couple of cats and a lot of family photos in spongy heartshape frames.

And Sissy. She was fluffy, too. Wearing a white terry cloth robe, her hair up in a pink towel. I guess she'd just come out of the shower or bath. Her delicate features seemed very naked, scrubbed pink and white. A vee of naked flesh was visible beneath the hollow of her throat.

There was a counter at the edge of the kitchenette. I sat on one of the barstools there while Sissy poured me a glass of wine. I felt very sophisticated, bringing my report to her when she was barely dressed like this. I felt like a real investigator, drinking wine with her, discussing a case. The coaster with Emma's phone number on it was in my back pocket, and I remembered the way Emma had put her hand over my hands and how I felt that everything was finally coming together in my life and making sense. And now, also thanks to Emma, I had done well in my work, too, and was giving my report to Sissy, my boss. I felt very sophisticated and successful and good.

Sissy perched on the stool next to mine, tugging the bathrobe together to cover her pink-and-white legs. She held me with her moistly maternal gaze while I told her about Arnold Freyberg, the Blake professor with a penchant for Wilfred K. Green. I told her how he'd been chased out of his job by the feminists—maybe by M. R. Brinks herself. I left Emma out of it—I didn't want to tell her about Emma—but I did mention that Freyberg was once seen drunk at an academic party, quoting Green in an attempt to seduce a much younger woman.

"Wow," said Sissy. "That's good. That's very promising. He sounds like he could be our guy." She cocked her head to one side, admiring me as if I were the backside of a newborn babe. Her scrubbed face practically beamed—she seemed just that enamored of my brilliance. "I'm so proud of you, sweetheart," she said ever so nicely. "I knew you could do it."

I shrugged, maybe blushed. She laughed and put her hand on my cheek again in that motherly way she had. This time, though, her hand lingered there. There was a pause, and her gaze turned meaningful. With a little self-conscious smile, she leaned over and kissed me. Just a gentle peck at first, but her lips remained against mine, and they were warm and giving. Soon I put my hand on the back of her neck and pressed into her and it was not a gentle kiss anymore and my tongue was in her mouth. We both stood up off our stools and my hands slipped into her bathrobe and I felt the shock of her skin and how soft she was.

The next thing I knew we were on the sofa, me with my pants off, her with her robe splayed open. She was the oldest woman I'd ever been with, and her breasts seemed very rich and ripe, her body very deep to me somehow. The pink towel had come undone and her golden hair was falling wet against her cheek. My face pressed into it. It smelled wonderfully of shampoo.

She shed tears when she came, which I had never seen before, and the way her soft, sweet, familiar, motherly whisper became a wild, high, yearning cry was incredibly exciting to me and drove me on to the end.

Then I was sprawled spent on the shag rug with Sissy curled up next to me making little-girl noises and calling me darling and sweetheart and asking wasn't I her baby, wasn't I going to be her sweet baby now, wasn't I?

I stared up at the ceiling and thought of Emma and I wished to God that I never had done it.

PART THREE China Basin

TWENTY-TWO

Weiss stood musing on a field of flowers. Dahlias, a carpet of yellow and violet and orange. Head hung, hands in his pockets, he gazed over them, all but unseeing. He was thinking about the letters, the e-mails to Professor Brinks.

Their phrases haunted him. *I will remake you into your body . . . The world doesn't need any more big ideas or grand theories . . . Why do you cling to them, woman? The moment of desire, Marianne! Don't try to sell your cant to me. The world craves you naked on your knees . . .*

He had reread the passages several times last night. He'd crept back to them as if they were an addiction. Their sensual images stayed with him, kept him awake for hours, blossoming into fantasies. Sometimes they were fantasies about Sissy or M. R. Brinks herself or other women he'd known or seen. Mostly, though, he imagined Julie Wyant, the angel-faced hooker he'd never even met. He lay in bed in the dark with his eyes open, thinking about her. Conjuring the touch of her body, the liquid silk of her red-gold hair. He would turn onto one side and onto the other. His pillow grew clammy with sweat. He told himself again that he could not try to find her because Ben Fry would follow him and hunt her down. But he felt if he did not try, he would die of his longing . . .

He lifted his eyes from the dahlia bed. The white dome of the Flower Conservatory rose out of the surrounding palm trees, the eucalyptus and the oak. Sunlight glinted on its spire where it touched the blue sky. He turned from it, looked down and west into the mistier depths of the park's forest. He saw Professor Brinks striding toward him along the path.

She was much as before, a sturdy little figure with a marching stride. A gray jacket this time, but just as angular and slashing as the last one, the navy one. And her black slacks were creased for the kill. Still, Weiss, with all those fantasies in his head, all those images from the e-mails, got a sexy little jolt from the sight of her. Her grim, pretty features between curtains of black hair. The clap of her heels on the macadam.

The world craves you naked on your knees . . .

"Mr. Weiss," she said.

She shook his hand briskly. With her free hand she adjusted the shoulder strap of her huge purse or briefcase or whatever it was. Weiss, hovering over her in that protective way he had with women, noted the tension at the corners of her mouth, at the corners of her eyes, too. She was worried about this meeting.

"Have you found him?" she said. There were no other preliminaries.

"I think so," he told her. "I have to be sure before I can give you a name. It should be by tomorrow, the day after at the latest."

"Well . . . good. Good, then." She looked up at him uncertainly. Wondering, obviously, why he had asked her to come.

But he didn't tell her. Not yet. He wasn't sure how to put it yet. He'd rehearsed a lot of tactful phrases, but now they all seemed stilted and phony to him. Stalling for time, he began to stroll along the path back the way she had come. She strolled beside him, anxious, waiting.

After a moment, his hands went into his pockets again. He flashed a smile down at her, a kindly smile. For all she was dressed up as a man—so he thought of it—he found her compellingly feminine this time. Again, it was probably the effect of those e-mail raptures floating around in his brain. *I will pour wine into the hollow of your throat and drink it as it spills down between your breasts and over your belly . . .* Anyway, he felt very tender toward her.

"I just wanted to consult with you before I followed up on this," he started. "I just wanted to confirm that you were . . . well . . . certain about going on."

There was a hitch of silence. "Well, of course," she answered then. "Of course I am. Why wouldn't I be?"

He didn't answer. They strolled together slowly, big figure and small, he, in his wrinkled houndstooth jacket, as disheveled as she was crisp. The lush summer trees pressed in on either side of them. The path became a narrow green gallery under a strip of sky.

"Well," he fumbled on. "There's the money, for one thing. There'll be expenses, more expenses, involved and . . ." His voice trailed off. "Uh . . ."

"And what?" said M. R. Brinks, her nervous, serious little face turned up to him.

"Well, you know. And the consequences," said Weiss. "I wanted to make sure you had a good idea of the consequences, of where this could go."

The professor's laugh was a surprisingly fluty trill. "Oh, what's the matter, Mr. Weiss? Are you afraid I'll kill him?"

"No," said Weiss firmly—this was the point he'd been trying to get to. "I'm afraid you'll be disappointed in him. I'm afraid he'll . . . well . . . you know: break your heart."

She stopped laughing, stopped in her tracks, stopped on what seemed the edge of a reply. She gaped up at him. Weiss gazed over her head, into the trees, studied the empty distance so as not to embarrass her. All the same, he saw her moisten her lips with the tip of her tongue.

"These cyber relationships . . ." he went on gently. "We've handled a few of them. They tend to end up badly in this sort of circumstance. I mean, when one of the people doesn't want to be found."

"What are you implying?" snapped Professor Brinks. Her voice dropped to a hiss as an ancient man and wife hobbled by on the path, going arm in arm. "What are you . . . Why are you saying this to me?"

And Weiss did look down at her now. His heavy features seemed all the heavier with the weight of his sympathy.

The professor seemed unable to bear his gaze, unable to bear the fact that, clearly, he had guessed the truth. She began to protest, but it petered out in a series of choking splutters. Finally, miserably, she just managed to say, "What business is it of yours? What business?"

"None," Weiss told her. "But since you were concerned about publicity and so forth, I thought it was my responsibility to warn you before I go ahead. I mean, if you think you've fallen in love with this man—"

"*Stop! Ssh! Stop!*" Panicked, she looked every which way around her. But the old couple was gone, and there was no one else in sight on the tree-lined corridor.

Still, for another moment or two, M.R. Brinks kept looking here and there—all over, only not at Weiss. She avoided looking at Weiss. Then—in a gesture that squeezed the detective's romantic heart—she brushed a fingertip quick as quick against the corner of her eye. Before a tear could fall there, before it could even form. She shifted round that huge briefcase of hers. Unzipped it. Rooted in it, her nose twitching.

Weiss, of course, being how he was, would've probably slayed a dragon for her at that point. But the best he could do was fish out the little Kleenex packet he kept in his jacket pocket; offer her a tissue. She took it and tamped fiercely at one nostril, then the other.

"How did you know?" she asked him. "Did you talk to him? Did he say something about me? How did you know?"

He shook his head. "To be frank with you, the whole story wasn't all the way believable from the start. Why would you let it go on for nine months like that and then suddenly hire me? Why was he the one who changed his address—unless he was the one avoiding e-mails from you? But basically, it was the letters—once I understood what they were. I mean, the first time you read them, sure, all the sex stuff sort of jumps out at you. But if you really go over them, it's pretty obvious they're half of a conversation or dialogue or what-have-you. You know? 'Why do you cling to your grand theories? Don't try to sell your cant to me.' It's one side of a . . . philosophical discussion, I guess you'd call it. It's pretty obvious that someone was answering back."

She sniffed harshly. Tartly, she said, "Well, I'm gratified you took the time to make such a close textual analysis, Mr. Weiss."

He couldn't help but lift one bushy eyebrow. She had no idea how close.

"I'm sure this is all just . . . very funny to you," she said. "I'm sure all the boys in your office got together for a good patriarchal laugh . . ." But the end of this faded away to nothing. Because she looked up into his face. His weary, ugly, hangdog face. And it must've been hard for her to imagine him laughing like that. The curses she brought down upon her own head in the dark watches—that she was a hypocrite, a fool, a masochist, whatever—none of that would've echoed back to her from Weiss.

"Oh!" She broke finally under the weight of his compassion. She had to dab at her eyes for several moments before she could go on. "I don't know why I ever answered him in the first place. That first letter he wrote me—well, it was just hate mail, wasn't it? I get letters like that all the time. I never answer, but . . . but there was something in it . . . something . . . out of the ordinary. I don't know." She frowned, shook her head fiercely. "It was harassment. Pure and simple. I told him it was harassment. I told him to stop right then and there. I did. But he wouldn't stop. He wrote back. And then I wrote back. And then, after a while . . . I didn't want him to stop anymore."

Weiss nodded. Sad-eyed, hands in his pockets. Hanging over her like some kind of great old tree.

"And it just snuck up on me, I guess," she murmured. "I thought I was being so clever, you know. Deconstructing all the sexist assumptions behind the things he wrote. But all the while I was deconstructing, the things he wrote made me feel . . . well . . ."

"Sure," said Weiss. "I understand."

She brushed this off impatiently. "Anyway," she said. "After nine months of correspondence, I thought . . . well, I thought it might be nice if we could meet, you know, in person. But he wouldn't. I tried to convince him, but he became . . . adamant. He threatened to break it off. To stop writing. Change his address. That made me . . . I panicked, I guess. Got confused. I was afraid of losing him, but at the same time . . . I wanted more, you know. I wanted to go beyond just . . . just words. At one point, I actually had a friend—a friend who knows computers—try to trace him, but . . ." Her voice failed her here a moment. "Finally, I just . . . I *pleaded* with him." She used the word purposely, glanced at the detective to see if he disdained her for it or pitied her. But there was just that face, that Weiss. And she found herself confessing to him: "I pleaded with him. These long . . . truly pitiful letters. Begging him. Literally *begging* him to please meet with me, to let me feel . . . anything . . . his hand on my face . . . anything. I guess that's what did it. Scared him off or whatever. Suddenly—without even saying goodbye . . ." She finished the sentence with a forlorn gesture: He was gone.

Weiss began to speak, then stopped. It was a young couple passing this time, he a reed in faded jeans and a torn T-shirt, she bursting like fruit out of her halter top and her cutoff shorts. Weiss waited till they were well out of earshot before he said, "Look, Professor Brinks, you're obviously a very smart woman—"

Professor Brinks snorted.

"You must've thought this through," Weiss went on. "If he doesn't want to meet with you he probably has a reason—I mean, it probably doesn't even have anything to do with you. He may just be—"

"Married," Brinks said. "Or gay or a woman or deformed or ten years old. Believe me, yes, I've thought of everything. And if anyone ever found out I was doing this . . . I mean, if, as you say, he ever made my letters to him public . . ." She stared down at the path, seemed to stare right through the pavement into the earth. "The things I've said. The things I've promised to do. My reputation . . . my work would be . . ." She pressed her lips together. Her whole narrow frame quivered like a plucked bowstring. "God, God!" she burst out, lifting her eyes now to the sky. "It's all so *fucking* pathetic!"

Weiss shrugged. That's all. As if to say, We are what we are. Then he paused for a moment. To let her settle herself. To let her run over again in her mind the consequences of going forward, the possible consequences to her work, to her life, to her dreams, the potential for catastrophe. Then, when he felt certain she had considered it all, held it up to the light, he asked her, "So what do you want me to do, Professor?"

"Oh, find him!" she answered without hesitation. Her eyes were blurry now, her face pinched, her mascara smudged. "Please, Mr. Weiss! I don't care about the rest of it. I don't care about anything anymore. I just have to find him. Please."

TWENTY-THREE

She walked away unsteadily on the gray path between the trees. He watched her, standing where he was, hands in his pockets still.

He envied her, the truth be told. He knew it couldn't have been easy for her to confess to him—even to confess to herself—the things she felt, the way she had betrayed her own philosophy. But at least she had the courage to go through with it, to make her move. At least she'd plunked her money on her passion, and to hell with the usual human charade.

The path curved in the middle distance. It vanished in the trees. Brinks, her steps dreamy and faltering, rounded the bend. Another moment, she was out of sight.

Weiss straightened with a breath. He turned away.

He drove back to the Agency, heavy-hearted. Letting his dull, gray Taurus coast through the swift flat avenues toward the denser traffic of the hills. There was M. R. Brinks, he thought, arched like a high-board diver in the oh-so-hazardous air, and here he was, earthbound, paralyzed. Sweating over his weird little obsession with a whore he'd never met, stewing in his helpless paranoia about a killer he'd never seen.

All he had to do, he thought, was turn the steering wheel. Guide his car to the freeway. Point it north toward Paradise. Julie Wyant would be long gone from there by now, but it would be a start, anyway. It would be something.

Sick of himself, he continued on into the city center.

He arrived at the Agency silent and louring. Thumped down the hall toward his office. He passed me in my alcove on his way. There was Sissy, perched on my desk. Beaming down on me moonily. Picking lint off my shoulder with a proprietary air. I was trying my best to pretend she wasn't there, or to pretend I was too busy stuffing invoices into envelopes even to notice her. Because how could I call Emma with her hanging over me like that? How could I call Emma at all before I'd extricated myself from this catastrophe?

As Weiss came by, Sissy quickly slipped away. But Weiss saw her. Of course he did. He saw and understood it all, the basics of it, anyway. He groaned inwardly as he went past. Sissy now, too, he thought. Sissy, whom he idolized. Whom he could never have approached himself. Christ, the whole summer world was just one big fucking love song today, wasn't it?

He stepped into his office, shut the door behind him. Lumbered to his desk. Dropped into his swivel chair. Jabbed the Internet key on his computer. There was a three-note chime at once: a waiting e-mail. From Bishop. What now?

He opened it up.

Just one big fucking love song, he thought.

Weiss, the e-mail began, *something happened.*

TWENTY-FOUR

Bishop woke up that morning wrapped around a naked woman—but who? And where, come to think of it. Where the hell was he? All he knew at first was that the woman's face was pressed to his face. And that her breath was stale and beery.

He drew back. Tried to force his eyes open to get a better look at her. She was a coarse-featured brunette, it turned out. Maybe part Mexican. Her arms and legs were draped all over him. Their torsos were together, loin to loin, as if he'd fallen asleep inside her.

He untangled their limbs. Rolled her onto her back. Watched her heavy breasts drop to opposite sides of her. Groggy, he cast an eye down over her thick waist, her broad hips, the lush patch of black hair between her legs. He wondered how much he'd drunk last night. Or smoked. Or snorted or swallowed.

He gave a soft groan. Dragged his hand down from his forehead to his chin. But damn it, the woman was still there when he looked again. Sleeping on, snoring quietly, her mouth wide open. Well, there'd been worse, Bishop thought. He'd woken up with a hell of a lot worse.

He propped himself up on one hand. Looked around. Yeah, okay, now it started to come back to him. He was on a mattress on the floor. And there was Charlie on another mattress against the opposite wall. Naked on his back. Like a statue of a dead guy with all those muscles. The blonde nestled on one side of him looked about fourteen. The dyed blonde curled in his other arm jutted her apple-round ass Bishop's way. There were dark gray stains on the bedsheet under her. Motor oil. Sure, it was all coming back. He remembered the business with the motor oil.

He remembered where he was now, too. In the gang's clubhouse. A big old two-story pinewood cabin at the end of a tree-lined lane somewhere. He was in a room upstairs. Nothing on the floor but the mattresses and the women, him and Charlie, a couple of bottles of beer. Nothing on the walls but splintering wood panels and a winged Harley symbol and a forty-mile-an-hour speed limit sign riddled with bullet holes.

Tequila, he thought. Beer and tequila, that's what it was. And a pipeful of meth. And then the Mexican girl gave him a tab of something before leading him upstairs. Maria, her name was. Or maybe he just called her Maria.

His head was starting to throb. His stomach felt liquid, churning. Slowly, he managed to sit up on the edge of the mattress. He massaged his temple. Squinted at one of the windows on the wall above his head. He saw treetops. Morning mist moving in the branches. Sunlight beginning to push its way through in misty beams. It was pretty. He forgot himself for a moment, looking up at it.

Then he remembered that he'd killed Mad Dog and he felt like shit.

He cursed under his breath. He wished that hadn't happened. Not that he was sorry for Mad Dog or anything. The fat son of a bitch had needed killing. It had probably improved his personality. Plus it was self-defense, there was no question about that. Bishop remembered that bazooka of a pistol pointed at him while he was cruising the edge of the canyon at eighty per. So fuck Mad Dog. Death was too good for him.

Still. He probably shouldn't have let it happen. He probably could've stopped it somehow before it got out of hand like that. Weiss would be pissed. Worse. He'd be disappointed in that silent, enormous Weiss-like way of his. *Don't cross the line,* he'd said. *Don't cross the line.* Well, Bishop had crossed it, all right. There'd been all that beer and Honey stealing glances at him and Mad Dog staring at him in the gnarly corner. He had felt that fine, clear feeling that always came to him with the nearness of man-to-man combat, and he had crossed the line, no question, no turning back.

He sat on the edge of the mattress, knees raised. He pressed the heels of his palms into his eyes. And oh yeah. He remembered standing at the side of the road. Looking down the slope to where Mad Dog's body lay. It had been quiet there for a few moments. There'd been

crickets and cicadas, the dying fires from the crash. It had been peace-
ful in a funny kind of way. Then the thunder of motorcycles had risen
again until it filled the woods. Cobra and Charlie—they had turned
around and come looking for him.

They pulled their bikes onto the shoulder next to him. Motors running, headlights on. He had to lift his hand to block the glare. He remembered how their dark figures had come out of that glare like
walking shadows. When they came closer to him, he could see they
were grinning like devils.

Cobra went down the hill with a flashlight. When he came back
up, his teeth glinted in the moonlight and his eyes gleamed.

"Looks like the Dog had himself a little accident," he said.

Charlie chuckled. "You gotta be careful on these roads for certain."

Cobra chuckled also. "Fucking A," he said.

So that was it. Mad Dog was dead.

Bishop said nothing. He watched the two others smirking and
chuckling. He felt the pistol Cobra had given him pressed into the
small of his back. He wanted to pull it out and put a couple of slugs
into the pair of them. He would do Charlie first, one in the forehead so
his grin froze on his dead face. Then he would put one into Cobra's
belly, low, so he would have a nice long time to get the joke.

But that was just a pleasant fantasy. There was really nothing
Bishop could do about this. He had let things go too far. He could've
stopped it, but he had crossed the line. Shit.

Here, in Cobra's clubhouse, sitting naked on the mattress, he raised
his face, shook his head. He remembered everything now. He remembered how, after a while, standing out there on the roadside, Cobra had
reached out and grabbed his neck and given him a playful shake. Cobra
had laughed, his V-shaped face creasing upward, and Charlie had
laughed beside him.

"Time to partay, my brother," Cobra had said to Bishop there on
the road above the canyon. "Time to celebrate, dude. You're one of us."

TWENTY-FIVE

Bishop snagged a half-empty beer bottle by the neck. He took a swig. It settled his stomach. He worked his way to his feet. Found his jeans on the threshold. Pulled them on.

He wandered down a dark hall. Found a bathroom. Pissed. He wandered down a dark stair. Found the living room: an epic wreckage. Bottles, bags, pizza boxes, CDs strewn all over the furniture. And Shorty, fully dressed, splayed out in a big old leather recliner, fast asleep. There was a dead soldier of tequila under his boot heels, an Xbox controller held loosely in his hand. He must've ditched his old lady at some point and joined them.

Tipping up his beer bottle, Bishop wandered on.

He came to the doorway of a room stacked with boxes. Computers, radios, TVs. Stolen shit. Jacked off some truck or out of some warehouse somewhere. Who the hell knew what these asswipes were into?

You're one of us.

Yeah, right. Bishop peeled off the jamb, slouched on into the kitchen. He sure wished he hadn't killed Mad Dog, though. It was a weight on his gut. He shouldn't have gotten so carried away in the moment. He shouldn't have crossed the line.

He came into an old-fashioned country kitchen. Big black gas stove. Black-and-white tiling on the floor and the walls. Kind of weird the way everything was in its place in here. As if it were the one room in the whole house no one had entered.

But there was what he was looking for: a door, a screen door to the outside. A chance to get some fresh air, yeah. He was going to puke or pass out if he didn't.

Thick-headed, weak-bellied, he rolled on through. Came out atop a short flight of concrete steps overlooking the backyard.

The air felt good, all right. Cool and damp and refreshing. He breathed it in gratefully. Sipping his beer, surveying the yard. It was a misty, shifting landscape. Twisted oaks stood ghostly in the fog. Yellow leaves stirred on the grass at his feet like autumn stirring. And pale, sturdy fingers of sunlight stretched down from the unseen sky, fading to nothing before they ever reached the earth.

He looked to the far side of the half acre. The mist was thickest there. It churned and drifted as if it were a living mass. Dark shapes rose out of it and sank away in a sort of dance of coming and going. He watched it a while in a morose and dreamy daze.

And soon, and slow by slow, he became aware there was a figure—a figure at the center of it. A human form, sharply present and then spectral and dim and then sharply present again, hunkered in the morass like a garden gargoyle. It took a moment before Bishop realized it was a living man.

Cobra.

Bishop came down the steps, ambled across the lawn toward him. Another memory began to nag at him. Something had happened. Something important. About Cobra. About Cobra and Honey . . .

That's right: They had had a fight. A bad one. A loud one, anyway. It happened when the other girls turned up. Everyone was stoned and the girls started grinding to some classic White Trash and Honey had seen how things were going and she started screaming over the blasting music, saying she wasn't one of Cobra's whores, she wasn't going to be treated like one of Cobra's whores. Cobra cursed her. He was drunk as hell by then. He said he'd fuck whoever he wanted, when he wanted. He was a free man. Honey had stormed out, her blonde hair flying behind her. Bishop remembered that: her blonde hair flying. A minute later, in the lull between "Let's Get It On" and "I've Got News," they'd heard her pickup's engine kick over. They'd heard the truck bounding down the long dirt driveway to the road below.

Well, Bishop thought. That was good. That was something anyway.

A memory to lift his spirits, a little counterbalance to the sorry-ass business of killing Mad Dog. Honey and Cobra had had a flame-out. That was excellent. Bishop's offer to take her away from all this might be looking a lot better to her now.

After Honey was gone, Bishop remembered, Cobra had started to party hard. He drank hard and prowled around the middle of the floor and made a speech about some bullshit or other. *We're, like, the edge, we're, like, the new thing, we're, like, the old, the oldest thing again. Like brothers, man, like all brothers bonded together against everything, against all the so-called rules and codes. It's just us instead now. From now on. Everything is us, just who we are. We're men. We're men.* Then he roared like an animal, shaking his two fists at the ceiling. Finally he staggered off to his bedroom with one of the girls in tow, a narrow-hipped teenager with a glance full of thrilling mischief.

And now here he was out here, squatting on his heels in the grass. Wearing only his underwear, his white briefs. His body was all ropy muscle, but it seemed gaunt and fragile somehow.

Bishop stood over him. Cobra didn't turn or look his way. He just went on peering out into the mist.

They were at the border of a ridge, Bishop saw. The ground dropped down steeply just beyond. Through the shifting gray curtain, Bishop caught glimpses of the city stretched out below them, the broad plain of white buildings colored orange and rose with the morning light. The bay lay beyond them. He got only a hint of it. And only a hint also of the blue sky that lay out there beyond the bay. But as far as he could make out, it was clear as could be on the flatlands and the water. It seemed the fog was all up here, all gathered on the high ground.

Now at last, Cobra looked up at him.

Whoa, Bishop thought.

The outlaw was ashen. His face was sunken, ravaged. It looked like a skull but with bloodshot eyes. The flesh of his cheeks hung slack as if it were melting off him. The vee of his mouth hung slack, and there was drool glistening at the corners. His head bobbed slightly on his neck as if he were an old man, too weak to hold it steady.

"Man," said Bishop with a gesture of his bottle, "you look like I feel."

"Oh, bullshit. Bullshit to that, *compañero*." Cobra sneered irritably. "You don't fucking feel like this. Believe me. You don't have the *insight* to feel this bad. *Comprende?* Mr. Vroom-Vroom Bang-Bang. This is deep, bleak shit here. This is dark-night-of-the-soul-style shit. You gotta know something to be where I am, dude. You gotta *be* somebody all the way down to the ground."

Bishop gestured again, by way of a shrug. "Well, 'scuse my ass," he said. "I thought you were just out here mooning over some pussy."

"Oh, fuck her. What, you think this is about Honey? What do you think? You think she's gone and I'm out here crying? You think I let my old lady tear out over a couple of spare hardbellies?"

"Beats me," Bishop answered mildly. "She didn't look too pleased, you gotta admit."

Cobra gave a single miserable snort. "Fuck her," he repeated in a mutter. "She can go if she wants. She can go anytime she wants. Long as she comes back when I call her. She comes back or I drag her back. She knows it, too." He pointed a finger up at Bishop. "And everyone else better know it. You hear me? You all better remember what I told you last night in the Alley. Don't give me that what-the-fuck stare, man, I've seen you eyeball her. And eyeball away. It's a free country. But don't you go near her unless you're tired of living. There aren't enough miles in the road to put between us, dude, so help me, you go near her."

"Whatever," Bishop said.

Cobra lowered his finger. Lowered his shoulders. Turned again, the energy gone out of him. In his gargoyle crouch, his forearms resting on his raised knees, he went back to brooding on the depths of the fog. "Man," he said heavily. "Man oh man. Everything I fuck turns to shit. Everything I touch gets fucked. What the fuck's the point? You know? You try to do something with your fucking life, you try to make your life about something . . . Why don't women get that? Why do they always wanna make everything small again? She thinks I'm just gonna live and die, just live and breed and die?"

Bishop rubbed his eyes. His head hurt and his brain was running on slow. What the hell was Cobra talking about, anyway? And what was he—Bishop—what was he doing here? He was supposed to be doing something, wasn't he? Sure he was. It wasn't as if all this were real. Him and the gang and Cobra. It was bullshit. It was just another assignment for Weiss and the Agency. What with Mad Dog dying and with the booze last night and the crystal and him and Charlie upstairs on the mattresses humping the hardbellies in syncopation, things had gotten all weird and dreamy for a little while there. It had almost started to feel as if he'd actually become part of this whole business. Like Cobra said: *One of us.*

But no way, not hardly. There was something else. Something he was supposed to be doing here. The job. That's it: the big job. He was supposed to find out about this big job Cobra was planning to pull off.

"A man wants to be . . . part of something," Cobra grumbled on to the shifting mists. "Part of something big, you know. It's not about . . . it's not about what you do. The little shit you do. Y'know? It's about—what it means. What it all means."

"I thought you already had this covered," Bishop said. "All this big-time shit. That's what you told me. You had some big job all lined up already. Big plan, big money, that's what you said. Shit, that's what *I'm* here for, I know that much."

For another moment, Cobra crouched there, muttering at the fog, wallowing in his exquisite dejection. Then, as if he'd just gotten the joke, he made a noise, a sort of chuckling noise deep in his throat. He laughed. Suddenly, loudly, hoarsely: "Ha, ha!" He slapped his knee. He pushed off his knee and stood out of his crouch, his ravaged face coming level with Bishop's. The fog vortexed behind him and haloed his head with a circle of sunlit sky.

"Jigger my zesty carbuncles if you aren't dead right, my brother," he said. His face was still an ashen mess, a skull of melting flesh, but now his bloodshot eyes were bright. He grabbed hold of Bishop's neck the way he had last night on the edge of the canyon. "Wiggle my mossy lingam if you aren't dead-on, one hundred percent correctamento. You bring me back to myself, dude. Big plan, big money. That's it. That's it exactly. Right?" The circle of sky opened, and the sunshine fell on both of them. "We have to get ready for that. Honey, too. She won't miss that. I know she won't want to miss that. And you—" His hand cracked smartly as he slapped Bishop's naked back. "I guess you've paid your dues, haven't you? Huh? With poor old Mad Dog? I guess last night you sure as shit paid your dues." He slung his arm around Bishop's shoulder. "It's time to tell you all."

TWENTY-SIX

It was still morning, just the tail end of morning, when Bishop got back to the apartment in Berkeley. There was a lot on his mind, a lot racing through his mind. Cobra had told him the plan for the Big Job and there was Honey to consider and Mad Dog's death—all of it jumbled together. He had to make sense of it. He had to figure out what he was going to do next.

He shut the door behind him. Trod wearily down a little hall. He dropped his leather jacket on the floor as he went. Stripped his T-shirt off, dropped that, dropped his jeans. He was naked by the time he padded into the bathroom. A trail of clothes lay in the hall behind him.

The bathroom was cramped, mildewed. The light here was pale and yellow. There was an old claw-footed tub in one corner. Bishop high-stepped into it. He turned the shower on. Stood under the nozzle. The shocking cold water spat down his back, turned shocking hot. He bowed his head and let it stream over him.

It was a difficult business, he thought. He had to get Honey away. That was the main thing. That was his assignment. But it wasn't enough. He had to get her out clean, out clear. If she just walked, Cobra would come after her. No matter where she went, no matter how long it took, he would find her, bring her back or kill her, just like he said. Then there was the law to worry about—they'd want her, too. And there was Weiss to worry about, with all his cop-style rules and cop-style justice. It was hard to know where Weiss would stand. It was all hard, all complicated. A difficult business.

He turned off the shower. Grabbed a towel off the stack on the hamper. Dried himself on his way down the hall to the bedroom, leaving a trail of water where the trail of his clothes left off.

He pulled jeans and a T-shirt out of an old dresser. Pulled them on. Padded barefoot back to the living room.

He set his palmtop up on the table again with its portable keyboard in place. He had to start with Weiss. He had to get Weiss in on it. He fetched his cigarettes while the little machine booted up. He sat down at the table. Lit a smoke. Set it to burn in a tinfoil ashtray. He positioned his hands on the palmtop's keys.

Weiss, he typed. And then he stopped. Drew back his hands. He would have to tell him about Mad Dog. This wasn't going to be easy.

He set his fingers back on the keys. Took a breath—

The door buzzer sounded. Bishop cursed. He took the palmtop off the keyboard. Dumped both pieces in the table's drawer. The door buzzer sounded again. Bishop went to the door and swung it open.

There was Honey, standing in the hall.

It was a thrill to see her. He let no sign of it cross his face, but it was a jolting thrill. She'd dumped the bare-bellied biker chick look. She was wearing a crisp white blouse, khaki slacks. She looked like the kid in her father's snapshots. The all-American girl. His feeling for her washed over him as if he had forgotten it. But he had not forgotten it.

He stood back. She walked in past him with a glance. He took a breath of her scent as she went by. Maybe she noticed. Anyway, she smiled.

He shut the door. Came out of the foyer to lean against the living room archway. From there, he watched her walk to his table. He watched the curve of her slacks as she bent forward. She took the cigarette from the tinfoil ashtray. She turned to face him. Perched herself on the table. Brought his cigarette to her lips.

"So what are you?" she asked him. "Are you, like, a cop?"

Bishop shook his head, his gaze moving over her. The big windows were at her back. From where he stood, she was framed in the rectangle of the billboard outside, positioned next to the gigantic woman in the bank advertisement, her gigantic smiling face.

She took a drag of smoke. Narrowed her eyes at him. "So then my father sent you." She sniffed, turned away, crushed out the cigarette in the ashtray. "I hope he's paying you well."

"Pretty well, yeah," Bishop said. "I guess he doesn't want to see his daughter go to prison."

"You mean he doesn't want the media to see his daughter go to prison. He doesn't want his daughter making any headlines that might mess up his chance at a Senate seat."

"Hey, listen, you want to give your Daddy a hard time? Pop some X and fuck your brains out like the other girls, okay? If you gotta do twenty-five just to get his attention, he's probably not worth it."

Honey laughed. It was low, throaty, mirthless. "Are you always such a prick?"

"Yeah," said Bishop. "Why?"

She didn't answer. She shook her head. Sat perched on the table with her hands braced against the edge. She considered her feet. She was wearing black straps. She scratched the instep of her left foot with the toe of her right shoe. "I was there, all right?" she told him. "I was at the Bayshore Market. I wasn't inside with the others. I didn't have a gun or anything. But I was there. I drove the truck."

Leaning in the archway, Bishop's expression remained as it was: arrogant, ironic, impassive. *Shit,* he thought.

"So what can you do for me?" she asked. "What's the deal?"

Bishop came off the archway. Moved across the room to her. Took a Marlboro from the box on the table. He tapped the filter on his wrist, packing the tobacco. He looked down into her face.

"I can take you back to Daddy," he told her. "His lawyers'll protect you. If they can't protect you, his money'll make you disappear."

"I could go back to Daddy myself."

"You could," said Bishop. "But what about Cobra?"

"That's right," she said. "What about him?" She was close to Bishop. He could breathe her breath. "I leave him, he'll come after me. If he finds me with someone else, he'll kill me. Nothing would stop him."

"I'll stop him," said Bishop. "I'm in on his big job. I'll set him up, have the cops take him down red-handed. By the time he gets his ass out of Pelican Bay, he won't remember his own name, let alone yours."

Her hair stirred, strayed across her cheek, as she made a little motion with her head. Her eyes were scared, the way they had been in the Alley. Her lips were glossy and dry the way they had been then. He felt the same feeling for her rising in him. Strong. Too strong. He tried to keep it down.

"That's not good enough," she said. "Prison's not good enough. You know Cobra. He'll find me. He'll get someone to find me."

"No. That's not the way it works."

"It is. It is with him."

"You go back to Daddy. He goes to slam. That's the deal."

"No. He'll find me. He'd never stop. My father can buy off the law, but not him."

"Then what?" he asked her. "What do you want?"

She studied him, tried to gauge him. The pink tip of her tongue showed at one corner of her mouth. Bishop watched it as it moved across to the other corner.

"You gotta kill him, Cowboy," she said finally. "That's the only way. You know it is. You gotta kill him. I'll only be safe if he's dead."

Bishop paused, the unlit cigarette half lifted to his lips. He didn't know why it made him so hot when she said that, but it did. He had to force himself to take his eyes off her. That fresh, sweet, elegant face.

He stuck the cigarette in his mouth. He laughed as he lit it. The smoke blossomed out around the both of them. "Man, that's cold. That's ice cold. You two have a spat over a couple of girls and now you want me to whack the guy?"

"It's not about that, about last night. I just know him, that's all. If I leave him now, if I let him go down, he'll never stop hunting me."

"So it's that easy, huh? Just 'Kill him.' After the way you used to crawl all over him, too."

Honey shrugged. "I liked him." Her eyes were on his. Her gaze was steady through the cigarette smoke. "I liked the way he did me."

"Yeah, the way you liked that drug dealer, that Santé?" Bishop's voice was harsher than he meant. His longing for her was back full force. He couldn't stop it. It made him angry again. It made him want to hurt her again. "I hear you used to crawl around in the mud for him, fetching his hundred-dollar bills."

Her cheeks went red, but she stuck her chin up at him. "I liked the way he did me, too."

Bishop smoked. He met her gaze. Every second he looked at her made him ache. But in the end, he shook his head. "No."

"You have to," she told him.

"No."

"Why not?"

"Because it's murder," said Bishop.

"So what? You killed Mad Dog."

"That was self-defense."

"Well, this can be self-defense, too."

Bishop hesitated. Brought his cigarette to his lips nice and slow, pulled off it nice and slow, let out a nice, slow breath of smoke. "No," he said.

She watched him. She watched him a long time. Then she smiled. "That's funny."

"What is?"

"You are. That you won't do it."

"What's so funny about that?"

"Because you want to."

He leaned forward. He crushed his cigarette out in the ashtray. He could feel strands of her hair against his temple as he did. He could feel the soft cloth of her sleeve brush his forearm.

"Look at you," she whispered. "You want to so bad."

"To kill him?"

"Oh yeah."

"Why would I want to do that?"

"To prove you're better."

"Better at what?"

"You know. Better at being what the two of you are." She laughed. It went through him. "So why won't you? He would."

Bishop didn't answer. He didn't have an answer. He was just look-ing at her. He just wanted to have her or hurt her or something.

"I could go to him tomorrow," she said. "I could go to him right now. Kiss him on the cheek and whisper, 'Kill him.' You'd be dead. So what's to stop you?"

Bishop's expression of irony and arrogance was still in place, but it was getting stale. It was simply plastered on now, as if he'd forgotten to take it off. A habit more than anything. He opened his mouth to an-swer her—he had to answer her—but there was no answer still. He still didn't have one.

And Honey kept at him. "It's like how you want me," she said. "It's the same thing. The way you just stand there and want me. Like a little boy, drooling outside the candy shop without a quarter to his name. Cobra would've just reached out and done me. In fact, he did reach out. That's just the way it happened. He did me hard, too. I like to get done hard. I like to—"

Bishop was not prepared for the strength of it, the pent-up power of it and its rushing release. It was as if he hadn't known himself how hungry he was for her. Holding her fast against himself, kissing her fast, it made him feel almost crazy, almost blind with the heat. He wanted to let her go and be himself again, but he couldn't let her go. He couldn't even let her go long enough to get to the damned bedroom. He was still kissing her, clinging to her as she wrestled the jeans off him. His hands were frantic at the waist of her slacks. The slacks' front button popped off as he worked them down. Dimly, he heard it patter on the floor.

He kissed her neck and the front of her blouse, and his hands went under her blouse. She struggled out of her panties while he kissed her. Then he hoisted her onto himself and propped her against the nearest wall, the living room wall.

He rammed into her crazy hard. He looked at her as he did. She was still in her blouse, her white schoolgirl blouse, and the sight of her dressed like that made him even wilder.

Bishop rammed into Honey, and she writhed as if in pain against the wall. He thought of the girl in the snapshots at her father's house and that was the end of it.

Later, when she had gone, he sat shirtless at the table by the window. He put his palmtop and the keyboard together again. He lit another cigarette and put it in the tinfoil ashtray just as he had before. He positioned his fingers on the keyboard. He thought a long time before he started typing.

Then *Weiss,* he wrote, *something happened.*

TWENTY-SEVEN

Weiss. Something happened. I'm getting the girl out. But we need SFPD in on it. Cobra's gotta go down or he'll come after her . . .

It was a strange e-mail, Weiss thought. The tone of it bothered him. That *Something happened*. That wasn't like Bishop. It was too agitated, too feverish. Instinctively, with that knack he had, Weiss knew it was because of the girl. And he figured—enviously—that Bishop must've shtupped her by now. But so what? He shtupped every girl. Guy was a walking shtup-machine. It never seemed to get him so jazzed up before.

Something happened.

There was more to it this time. This time, the girl had gotten to him . . .

Weiss was still mulling it over the next morning. Silent as he rode shotgun out to China Basin in Ketchum's battered Impala. The e-mail had gone on to describe Bishop's plan for bringing down Cobra. And it was a good plan, but it left a lot of questions. Like: Was Beverly Graham at the Bayshore Market? Bishop didn't say, but what if she was? What if Cobra implicated her after his arrest? Would she cut a deal with the DA and testify? Would Philip Graham agree to that if it meant she did time, if it meant he lost an election?

And then there was the other little matter, the last two lines of the e-mail.

BTW, that guy Cobra wanted whacked took care of himself, drove off the Wildcat into the canyon. You might want to tell Oakland to fish him out of the woods.

Oh, Weiss had all kinds of questions. He just wasn't sure he wanted any of his questions answered.

Ketchum slid the car to the curb next to a construction site. A framework of concrete and rebar spread over an acre of rubble and dust. He came in too fast as always. The tire struck the curb hard; the old blue junker jolted. Weiss sighed.

"What?" said Ketchum angrily.

The two men unfolded themselves on their opposite sides, their doors clunking shut in turn.

The sky was clear today. The sun was a jagged medallion burning low over the water. But it seemed almost a decoration out there, an indifferent fire that gave no heat. The wind came off the basin hard and cold. Litter danced and rattled over the chunks of stone strewn along the ground.

Weiss and Ketchum walked side by side, cutting across the corner of the site. They were dressed almost alike, like cops, dark jackets and slacks, white shirts, striped ties. One of them huge and hulking, the other small and wiry, one white, one black, they moved in step. Their hands were in their pockets, their shoulders hunched. Their jackets flapped in the wind. Their black shoes crunched on the gravel.

Ketchum was still with the SFPD, an inspector. Still pretty much the man he was when Weiss and he were partners. He still scowled most of the time, still cursed the world and all its creatures in his guttural rasp of a voice. He was scowling now. He was pretty much always scowling.

The two men went without speaking about half the way. Then Weiss said, "So? Did Oakland find the body?"

That was all it took to set Ketchum off; that was the match to the tinderbox. "Fuck yes, they found the body," he snarled. "Punk weighed three hundred pounds, he was kind of hard to miss. They brought him out of the woods this morning; said it was like hauling a dead cow up a mountain."

Weiss nodded, no expression, just the usual brooding hangdog of a face.

"You wanna know where you went wrong?" Ketchum went on. "I used to think your mistake was letting Bishop off with a beating. But now I think: You just didn't beat him hard enough. Prick was still breathing when you walked away—*that's* where you went wrong. I told you, Weiss, you spare the rod, you spoil that boy."

"It's not Bishop's fault," Weiss said, without much conviction, with his stomach starting to churn over the whole affair. "The asshole drove off the road. Bishop just reported it."

"Oh. Okay. Okay. I believe that. Why wouldn't I? Why wouldn't I take the word of a psycho dirtbag piece of shit like Bishop? Asshole drove off the road. Right. So how come there's two pairs of skid marks? How come there's a gun like a cannon with a bullet discharged?"

"Who the fuck knows, Ketch? I don't know. The guy was biker trash. He shot a gun off. He drove into the canyon. He was probably stoned halfway to kingdom come."

"That's not the point. I'm not saying the Bay Area lost one of its finest citizens—"

"His handle was Mad Dog," Weiss said. "What do you have to do before a bunch of bikers call you that?"

"So what? So Bishop can kill him? That's good, Weiss. I like it. Something pisses Bishop off, he kills it. 'Less it has a cunt, then he fucks it. It has a cunt *and* pisses him off, I guess he fucks it then kills it. The Bishop Plan for a Better Tomorrow. Man, I'm trying to tell you something: You gotta cut that dickhead loose before he drags you into a world of pain."

Weiss gave a dismissive groan. Trudged along. He didn't need Ketchum for a conscience. He had his own conscience. Saying pretty much the same things.

But Ketchum kept going all the same, shaking his head, grumbling half to himself in his rumbling voice. "Think you're gonna lead him to the light of righteousness. Think you're gonna turn him into you. He's gonna turn you into him, that's what's gonna happen. Punk's a fucking animal . . ."

Which sent Weiss's thoughts, meanwhile, off on their own tangent, a private guiltfest. About Bishop's e-mail. About the questions he didn't want answered. And about how Bishop was counting on that, on Weiss not asking, not wanting to know. Because if Beverly Graham did go home to her father, and if she wasn't implicated in the Bayshore Market killings, and if Randolph "Cobra" Tweedy went to prison for life and couldn't bother her anymore—well, then Philip Graham would surely be one satisfied customer, and Weiss would surely be able to look forward to a lot more business from a lot more VIPs. Which was a pretty damn miserable piss-poor excuse for giving someone like Bishop a free hand.

"A man is what he is," muttered Ketchum, as his rant and Weiss's parallel meditations turned back into each other. "You can't change that."

They reached the far edge of the site. They stood together on the border of the rubble-laden field. They were looking down a street that led to the water. It was lined with a few low buildings, old structures that sagged toward each other, making a narrow corridor between. At the end of the corridor, there was a wharf. To the left lay an empty lot with, behind it, a plain of mud and marshland, a barren stretch of dirt and tidewater set against the sea. Broken posts and boards and stretches of old piers slanted up from its black, unstable earth: the ruin of a harbor. The open water glimmered in the distance beyond.

Shivering off a chilly blast of wind, Weiss lifted his chin toward the street across the way. There was a gray warehouse on the corner. A big one. It had a sign on the side of it, the paint peeling. CHINA BASIN STORAGE.

"Okay, so what's this shit now?" Ketchum asked him. His coat made a loud snapping noise as the wind whipped it.

"Bishop says they're going in here midnight Thursday night," Weiss told him.

"And these are the Bayshore Market doers."

"That's what he thinks."

"But he's not sure."

"He's pretty sure, Ketch."

Ketchum snarled in disgust. "Okay. So they go in."

"There's supposed to be a locker full of cash. A dropoff. A link. Cigarettes, money, drugs. There's a one-day lag before the pickup to make sure it's safe. That's when they go in. There's supposed to be millions."

"Yeah, there's always supposed to be millions. What about security?"

"They've got the alarm codes, the lock codes, everything. It sounds like an inside job. That's why Bishop thinks we should hang back. We go in early, the gang might get word, call it off."

"Any guards?"

"Two, sometimes three, armed with nightsticks. The gang plans to kill all of them."

Ketchum let his breath out in a long *ssssshhh*. "I don't know. I don't like it, Weiss. I could just pick these motherfuckers up and sweat 'em on Bayshore. One of 'em would crack."

Weiss shrugged. "Maybe. Maybe not. Take them in the act, you get a lot of leverage. You're gonna need it to get someone to roll over on Tweedy."

Ketchum studied the warehouse, narrow-eyed. And Weiss—who wanted like anything for the Bayshore killers to go down—could tell that his old partner wanted them, too, wanted Cobra especially with a great want.

Still, he hesitated. Gave Weiss a canny sidelong glance. "What the hell kind of case is this anyway? What's Bishop on?"

Weiss answered with a noise: *puh*. He wasn't telling that. "It's something different, something else. He just stumbled on the Bayshore angle. Figured he'd give you a chance to nail these guys, that's all."

Ketchum sneered. "Yeah, he just bubbles over with generosity, that Bishop. He's a giving, bubbly kind of guy, if ever there was one."

Weiss didn't bother to answer that.

The two men stood silently. They gazed at the warehouse across the way. Weiss's mind drifted to the e-mail again. *Something happened*. A lot of questions . . .

But the low thunder of Ketchum's voice broke into his thoughts.

"One day, I'm gonna do you a favor," the cop said. "One day, I'm gonna take Bishop down. I'm gonna get him on some of this bullshit he pulls, and I'm gonna send him away. Five years, maybe ten, maybe the whole quarter. For your sake and for the sake of the city of San Francisco."

Weiss stood silent. He kept his sad eyes on China Basin Storage.

"But for now," Ketchum said, "tell him we'll do it. When these bastards break into the warehouse? Tell him we'll be there."

TWENTY-EIGHT *Something happened.*

Weiss drove alone across the Bay Bridge. Eastward, out of the city. It was only early afternoon, still bright outside, but down on the lower deck, with the upper roadway blocking out the sky, it was shadowy and somber. Traffic was unbroken, slow but steady, five lines of cars in five lanes. Weiss's Taurus chugged along in the queue at a deliberate pace so that the bridge's side rails whisked by the window in a soporific rhythm and the natural light flickered over the dash in a monotonous counterbeat and the upper tier flashed past the top of the windshield, all very hypnotic. After a while it seemed as if the car drove itself. Weiss was barely there in spirit, pensive behind the wheel.

Something happened. I'm getting the girl out. . . .

But what? he wondered. What happened? Was it, as he suspected, the girl, in fact? Had Bishop fallen in love with her? Weiss liked to think that that was possible, that Bishop could fall in love, make a life with some nice girl. But under the circumstances, he had to admit, it was a whole lot easier to imagine him simply snakebit by someone as hellbound as himself. Especially if another man had her first. Especially if it was a man like Cobra.

The Taurus rolled on and the side rails whisked by and the light flickered and the upper tier raced overhead. And Weiss in his Weiss-like way did not so much analyze the situation as get a sense of it, a general inner impression. He saw Bishop on one side—on his side—and Cobra on the other, like a shadow soul. And the girl in between the two of them. And what a girl. A girl like that? A ruined princess like Beverly Graham? She might've been the woman Bishop would've won if he were the man he might've been. And Weiss could almost feel—he *could* feel—Bishop's yearning not just to have her, but to win her away from his rival, to win out yet again in that man-on-man competition that seemed forever undecided in some arena of his mind.

He did not think but somehow knew that the death of Mad Dog had been part of that competition. And he did not know but somehow feared that this plan to take down Cobra—this plan he had just helped arrange with Ketchum—was part of it, too.

The car broke out from under the roadway. The sky was suddenly dazzling in the windshield. The boxes and modest towers of the city's lowlands fanned out around him. The white stone and red slate rooftops of the university campus rose before him into the misty hills.

Weiss blinked as if awaking. His thoughts or his intuitions or whatever they were became scattered, fragmented. One minute he was thinking of Bishop and Honey Graham and Cobra—a sort of tableau with the men on either side and the girl in the middle—and then the tableau was himself and Julie Wyant and Ben Fry, the Shadowman. He fell into a daydream, one of his usuals: about running up a flight of steps, kicking down a door, trading gunfire with the Shadowman and carrying Julie to safety. From there, the scene shifted to the predictable clichés, Weiss and his missing whore locked together—as he'd imagined it now for days—in several positions inspired by those erotic letters, those e-mails to Professor Brinks.

In that way, Weiss's reason for coming here to Berkeley slowly swam back to the forefront of his consciousness. The letters. Brinks. Arnold Freyberg.

Library research by Sissy and some expert tracking by Hwang the Computer Guy had now more or less confirmed my lead. It was all but certain that Freyberg, the disgruntled professor of William Blake and Wilfred K. Green hounded out of his job by Marianne Brinks, among others, was the e-mails' author. If Weiss had wanted to, he could've simply delivered this information to his client at this point. He could've left it up to the lovelorn Professor Brinks to decide what to do next. He should've, probably, according to the rules of the trade.

But he wasn't going to. He told himself he had to make sure first. He had to confront Freyberg in person and make absolutely certain he had the right man. That's what he told himself. But really, it was that protective routine of his again. He was positive Brinks was setting herself up for a heartbreaking rejection, a big-time romantic disaster, and he wanted to be able to prepare her for it if he could, even talk her out of going forward if he had to.

So here he was in Berkeley, and the Taurus coughed and cruised through the corridor of traffic lights to the western edge of the university. Weiss turned to the north, rolled closer to the professor's address on Euclid Avenue. He became aware of a little hum of excitement under his skin. He was kind of looking forward to meeting this Freyberg. He'd been living with the professor's sex fantasies for days now. He'd even acted them out once with a couple of Casey's whores. He was curious—even eager—to find out what the man himself was like. Sissy had found a photo of him on one of his books. A narrow, handsome face, fiftyish, with a serious mouth and an intense gaze. Weiss imagined him as energetic, brilliant, and vital, in touch with his Natural Being. A little rakish, maybe, but wise to the ways of men and maids. And what with Julie and the Shadowman and the whores and his loneliness and so on, he felt he could use some wisdom on that subject right now.

I will remake you into your body. Only flesh, only sensation. The moment of desire! The moment of desire!

The Taurus turned onto Euclid.

TWENTY-NINE

The house was a few miles north of the campus, up where the road began to curve hard and climb hard into the foothills. The lots here were nestled side by side, but private, each building hidden on its own quarter acre of dense foliage. In the warm of the afternoon, the birds were singing loudly in those leaves and the cicadas buzzing in them and woodpeckers were working at the telephone poles—and every minute or so all those noises were washed away by the whooshing of the cars that went busily rushing up and down the street.

Weiss parked at the curb. Looked up a hump of grass to the house. It was a two-story brown shingle, the lower floor obscured by a broad olive tree, the upper floor an airy cube of latticed windows rising above the tree's crown. The big detective lumbered toward it over the slate walk. Him and his expectations

I will remake you into your body. The moment of desire!

It occurred to him that Marianne Brinks was waiting to hear from him and that she had her expectations, too, her hopes and dreams and expectations about the man who had been writing to her.

Now in the shade of the olive tree, he came to an open door. He knocked at the frame of the inner screen.

Freyberg appeared within. And for a second, Weiss was speechless.

The man was dying. The investigator could smell it wafting out into the summer air. Freyberg had probably never been particularly brilliant or vital or in touch with his Natural Being, but he was nothing now, eaten to a cancerous nothing. His flesh hung like a wrinkled overcoat on a skeleton two sizes too small. He was slumped and quivering, with a wide, frightened, querulous stare. Through the mesh of the screen, he seemed almost insubstantial. Shadowy and transparent as a specter, his own specter.

"Who is it?" he said. His voice was a death rattle.

"My name is Weiss. My secretary called you? Earlier?"

"Oh yes, the private detec—" It was all he could say. He started to cough, a thick, wet, strangling cough that seized his body like an inner fist. It made Weiss wince to watch it happen. He half expected blood to come gouting out of the man's mouth. Finally Freyberg managed to stop, managed to rasp, "All right, well, come in."

He turned away. Weiss pulled the screen open, stepped over the threshold. He followed Freyberg's shadow through a murky foyer. With every step, the smell of his dying grew stronger. It was the smell of medication and closed windows and weeks without a visitor and the stagnant dark.

They came into the living room. Blankets spilling off the sofa to the floor. Crumpled tissues, some of them bloody, in a line of piles along the sofa's skirt. A bedpan with lamplight reflecting off the piss in it. Medicine bottles, morphine flasks, an oxygen tank. And books everywhere—on tables, chairs, the floor—open and facedown most of them, some closed, some it seemed just flung away. The room had probably always been shabby. Just frayed armchairs facing the sofa over a frayed rug. But with the curtains pulled across the garden doors and the windows shuttered and the one lamp on, and with that smell of days, maybe weeks, of loneliness, Weiss found it suffocating.

"What a mess, what a mess," said Freyberg. He looked around as if searching for a place Weiss could sit. Then he seemed to give up and sank down weakly on the sofa. He had to take hold of the armrest while he lowered himself to the cushions. And when he was down, the way he slumped and sagged, his corduroy pants and plaid shirt seemed to billow around a ghostly emptiness.

He made a feeble gesture toward the armchair across from him. Weiss removed a splayed copy of *Don Juan* from the seat, sat down.

"Cancer," Freyberg said hoarsely. "If you're wondering. Maybe being a detective you already detected it. Started in my eye, of all places. I thought it must be glaucoma . . . But they tell me it's everywhere now. Lungs . . ." He waved a branchlike hand. "Bones." He coughed, softly this time but still a deep, painful sound. "The last few days, I've been getting these spasms in my thigh—damned if I know what that's about."

Weiss, his hands clasped in his lap, inclined his head politely. He was listening—but he was also thinking about how awful this was, what a disappointment for poor Professor Brinks.

"I don't suppose it matters, really," Freyberg was saying. "I mean, if it's everywhere, what difference does it make? But I just wonder. I mean, why my thigh? What would make it spasm like that? You think it's in my brain now? You think that's it? Or in some nerves or something?" He snatched a Kleenex from a box on the sofa, held it to his mouth. Hacked into it, wiped his lips with it. Weiss thought he saw a red blot on the sheet before Freyberg stuffed it into his pocket. "It's strange, that's all. Strange . . ."

With that, he subsided into abstraction, his chin almost to his chest, his gaze somewhere in the dim middle distance. Weiss, sympathetic, let him be. Still thinking of Brinks. Remembering how she'd worried that her e-mail seducer would turn out to be "married or gay or a woman or deformed or ten years old." She hadn't thought of this.

Freyberg breathed in, wheezing softly. Worked his lips like a toothless old man. He came out of his fugue and looked at Weiss as if he only now remembered he was there. "I'm sorry, I . . . What did you want to see me about? I assume it's about my insurance claims. Your secretary wouldn't say."

"It's not about insurance. I've been hired to find the author of some e-mails," Weiss said.

This clearly took Freyberg by surprise. He narrowed his eyes at Weiss as if trying to make him out from a distance. "E-mails?"

"Yeah. They were written to a woman, a professor like you at the university here."

And still, Freyberg stared at him in that quizzical way, his glistening lips parted. It went on so long that Weiss began to wonder if maybe the Agency had gotten it wrong. Maybe this sick, suffering man hadn't written the letters at all; maybe he had no clue what Weiss was talking about.

But then Freyberg said—said as if amazed, "Marianne? Marianne Brinks hired you to find me?"

"You did write them, then?"

The withered creature gestured in helpless confusion. Looking this way and that way into the shadowy room as if for help, as if for someone who would explain what was going on. "Jesus. Does she know yet?" His lips started trembling. "Have you told her? Have you told her it was me?"

Weiss shook his head. "Not yet. No."

The professor's skeletal hand fluttered over his face. "Oh Jesus. Oh Jesus Christ. This is—" Then, when the hand had passed, there were the eyes, rheumy now, protruding, staring, scared. He tried to laugh the whole thing off. It made a dreadful sound. He settled for a damp smile, sickly pink. "Well, it's not going to be pleasant when she hears."

Weiss hesitated a moment. "You mean because you two had arguments at the university."

"Arguments? She hates my guts. It's like a bad comedy, isn't it?" He wheezed. "Uptight feminist gets an e-mail from a stranger. She falls in love with him. And all the while it's the chauvinist male she despises, a man she practically hounded out of his job. Hollywood couldn't do worse."

He grabbed a fresh Kleenex and hocked some more blood into it. Weiss sat and watched, bemused. He'd been right about one thing, at least. This was a big-time romantic disaster in the making, there was no question about that. "So on your side, it was hate mail," he said. "You were angry about losing your job, so you wrote Professor Brinks hate mail. That's why you took the trouble to disguise yourself and block a trace."

Freyberg, groaning out of his conniption, nodded wearily. "At first. It was hate mail, at first. But then she answered. I never expected that. And so I answered and. . . . Well, she's not a stupid woman, after all. I could just never get her to *listen* to me before. She was always too busy shouting me down, rattling off her nonsense . . . And now she *was* listening. Not just listening . . ."

After a while, when he didn't go on, Weiss shifted, uncertain. He scratched his head. "So . . . where are you on this exactly?"

"Hm?" said Freyberg. "Me?"

"Yeah, I mean, how do you feel about her? She says she wanted to meet with you. She says you refused and then stopped writing to her. Is that because you still hate her or what?"

"No. No. I don't still hate her. Not the way she is in her letters, anyway."

"You like her."

"Yes."

"But you're afraid if she found out who it was writing to her, she'd just go back to hating you, the way she did before."

Freyberg answered with an almost imperceptible shake of his head. "There's that, yes. I guess."

"Or was it just because you didn't want her to see that you were sick? Is that it?"

Freyberg sat rigid, but his lips convulsed into a frown. "Well," he answered miserably, "look at me. Look at me."

Weiss did look—and Freyberg looked away. For a moment, it seemed he had gone abstract again, gone off into another abstract study of the death-scented dark. But Weiss soon noticed the way his head was quaking up and down, the way his shoulders were quaking. Then Freyberg made a noise, a low stuttering chuckle. It came from so deep inside him it sounded as if it were drifting up from the bowels of a cave.

His tears were more horrible than his laughter. They wracked him, but they never really fell. He shook and quaked and moaned and his face crumpled like a child's and spittle gathered at the corners of his open mouth. But it was as if his illness had left him arid inside so that even his misery was so much dust. He sobbed painfully, his eyes dry.

Weiss was silent. The outburst seemed to go on a long time.

"Don't tell her!" Freyberg cried out hoarsely at last. "Don't let her come here. Don't let her see me like this. Please!"

The professor buried his face in his hands. He made noises Weiss had never heard before. Weiss sat and watched. His heavy features were impassive except for that sad, weighty expression already written into his sagging cheeks, his deep-ringed eyes.

At last, exhausted, Freyberg raised his head. He wiped the snot and blood off his mouth with his palm. "Just for a little while," he said. "Just keep her away for a little while. A few more weeks and it'll all be over. Let her go on the way she is, picturing me in her head. Don't let her see me like this, the way I am."

Still Weiss didn't move. Still Weiss only listened.

The professor reached a shivering hand out to him. "I don't want to die unloved," he whispered. "Dear Jesus Christ in heaven. I don't want to die unloved."

THIRTY

That night, she slipped away and came to him again. Walked in without a word and pulled herself close against Bishop's body. Her breath was hot in his mouth. The smell of her was all around him. One of his hands slipped down the back of her jeans and one ran across her shoulder and up into her soft hair. His feeling for her was fierce. He carried her into the bedroom without speaking.

It was one of his moments. One of those times that took him out of himself. They happened usually on his motorcycle, moving fast. Or dodging thunderheads in a small plane or dropping it on instruments through a storm at three hundred feet onto a sudden runway. They happened in the final seconds before a fistfight or during the minutes when he was inside a woman, in motion through a medium of indifferent sweetness. They happened, and the knot in his chest would loosen and the red atmosphere of fury through which he saw the world would turn clear for a little while.

But this was something else with her, a whole other level of mindlessness. If it had only been the elegance of her features or the photographs in her father's house or the silken softness of her naked skin or the way she thrashed and cried almost as if she were dying into the action between them, it might've seemed to him just the usual business, the usual bridge of dumb pleasure between tedium and anxiety, or anxiety and pain. But it was more than that. He went inside her and inside her with such ferocious awareness that there was almost a kind of music to it, a kind of music even to his interior silence.

Just before the end, Bishop placed his palm against her cheek and looked down at her with what for him was rare seriousness. And when she closed her eyes and pressed her cheek against his palm, he felt it come up from the core of him into his chest, He felt a fullness in his chest, and the finish was bright and blinding.

He lay on his back and she lay curled against him. The sheets and covers were bunched at their feet. He looked down the white length of her. He kissed her hair.

"Is it on?" she asked after a little while.

"Yes," he told her.

He had gotten the e-mail from Weiss that afternoon: *Ketchum is in. The girl is up to you.*

"What will I have to do?" asked Honey.

"Just get away, just come here. Your father will pick you up."

She moved a slender hand across his skin. She toyed with the small hairs around his nipple. "And will you kill him, Cowboy?" she whispered. "Cobra, I mean. Will you?"

He smiled a little, shook his head. "I told you. He'll be in prison forever. You'll be fine."

"But it's not that. It's not just that."

He waited for her to go on, breathing the scent of her in deep, not just the scent of her perfume but the scent of her and of the sex with her.

"In my house, my father's house, we go to church every Sunday," she said quietly. "My sister Tara's in the high school choir, my sister Zoe's on the soccer team; she won first prize at the science fair last year. My mother works at a children's hospital. She raises funds for them. She loves my father and he loves her. They tell each other all the time. They tell us, too, me and my sisters, and my sisters tell each other."

Bishop laughed. "Jesus."

"I know," she said. "It's a fucking nightmare. My father wants us all to be perfect all the time. His perfect little girls."

"I'd say you've pretty well scotched that plan, don't worry about it," said Bishop.

He felt her smile, her lips against his flesh. "I feel like I'm in a coffin when I'm there. In a coffin buried alive. Or like . . . I read somewhere that in the old days, pregnant women sometimes used to give birth in their coffins after they were dead. They'd start rotting, you know, and the gases would build up and the baby would get pushed out into the coffin, even though the mother was dead. That's what I feel like when I'm home. Like I'm a dead pregnant woman in a coffin. It's like I'm dead only there's something alive inside me. And the gases build up and build up until this thing that's alive has gotta explode out of me. And I feel like when the living thing explodes, it's gonna be, like, this . . . this crazy, angry monster. And it's gonna rip its way out of the coffin and just tear everything apart, just kill everyone and rip them all to pieces with their fucking Sundays and their science fairs and I-love-yous all the time."

Her head was on his chest, so Bishop couldn't see her face. He was surprised when he felt a tear work its way through his chest hair to touch his skin.

"You're like that, too," she told him after a minute.

"Like a dead pregnant woman in a coffin?" he said.

She sniffled and laughed. "Oh, fuck you, Cowboy."

"I'm just trying to follow you here. It's a complicated thought."

"No. Well, yes. You're like, you wanna explode like I do. You're like, somebody told you you're supposed to be the good guy, so you're trying to be the good guy, but you just want to explode out of it and . . . and tear off and . . . tear things up and go wild. And you think you shouldn't. Everybody tells you you shouldn't, so you think it's wrong, but you want to anyway."

Bishop rested his cheek against her hair. He listened to her voice and breathed the scent of her. There was something to what she said, he guessed. He thought about Weiss. About the things Weiss wanted from him.

You wanna be a piece of shit your whole life? A man like you.

He thought about Weiss writing him that e-mail before he killed Mad Dog: *Don't cross the line.*

"You don't know me," he told her.

"I know you," said Honey, in his arms. "Because you're like me. It's like you've always got to choose between doing what's right and being who you really are. But it's not what's right, Cowboy. It's just what they say is right. It's all about what they want, really, what they're after in their lives. You know? I mean, my family goes to church and plays soccer and raises money for charity so everyone will say how wonderful they are and my father can make a lot of money at his business and win his fucking election. Well, I'm not gonna change who I am just so my father can win some fucking election."

Bishop drew in that scent, that scent of her and of her sex, and considered what she said. And there really was something to it. People told you what was right and wrong, but everybody was running his own game somehow. Hell, Honey's father could go to church all he wanted. When he needed to get his daughter back without the press finding out, he'd hired Bishop to seduce her. What would the minister have to say about that?

And Weiss. He was no different. It was all well and good for Weiss to say *Don't cross the line.* But the truth was he could've pulled Bishop off this case before Bishop had had to kill Mad Dog. He could pull him off now before this warehouse job went down and Honey dodged the law and whatever happened to Cobra happened. But Weiss didn't pull him off; he wouldn't. Because he wanted Honey's father to be a happy customer and to tell all his rich friends about Weiss Investigations. Weiss was looking out for his business, for himself. Everyone was. Honey was definitely right about that.

"What's this got to do with killing Cobra?" he asked her.

She moved, drew away from him, lifted up so she could look at him, so he could see her face. The room was dark, but the glow from the streetlamps on Telegraph came through the window, and he could make out her features, smooth and sweet-looking. It was easy to imagine her in church or in the high school choir.

"If Cobra was dead, I wouldn't have to go home," she said. "I mean I *would,* you know. I'd go home so you could say you'd done your job, so you could get paid and everything. But I wouldn't have to stay. Because I wouldn't need my father to protect me."

"How the hell do you figure that?" Bishop said. "There's still the rest of the gang. I mean, they won't come after you like Cobra would. But someone's sure to cut a deal with the cops, spill his guts, tell them all about you. You were there at the Bayshore, Honey. It's felony murder, like I said. You'll need your father to buy your way out of this, one way or another."

"Not if I had my own money. I mean, I couldn't run away from Cobra. Even if he was in prison. He'd find me wherever I went, whatever I did. I'd need my father then. He'd hide me out of the country somewhere, hire bodyguards and all that. But if it was just the law, just the law looking for me, just the cops or whatever, that wouldn't be so hard. I could run, I could get away somewhere myself—if I had money of my own."

"But you don't," said Bishop. "Your father told me. He cut you off after you ran off with Santé."

Honey's eyes glinted in the dark. "Cobra does," she said. "Cobra has money. A lot."

Bishop propped himself up on his elbows. "He does? Where?"

"Hidden. I know where. It's all the cash he's saved from all his stuff he's got going. Not just the robberies, you know, and the hijacks and stuff. Also meth labs, coke connections, all kinds of shit the other guys don't know about."

"How much is it?" said Bishop.

"I'm not sure. But close to a million, I think. That's what he told me, anyway. He said after he did the warehouse job, we were gonna leave the country. Go down to South America. Just blow out and fucking . . . just . . . you know."

Bishop nodded.

She touched his cheek. "It could be us instead, Cowboy. Shit, I'd like it even better if it was us. I mean, with you, I wouldn't have to listen to all Cobra's speeches all day and pretend to give a shit what he thinks about anything. And you wouldn't have to waste your time with all the boy-girl crap, pretending you want me for my little pink soul or whatever. There wouldn't be any of that. There wouldn't be anything, just the money and fucking. And you gotta admit, the fucking rocks."

He nodded again in the dark. "The fucking rocks," he said.

"So we do it till we're sick of each other, then walk away, no hard feelings. A million bucks would take us places, Cowboy. And when we're done, we walk away."

Bishop stayed where he was, propped up on his elbows, looking at her. Her eyes still glinted with the tears gathered in them. And that scent, that mingling of perfume and sex and her, was like a cloud all around him. He looked at her lips and felt her breath against him when she spoke.

"It would be so cool," she said. "Everything would just be us, just us the way we are. Wouldn't that be so cool, Cowboy?"

After a while, Bishop laughed again. He laughed and lay back on the bed. She swarmed over him. She stroked his face.

"Wouldn't it?"

"Sure," he said up at her. "Sure, it would be cool."

She laughed once, too, gazing down at him.

"If Cobra died," he said.

THIRTY-ONE

Another summer's day went by, and then it was the twilight of the crime.

Bishop waited for her as darkness fell. He paced at his apartment window, smoking one cigarette after another. He glanced outside from time to time, past the bank advertisement on the billboard, at the sky. He watched the slender moon rise above the city.

It was ten o'clock, then ten fifteen. Then the buzzer sounded. There she was in his doorway, breathless. Her cheeks were flushed. Her eyes were bright. She had a suitcase with her, a small red bag stuffed fat.

She dumped the bag on the foyer floor. Stepped to him, and kissed him. He pulled out of it, looked at her. Stroked her hair from her face. She was nervous and frightened and beautiful, so beautiful it made him ache. And if he did not kill Cobra tonight, he thought, he would never see her again. He hadn't put it that plainly to himself before, but now he did. As long as Cobra was alive, she would be afraid like this. She would let her father spirit her away somewhere and surround her with guards, and he would never see her.

He stood there and held her and looked at her face and she looked up at him and she was flushed and breathless and for a moment he forgot everything else and he did not know what he would do.

"What did you tell him when you left?" he said.

"I just ran," she said. "I wrote him a note."

"Okay."

"To make it look natural, like a breakup, so he won't suspect about tonight."

"Sure. That's good."

"He'll know, though. When the police show up, he'll know I was in on it."

Bishop didn't answer. He already knew what she wanted from him.

After a while, they moved apart. They went to the table by the window. They sat on the wooden chairs. They smoked cigarettes. They touched each other's hands, played with each other's fingers. He looked at her fingers with his and thought that he would never see her again.

Ten-thirty sharp. The buzzer. Honey sucked in a last drag of smoke, crushed out her cigarette quickly. Bishop went to the door. He pulled it open. Philip Graham stepped in.

Honey stood up out of her chair. Father and daughter faced each other across the room. Graham, with his perfect hair and his forthright chin and that never-changing look of disapproval behind his big glasses, looked almost unaffected by the meeting except that he seemed somehow to vibrate inside with suppressed emotion.

"Look—" he said with a quick frown. And he raised his hand as if about to continue, to make a pronouncement. But he didn't continue. That was all he said.

Honey picked up her suitcase. "Whatever," she muttered. "Could we just go?"

Graham lowered his hand. He released a breath. He nodded unhappily.

At the door, he stopped to speak to Bishop. "Thank you," he said. "I'll tell Mr. Weiss I'm pleased with your work."

Bishop smiled a little at that. He liked the way Graham said it: straight, looking right at him. They both knew he had hired the detective to seduce his daughter away from Cobra, and they both knew Bishop had done it and Graham would not pretend otherwise. Bishop liked that in him. It reminded him of Honey.

"I'll wait in the hall," Graham said, and he went out.

Honey came to Bishop and kissed him. A light, soft kiss, the last kiss. She didn't say anything but it was all in her glance. If he did not kill Cobra, he would never see her again. Bishop kissed her back and tried to hold the taste of her on his lips.

He watched her go and he watched the door close. Then he stood in the center of the room alone and watched the closed door.

He was still standing like that a few minutes later when the phone rang. Reluctantly, he turned from the door, went to the phone on the table, snapped it up.

It was Cobra. His voice was harsh and tense.

"Twenty minutes" was all he said. "Shotgun Alley."

THIRTY-TWO

The bar was packed. The juke played country, loud. To the right, on the stage, a woman was dancing. She was wearing a short denim skirt and a white T-shirt. A red spotlight was on her. Her dance was slow and ecstatic. She swung her hips and ran her hands over her torso. The bikers thronged on the dance floor below her to watch. They clapped and whistled and raised their beer bottles. They shouted at her to bare her breasts.

Across the rest of the bar, the tables were full. A haze of cigarette smoke hung over them. Conversation was loud, and there were rising bursts of laughter. There were also cheers and whoops from the dance floor as the girl onstage slowly lifted her T-shirt to her throat.

Bishop walked slowly through the smoke to the gnarly corner. He was the last of the gang to arrive. The others were ranged around their table. Shorty was standing with one foot on a chair. His shaved head glinted in the hazy light. He lifted his chin to Bishop by way of hello. Charlie, the muscle boy, was tilted back in his chair, smoking. Steve leaned against a wall, his arms folded. His scarred face was expressionless. He watched Bishop approach through heavy eyelids, through canny, clouded eyes.

Cobra sat hunched at the table's head. He was rolling a cigarette, working it with the fingertips of both hands. There was a map laid out in front of him, tossed there aslant. A tobacco pouch lay on top of it spilling scattered strands of shag. Cobra frowned down at the cigarette in concentration.

Bishop reached him, stood by him, resting one hand on Mad Dog's former chair. The outlaw didn't look up. Bishop waited, holding his helmet down by his side.

Finally Cobra was done. He moistened the cigarette paper with his tongue and sealed it and wetted the end between his lips. Now he did glance at Bishop. He smiled around the weed. It was a dead smile. The V-shaped crags of his face never lifted. His green eyes were dull and furious. His skin was papery, pale.

He'd found the note from Honey, Bishop thought. He knew she was gone.

"Change of plans," Cobra said.

"All right," said Bishop.

"We go in without the truck."

Bishop made a show of looking round at the others. "Where's Honey?"

"Honey." Cobra drew the name out. He filled it like a vessel with the acid sound of his hurt and anger. "Honey's gone." He lit a match. It flared as he touched it to the cigarette's twisted tip. "Honey left a note. 'Can't stand the heat. Bye-bye.'" He made a kissing noise, then blew smoke out in a gust.

The other men stood in silent sympathy—sympathy tinged with quick-eyed fear. They were afraid of Cobra's sudden temper and his sudden bayonet.

But Cobra shrugged. "Well, the women. They do come and go. But we are who we are. That's the way of it. They think they want in, then they go, and we do what we have to do. Yes? No? A show of hands?" He laughed flatly, joylessly. He studied the red-hot tobacco. He nodded as if at his own deep wisdom.

Then he looked up, and he was all business. "Here's how we'll do it now. We come in on our exit routes, five different directions. Park separate. Look at the map. It shows you where to go. We come together on foot at the warehouse corner. Just like before: I key in the code, we go in all at once. Guards give us trouble, we kill 'em then and there. They play along, we tie 'em up and cut their throats quiet before we go. I'm saying it again, okay? No witnesses. It's not just the cops we gotta worry about on this, the dealers'll be looking for us, too." He checked their listening faces to make sure they'd heard. "Okay. Then we walk out. Separate. Nobody rides together till we hook up at the clubhouse and divide the cash."

Bishop tilted his head to look at the map. He saw where he was supposed to park his bike. Saw where the others would park. "Sounds good to me," he said.

The other men nodded.

Cobra breathed in more smoke. Held it, savored it. Let it drift up out of his lips. He studied the others, man by man, through the rising tendrils.

"Christ," he said. "Look at you dickheads. You don't know." He smirked at them bitterly. "You don't even give a shit. Do you? Nah. Just some money in a warehouse, right? Who cares? You don't have a fucking clue." He shook his head in pity for them. Leaned forward on his elbows, his hands wrapped together, the cigarette poking up through his fingers. "It's the *assumptions* we're going after. See? The assumptions we're stealing away. Because it's drug money from the oh-so-mysterious East. It's a payoff. For smuggled cigarettes from the oh-not-so-mysterious West. Now do you get it? The drug boys wash their money and the tobacco companies beat billions in taxes. And you think the governments here and over there don't know? They know. Sure they know. They go about their business, all very respectable, all very shirt-and-tie. But it's all of a piece. Corruption, respectability. Hypocrisy, the status quo. All of a piece the whole world over."

Cobra tilted his head, a coy, catlike gesture of superiority and secret knowledge. "Well, we are taking that piece apart tonight. We are taking that piece apart piece by piece until it's all in pieces. And *that's* what this is about. Okay? The assumptions. They assume their privileges, they assume the lowdown bedrock of their upright lives, they assume the whole system is clicking over and in place, and we are taking that apart. We're injecting ourselves into the mix, we're—" Then suddenly—since Shorty and Charlie and Steve and even Bishop were nodding openmouthed like husbands half-listening to their wives—he slammed his hand down— *wham!*—on the tabletop. *"This means something!"* he growled from deep in his throat. He glowered darkly at them all. "It's important. *We're* important. We're the leading edge. The leading fucking edge of the new thing, you hear me? We're . . ."

His shoulders sagged and his gaze grew vague and for a moment it seemed he had lost track of himself, lost track of everything. "The bitch," he muttered. Then he went taut. Cast a sharp look at them, one by one. Shorty, Charlie, Steve. They had all gone ramrod straight at the sound of his slamming hand. They all went on nodding as Cobra's eyes went from each to each. Then he got to Bishop—Bishop, resting a hand on Mad Dog's former chair.

Bishop looked down at Cobra steadily. He understood that all this talk was really about Honey somehow. All this blather about what things meant and how important they were: It was all about Honey and the fact that she had left him, and the fact that he loved her, in his own way. Bishop looked down at him and there wasn't much but scorn in his heart, scorn for Cobra's weakness and the nonsense he rattled off, and scorn because he, Bishop, had taken the man's woman from him and she had cried out under him and her tears had pooled on his chest. One way or another, Bishop thought, Cobra was over. Cobra was over this very night.

As for Cobra, he went on searching Bishop's face. He searched his expression a long time. How much of these feelings he saw in Bishop's heart, it's impossible to say. In the end, he just answered with a grin—and managed a real grin this time, full of wickedness and irony, with the devilish angles of his face all raking upward in the force of it.

He shoved his chair back from the table.

"Let's go," he said.

THIRTY-THREE
Midnight then. China Basin. They came together out of the dark.

A film of mist from the water hid them first. It turned and drifted silently in the glow from the city and the light of the crescent moon.

Then there they were, Cobra and the others. Striding out of that mist from every direction. Each wore a leather jacket, a T-shirt, jeans. Each carried a gun held down by his side. Steve had a ball-peen hammer clipped to his belt. The hammer slapped against his thigh with every step. It kept time as the five swaggered toward each other.

Bishop came across the construction site—the same one Weiss and Ketchum had crossed. His boots crunched on the broken stone as he passed under the silhouetted framework of steel and concrete with its weirdly twisted offshoots of rebar. He saw the other outlaws converge at the street corner. He stepped off the sidewalk and crossed the broad avenue to join them.

They stood all together, a loose circle of them. Cobra had his .45 in his hand, and Steve and Charlie had their Glock semis. Shorty had a shotgun propped up on his hipbone. Bishop went for his belt, drew out his .38. Cobra smirked at the measly snubnose.

"Don't hurt anybody with that," he said.

He gave a wink to the others and strode to the warehouse.

There were two doors in the hulking gray box of a building, plus the wide bay entrance blocked by a security screen. Cobra took the near door. Bishop and Shorty pressed to the wall on either side, ready to go in. They waited while Charlie and Steve marched on across the bay entrance to station themselves outside the far door. Charlie nodded when they were set, a gesture just visible in the mist and city glow and moonlight.

Then Cobra moved. There was a small number pad to the right of his door. There was a small red light on the pad. Cobra pressed the buttons on the pad. Each button made a small beep as his finger stabbed at it. When he pressed the fifth button there was a longer beep. The red light turned green.

That was it. Cobra stood back, lifted his weapon, took aim at the lock, and fired. Charlie did the same at his door and the two shots went off at once, made one muffled blast in the night.

Cobra lifted his leg and Charlie lifted his and they kicked out, their heavy boots striking the doors just beneath the knobs. The doors flew open. Cobra charged in. Bishop and Shorty peeled off the wall and went after him. Across the bay entrance, Charlie rushed in with Steve right behind.

Bishop looked around, looked everywhere, his head moving in quick, staccato jerks, his heart pounding. It was shadowy in here, but there was just light enough for him to see by.

They were in an office. He could make out the shapes of the desks and filing cabinets. He could make out the open doorway into the main bay. There were bulbs burning dimly above the bay door; that's where the light was coming from. But there was no sign of the police ambush in there. Just the shadows and the quiet.

Cobra led the way through the open door. The tall, broad figure of Shorty followed. Bishop went in last.

The warehouse bay was wide and high. Rows of towering lockers and towering shelves, one towering row after the next, rising into rafters and scaffolding and darkness. Forklifts and stepladders stood against the wall or by the security curtain. Between the curtain and the edges of the lockers, there was a broad corridor of open space.

Moving fast, breathing fast in their excitement, Cobra and Bishop and Shorty met up with Charlie and Steve in the center of that corridor.

They were in a pool of light from the bulbs over the door. Bishop kept his expression wry and cool as always, but he was wound tight; tight. His pulse was hammering even quicker. The suspense was like a metallic glow in his head, almost too bright to bear. He expected the police to jump them—now, right now. He expected to hear their shouts and see their guns and their tense faces. But still it was quiet. There was nothing.

"Where the fuck's the guards?" Charlie grunted.

Cobra shook his head. "Off, maybe. Who the fuck knows? Let's just do it."

He gestured to Bishop and Steve to follow him. They started up an aisle between two walls of lockers. Shorty with his shotgun and Charlie with his Glock stood guard in the corridor, watching the doors.

In the aisle, the shadows were deeper. At first Bishop had to strain to see. Then Cobra dug a miniature Maglite from his jacket pocket. The three men followed its powerful beam deeper into the bay.

The locker they wanted was midway down. It had a man-sized gunmetal door on it, and there was another keypad beside the door. Cobra had the code to this one, too.

While the outlaw punched the buttons, Bishop scanned the aisle, back and forth. He lifted his gaze to the locker tops, and higher to where the rafters faded into blackness. Where the hell were the cops? Where was Ketchum? If there'd been some mistake, if Cobra walked out of this, if he went looking for Honey—Bishop began a rushed, rough, fragmented estimation of the disaster.

But there was no time for it. The keypad gave its long beep, breaking in on him. The light on the pad went red to green. Cobra yanked the locker door open. His face was arching and eager, his gaze a bright emerald in the Maglite's glow.

Three large duffel bags lay piled together on the locker floor. The Maglite's beam played over them.

"Check 'em," Cobra said.

Steve knelt down quickly. Bishop looked away, peering into the surrounding darkness. No, there was nothing moving, there were no cops, there was no one. He heard the rip of a zipper.

He looked down. Steve had one of the duffels open. The Maglite beam was dancing over the contents. Steve looked up at Cobra with a grim smile on his pitted face. He gave a dull grunt of approval. "Huh."

There were heart-stopping millions in there, stack upon stack of pale green cash.

Cobra nodded. "Zip it up. Let's go."

The three tromped back up the aisle, Cobra in the lead. Each had a duffel over his left shoulder, a gun in his right hand. They stepped out into the corridor.

Shorty and Charlie wheeled from either door, met the others on either side. Cobra grinned at them.

"Yeah," he said.

"All right!" said Shorty, clenching his fist.

The others laughed in triumph.

Then all hell broke loose.

THIRTY-FOUR

Even Bishop never saw them coming—but suddenly there they were. Two helmeted men in black armor at the office door, one leveling an HK, the other handpumping a round into the chamber of a Super 90 12-gauge. Two more with CAR-15 assault rifles were at the far door, closing in. And from up the dark aisles came even more of them, stalking out of the shadows like killer phantoms. Red target lights lanced out and pegged the outlaws' chests. The bay fluorescents flickered on above to reveal the snipers on the locker tops: three men kneeling up there, each training a Remington on the group below.

Finally, Inspector Ketchum strolled in from the office. He stepped casually between the two cops flanking the door. The wiry black man seemed small next to the others in their helmets and bulky Kevlar vests. He himself wore only a suit, it seemed, and a trenchcoat against the night mist—and of course his usual scowl of disdain for all mankind, particularly these dickheads.

"You're fucked, boys, lay 'em down," he rasped softly.

Shorty, with a guttural noise of rage, clenched his teeth and tensed to move, his shotgun stiffening. There was a whispered spit of air, a wet impact. Shorty's shaved head exploded, sending a spindrift of blood over the face of Charlie nearby. Shorty, already dead, tilted back, then crumpled down. He made barely a sound in falling. Nothing, in fact, had been louder so far than Ketchum's quiet rasp.

Charlie, his features sprayed with red, gaped, trembled. Piss darkened his jeans, pattered onto his boots. He let his semi slip from his lowered hand. It clattered weakly on the cement floor.

Steve raised his arms. The duffel bag fell off his shoulder. The Glock tumbled out of his limp fingers. It spun down, bounced off the cement end over end, and lay still.

All this seemed to happen in a single moment, and in that moment Bishop noticed something. The red target dot had gone out on Cobra's chest. Steve, with his raised hands, was in front of him. He had blocked the sniper's shot.

Cobra must've seen it, too, must've seen the way Steve was placed and how it shielded him. He shifted, just a little, but enough to move the duffel bag and hide his expression from Ketchum. Bishop's glance went down. He saw Cobra's hand begin to tighten on his .45.

Bishop dumped his duffel bag, raised his pistol to the side of the outlaw's head.

"I'll kill you, Co," he said evenly. "Try it and I'll kill you."

Cobra turned to him—turned and looked, first into the barrel of the .38, then past the barrel into Bishop's eyes. There was no surprise in that look. It was clear that in that instant he realized everything, the whole story, but in some part of his mind he must've already known, because there was nothing like surprise. He merely straightened where he stood, went taut with the betrayal. Thrummed with the force of his hatred. And he smiled, his craggy features arrowing upward.

"You're dead," he said.

Bishop answered by lifting his chin a little—as much as to say *just drop the gun.* And Cobra did drop it. Slung it away like an empty cigarette pack so that it hit the floor flat and spun across it to the feet of an oncoming rifleman. Cobra shrugged off his duffel bag, too. It dropped heavily with all its millions. But the outlaw never took his gaze away from Bishop—not his gaze or his hatred or his smile. He just nodded and went on smiling—as much as to say yes, yes, now he knew, and he was not surprised.

The cops, at the same time, were closing in, a tightening semicircle of gun barrels and unwavering stares. They were shouting.

"Hit the dirt, scumbags!"

"Down, down, down!"

And now they attacked.

One grabbed Charlie, knocked his legs out from under him with a sweeping kick.

"Get your fucking balls to the cement!"

And two grabbed Steve and slung him to the floor, screaming.

"Hit the fucking dirt!"

"Get down!"

The outlaws were forced to their bellies under a swarm of armored men. Their hands were wrenched behind them; their wrists were cuffed. Ketchum stood watching quietly, his hands in his pockets.

And at some point during all the chaos, someone made a mistake.

He was a big cop named Rittenbacher. While the other cops were going for the other bikers, he went for Cobra. He had an HK MP5 sub-machine gun trained on Cobra's head. His voice was an animal snarl from under his helmet visor.

"On your dick, you piece of shit, or I'll bust a cap in your fucking brain!"

Hands in the air, Cobra took a step back. To reach him, Rittenbacher pushed in front of Bishop, coming between Cobra and Bishop's gun, cutting off Bishop's shot. Holding his weapon in his right hand, he reached out and grabbed Cobra with his left. But by then Cobra had turned, had maneuvered himself so that now Rittenbacher had to step in front of him, which blocked the beads of the snipers, too.

Bishop saw what was happening. He shouted, "Blade!"

But it just went sour too fast.

Cobra's right hand flashed down, flashed up—and now he had the long bayonet in it. He whipped the point of it into Rittenbacher's side, into his heart and out, that quick. Rittenbacher stiffened. His eyes went wide. Any noise he made was lost in all the shouting.

In a single movement, Cobra grabbed Rittenbacher's HK and shoved the big cop backward into Bishop. Rittenbacher dropped, a dead weight knocking Bishop to one side.

Cobra, meanwhile, ripped the HK's strap clear of Rittenbacher's shoulder. The gun was his.

Before anyone could react, he was charging at the door, charging straight at the startled Ketchum. He swept the machine gun over the room as he ran, sending a fusillade in every direction.

Bullets sparked off the concrete, off the metal lockers. Cops dropped to the floor as one. The snipers on the locker tops ducked their heads. Ketchum went for his Glock, but he was too late. Cobra barreled into him, shoved him aside.

The outlaw raced through the office door. Behind him, only Bishop, who'd struggled free of Rittenbacher's corpse, was still standing. Bishop leveled his .38 as Cobra plunged into the office shadows.

But it was no good. There was no shot. Armored cops jumping to their feet blocked him. Ketchum blocked him, trying to get off a shot of his own.

Bishop cursed. He fought his way forward, weaving around the cops. He reached the office door just behind Ketchum. Ketchum went through, and Bishop followed.

By then Cobra had reached the door to the outside. He yanked it open. Ketchum raised his pistol quickly and fired. There was a white flash, a deafening blast.

But Cobra was gone, out the door, rocketing headlong into the night.

Bishop went after him.

THIRTY-FIVE

There was an army of cops outside the warehouse by this time. A perimeter of cars and guns and officers watching, waiting. Not one of them saw Cobra escape. By the time they got the alert from inside, there were half a dozen people bursting through the warehouse doors, no way to know who was who, where to aim, when to fire. Cops jumped into their cars and set the red lights flashing. Sirens started to howl like hunting dogs. Other cops, in armor and armed, began ducking and dodging through the city-lit mist. But Cobra was already out of sight. No one had a clue which way he'd gone.

No one but Bishop. Bishop was sprinting toward the construction site, his teeth clenched, his eyes blazing, his arms pumping, his hand gripping his .38. He was through the perimeter in seconds, never slowing. His heavy boots flashed over the pavement. It seemed he willed them to be weightless in his rage to outrace the fugitive.

Because he knew where Cobra had parked his bike. He had seen the mark on the map in Shotgun Alley. He knew Cobra would reach the machine and be off before the cops could organize, be gone before the cops could marshal their unwieldy cages and head after him. He knew that Cobra would get away unless he—Bishop—could get to his own bike first, unless he could cut the outlaw off. He knew he was the only one who had even half a chance to stop him.

He pumped harder, ran faster, leapt over the curb, off the pavement, into the rubble of the construction area. His boots smacked onto the broken stone as he pistoned past the rising network of girders and concrete. Still, it seemed a slow, slow journey, a long, long run. Crazy, horrible, bloody images in his mind the whole way. Cobra on the loose. Cobra springing out of nowhere, Honey hunted, Honey seized in the dead of night. She flashed before him, tortured, mutilated. Bloody on the floor with Cobra standing over her, howling in triumph. The outlaw knew everything now, and he would live for revenge. He would live to kill her. She would never be safe again, if he got away. She would never be safe, unless Bishop could bring him down.

There it was, finally: his own bike, his black-and-chrome Fat Boy, standing tilted at the edge of a streetlamp's glow, at the far border of the construction site. He cranked himself harder, went faster, was there. Too motored up to slow down, he had to grab hold of the machine, grab the seat, the bars, to keep from barreling right over it. The bike was jolted. His helmet was jarred off the brake lever. It fell clattering onto the stones. He didn't care. He didn't pause. He jammed his gun down into a jacket pocket. Swung into the saddle. Flipped the bike on. Throttled it high.

And in the selfsame moment, he spotted Cobra. He saw the streak of his silver Softail under a streetlamp straight ahead. The outlaw came racing around a corner on the opposite side of the construction site. He turned onto the street, heading away from the Basin. The chopper's headlight was off, and as the bike sped out of the lampglow it became a featureless blur of motion in the mist. But Bishop could track it as it raced perpendicular to him, raced to cross his path, to pass him by as it vanished into the city.

Bishop worked the Fat Boy into gear. The bike shot into motion so fast he damn near lost it. It hit the dirt. It left the ground. It leapt through mist and darkness and dove down into rubble and dust. The earth seemed to slide out from under its tires. For a moment Bishop felt as if he were riding on his side. Then the bike sliced forward, slowly rising, righting itself. He gunned it, angling across the site, trying to get to the other side before Cobra got past him.

Bishop went faster, then even faster over the rough terrain. He felt a wild and reckless stillness in him. He felt distant from himself, another man. Something drifted through his mind: dreamy murder like a wisp of smoke. He wanted—he didn't know what he wanted. There wasn't time to know. The idea was already gone and he was thinking nothing, just working the Fat Boy through a brutal acceleration, trying to feed the cold fire from his veins into the machine.

The bike struggled, bucked, jackknifed over the broken field. He wrestled it down, forced it forward, forced it on. There was Cobra on the street ahead, nearly past him. But now, at the corner of his vision, he caught sight of an obstacle, an outcropping of the half-finished building here, a girder slamming through the darkness directly toward his face.

There was no time to swerve. He didn't want to swerve. He wanted Cobra, that's what he wanted. He bore down on the outlaw even as the girder filled his view. He ducked low, pressed himself hard against the shuddering bike. He felt the engine's vibrations in his chest. He felt the steel beam brush over his back, whisper over his leather jacket. Then he was under it. He raised his head, looked up. Cobra was gone.

No, wait—not gone. Just past the point of interception. But still there, still streaking through the mist and toward the corner.

Bishop angled after him. His bike hit flat ground, seized some kind of traction. It exploded forward, off the rubble, onto the pavement, onto the road behind the silver chopper. The Fat Boy slid wide as Bishop brought it to bear on the outlaw's tail.

As he did, Cobra slanted round the bend, out of sight. Bishop got a good glimpse of him as he made the turn. He saw the gleaming bike leaning under the intersection's streetlamp. He saw the outlaw, his angular face bare to the wind, his hair swept back, his craggy features flattened with the force of his speed.

Then he was gone and Bishop was swerving after him.

They roared down a side street, machine after machine. It was tight here, dark. A narrow canyon between empty buildings. Headlights off, the bikes plunged into shadow. Bishop felt the onrushing air pull at his cheeks, bite at his eyes, blur his vision. But all the same, with a surge of animal joy and hatred, he made out the dim shape of the silver chopper and saw he was gaining on the rear tire inch by inch.

They broke from the street onto a broader avenue. The scene before them fanned wide. Bishop glimpsed a gravel pit to his left, gray as ash, its monstrous elevator piercing the mist to rise against the stars. Ahead, at some distance, was the curving line of the baseball stadium. And to the right, under the sliver of moon, were broken piers and an expanse of night-black water. Beyond it all rose the city skyline, a jagged panorama of pinnacles and higher pinnacles etched in light and more golden light. Cobra streaked into this backdrop and then turned right, heading for the water.

Bishop was just behind him. He pressed down, pressed himself nearly flat against the handlebars, trying to pick up speed, trying to pierce the wind. He took the corner wide, making a broad arc out to Cobra's left. He barely slowed. He twisted the throttle. He spurted forward again, his front tire beginning to draw level with Cobra's rear.

That was what finished it: Bishop pressing in to Cobra's left. The outlaw must've been hoping to break in that direction, to cross the marina, find the freeway, the bridge. But Bishop was there.

A second later, a road opened to the right. Cobra began to go for it. But he saw—and, drawing level with him, Bishop saw—the whirling red flashes of the hunting cop cars down that way. Cobra hesitated—and he ran out of room.

The avenue ended. There was a curb, an empty lot, and then the ruined piers and the water. Bishop saw it. He wrenched his bike away, away from Cobra, away from the onrushing gutter. He braked hard. The tires skidded out from under him. The Fat Boy laid down a curling line of smoke and rubber as he tried to right it, to rein it in. He almost did, too, he almost stopped it. But not quite. At the last moment, he lost his hold. The bars slipped from his hands. The bike spun out from under him. He was pitched sidelong through the air, an awful instant out of all control. Then the pavement; the impact jarred him to the bone. His body slid over the tearing macadam. He rolled to absorb the impact. There was another terrible second when he didn't know if he was hurt or if Cobra was getting away or if Cobra was there, right there, moving in to attack him—

Then he was up, he was on his knees, scanning the darkness wildly. He found him, found Cobra. Cobra was down.

The silver chopper hadn't stopped in time. It had hit the curb head-on and flown forward. Cobra stayed in the saddle, riding over a black rainbow of empty air. He and the motorcycle came crashing down together into the vacant lot that fronted the water. His rear tire blew. The bike whirled away from him. Cobra was hurled across the lot's broken concrete. The machine gun, which had been strapped to his shoulder, tore loose, tumbled into the rubble. Cobra rolled, and when Bishop saw him, he had come to rest on his back, spread eagle. He was lying still, one hand extended toward the weapon, the weapon inches out of reach.

Bishop, rattled, struggled to his feet. He felt dazed and dull. He felt the stinging scrapes on his forehead, on his hands. He felt a line of hot blood touch the corner of his eye, running down.

He heard the sirens baying. They were coming closer. He sensed the cop cars searching the area, saw their red, rotating glow begin to tinge the mist. He saw the mangled wreckage of the chopper in the vacant lot. He saw the downed biker splayed out beside it. The gun. He saw where the lot ended beyond them and went down over a dirt hump into blackness, the blackness of the water. He made out the gnarled shapes of what had been piers and posts out there. They rose above the gently lapping surf, above rippling reflections of moonlight and city light that surged and ebbed under the red mist's drifting tendrils.

Now, as Bishop stood there, he heard Cobra moan where he lay. He saw the outlaw shift slightly, his chest rise and fall. He was still alive.

Some sort of choking thrill, some sort of choking urgency, rose from Bishop's chest to his throat. But he didn't know what he was thinking. He wasn't thinking anything. He just knew Cobra was still alive and he knew he had to get to the HK first. That's all.

He started forward. He moved wearily, stiffly. His body felt hollow and strangely precarious, as if something had been knocked loose inside it. But he didn't hurt much yet; nothing had been broken, he could move. He stepped up onto the curb. He walked over the rubble toward the outlaw and the weapon.

He was a step away when Cobra stretched his arm out, fast, and seized the machine gun with one hand.

Bishop reacted on the instant. He kicked. His boot struck Cobra's wrist, and the gun skittered over the gravel. He jammed his own hand into his jacket pocket, felt for his .38.

Cobra twisted off the ground and lunged at him. Grabbed his legs. Brought him down.

Bishop grunted as his back hit the concrete, as the air rushed out of him. He had his gun half drawn, but he lost it—it was knocked from his grasp—as he struck the earth. Cobra was on top of him, was clawing his way up him to strike a crippling blow. With pulsing desperation, Bishop realized he was about two seconds away from dead.

He lifted his torso—like a man doing a sit-up. He caught Cobra as he came on. He glimpsed the outlaw's contorted, striving face and drove his stiffened fingers into it. He was aiming for Cobra's eye. He was close enough. Cobra let out a high-pitched scream and tried to recoil. Bishop grabbed him by the hair, struck again, hammering the heel of his palm into his nose. Blood burst out from under Bishop's hand, spit over Cobra's cheeks. Cobra screamed and wrenched himself away, rolling and stumbling across the lot.

Bishop rolled in the opposite direction. He jumped to his feet. There was no time to look for the gun. Cobra was on his feet, too, crouching low, pissed off and coming at him. Blood was pouring from the outlaw's nose, running down over his mouth. He grinned at Bishop and the blood stained his teeth. His emerald eyes were shining in the night.

Bishop grinned back at him. There were sirens growing louder in the air all around them. There were red flashes growing brighter, coming closer. But Bishop didn't hear or see them anymore—them or the night or the skyline or the glimmering water, either. He saw Cobra, Cobra's crouching body, his grinning, bloody face. He felt his own body coiling and full of clean fire, perfect for the task at hand.

The two men circled for a second, then Bishop went in. His kick to Cobra's knee snapped out and back like a whip, and though somehow Cobra managed to dodge the worst of it, Bishop followed after it, jabbing and slashing with his open hands. He felt his fingertips sink into the soft flesh of Cobra's throat and felt his elbow sweeping across the mess of blood beneath Cobra's nose. He felt his boot, in tight now, driving down into Cobra's instep and then his knee coming up into Cobra's groin.

And it felt good. It felt good as good to hurt the other man. He was in a place inside himself of blazing light and high silence, immensely present in a sweet, white killing zone. He felt invincible and murderous and fine. This—the destruction of his rival—seemed to him everything he had wanted forever. He attacked and attacked with a sense of pure release, as if he were the energy blasting out of an atom.

And now Cobra was on the ground, gagging and bleeding. Scrabbling across the gravel—*like a beetle,* thought Bishop in triumphant scorn. Bishop, pale-eyed, dreamy-eyed, was stalking after him—slowly, relentlessly, stoked and stoned on the rush of violence, on the pleasure of watching his enemy crawling and then staggering in a panic to get away.

Bishop, implacable, pursued him step by step. As he came, he caught—or thought he caught—a whiff of something, a dense and floral scent drifting beneath his nostrils, a smell so achingly sensual it nearly made his eyes roll with the pleasure of it. He knew what it was. It was Honey. It was the way she had smelled lying next to him in bed, fresh from sex, her perfume mingled with her sweat. It came back to him and she was almost there, he could almost feel the touch of her, almost hear her whispering to him, whispering, *If Cobra dies, we can be together . . . we can be together, if Cobra dies . . .*

In that moment—that moment when Bishop lost his focus—Cobra scuttled suddenly slantwise, found his lost machine gun, and grabbed it.

Bishop moved fast. He was on the other man in an instant. He drove his boot into Cobra's side. Cobra grunted and went over. He hit the ground hard and rolled. He was at the edge of the dirt mound beyond the vacant lot, and then he was over it, rolling down the dirt slope, tumbling into the water. He landed on his face with a splash. He fought to his hands and knees, gagging and retching salt sea and blood. The gentle surf rose and fell around him. He gasped for breath, then gagged and retched again.

Bishop was still coming on. From the corner of his eye, he caught sight of his .38. He bent and swept it up and kept walking to the top of the dirt mound. He planted his feet. He lifted his gun in an outstretched arm and aimed it at Cobra below.

Cobra was still on all fours down there in the water. Up to his ass and shoulders in the shimmering Basin tide. Bishop looked at him in disdain from on high. Calmly, he aligned the gun barrel with the out-law's head. Once more, he smelled Honey. He felt her flesh against his flesh.

If Cobra dies, we can be together . . .

Bishop's finger tightened on the trigger.

On his hands and knees, Cobra turned to look at him. He saw the bore of the weapon trained on his face. He smiled. He nodded and smiled as if he knew it all, understood it all, even to that faint woman-scent at Bishop's nostrils.

"Go ahead," the outlaw shouted. "She's worth it."

"I know," Bishop shouted back.

Cobra laughed and Bishop laughed, and the two men understood each other.

But for another second, Bishop held his fire. He didn't know why. His finger squeezed the trigger, but not quite hard enough. Another second went by and another. Still, Bishop didn't fire.

We can be together, he thought.

He thought, *Don't cross the line.*

That was the end of it somehow. Somehow, in that last moment, he came to himself on a trembling breath. He blinked. His homicidal smile faltered.

"Fuck!" he whispered—as if he were his own better angel stum-bling in horror on the scene.

His gun hand grew unsteady. For a few more seconds, as Cobra grinned up at him, he wrestled with the impulse to shoot him dead. He frowned, half convinced it was a weakness in him not to just blow this useless piece of biker trash away.

But it would be murder. With the guy just kneeling there, helpless like that. It would be cold-blooded murder. And Weiss—fucking Weiss— would never forgive him for it.

"Oh hell," he muttered.

His trigger finger relaxed. His arm began to lower. The impulse to destruction passed like drunken madness. That was it, that was all. He was himself again. He was going to walk away from this. He was going to walk away from Honey and the killing passion and the entire business. And as for Cobra, fuck him. He would leave him to the cops. He would leave him to the law of the land.

Cobra, panting, smiling up the hill, was witness to Bishop's moment of recovery. He seemed to understand this, too, to understand the whole thing. His body buckled with relief. His features flooded with comprehension and even a kind of inspired gratitude. It was an event on the order of the religious, of the miraculous. He'd been about to die like the dog he was, die as he deserved, and in an instant of unlooked- for redemption, he'd been spared.

He rose up onto his knees as if to sing in thanks and praise and hal- lelujah—and instead yanked the machine gun up out of the sand and seized the opportunity to open fire.

The HK sent a burst and then another burst of bullets into the night as Cobra swept it around in one hand to bring the flaming barrel to bear on Bishop's chest.

Bishop let out a cry of surprise and fear. In a panic, he pulled the trigger of his pistol six times with lightning speed.

Only one of the slugs from the .38 hit Cobra, but it hit him smack in the face. His sharp, arched, craggy features seemed to implode into the red-black hole. The light went out of his eyes and his gun hand flew up and the HK discharged harmlessly toward the sky.

Then the outlaw tumbled sideways. He crashed down into the water. The surf bubbled and churned and closed over him. His body sank beneath the waves.

Another moment and he was out of sight. Bishop lowered his arm to his side. He hung his head.

The mist went scarlet and dark, scarlet and dark around him. The air was full of sirens. There were doors, car doors, opening, shutting. There were heavy shoes tramping over the broken cement.

By the time the cops reached Bishop at the top of the mound, Cobra was gone. There was nothing left below them but the plash and recession of the moonlit tide.

PART FOUR The Dead in the Water

THIRTY-SIX

Weiss moved heavily through the rain. He pulled his collar up. He hunched down inside his trenchcoat. He didn't have a hat, so the water matted his salt-and-pepper hair, ran into the folds of his saggy cheeks like tears.

It was a miserable rain, thin, steady, cold. It carried the pungent smell of fallen leaves in it, the first whiff of autumn. He had parked a full block away, the only space he could find. By the time he reached the old white brick building, the legs of his pants were soaked; his skin felt clammy. He pulled the wood-framed glass doors open and was grateful to step inside.

At the elevator, he pinched his coat and shook it. The excess water puddled on the marble foyer floor. He slid back the old-fashioned elevator cage. He got in and it rattled shut. As the box ground upward, he stood gazing at the sinking walls, his hands in his trenchcoat pockets. His hangdog face was impassive. His sad eyes were distant. He felt the low boil of anxiety in his belly, but what the hell. There were a lot of things to worry about just now and not a damn thing he could do about any of them.

Bishop was irritated the minute he saw Weiss in his doorway—standing there gigantic and dripping wet, his eyes full of sorrow. That's what annoyed Bishop most: that look of pity Weiss lugged around with him like a suitcase. Bishop read it as pity, anyway—pity for all mankind, which was idiotic enough, and pity for him personally, which just pissed him the fuck off. It meant they hadn't found the body yet. Which sucked, all right—and Weiss being all compassionate about it only made it worse.

Bishop grunted a greeting, turned away. Walked back to the table by the window, leaving Weiss to come in behind him. Well, he was edgy to begin with. But his boss was the only man on earth who could get under his skin like this just by showing up.

Weiss stripped his coat off, draped it over a chair. The water dripped from it, pattered on the wood floor. He felt chilled and uncomfortable in his damp clothes. But then, he didn't feel all that comfortable just being here, under the circumstances.

"Crap day," he said.

Bishop didn't answer. He plunked down into one of the chairs by the table. He snatched up his cigarette box, snatched a cigarette, lit it.

Weiss watched him, read his temper and his nerves. Winced to see the angry bruises on his face and hands. Purple stains in the flesh, spreading out, becoming yellow stains. As Weiss lumbered toward him, he saw the deep rings, too, under his hollow, sleepless eyes.

Poor bastard, he thought.

He sank into the table's other chair with a heavy sigh.

Oh, fuck Weiss, thought Bishop. *And his pity and his sighs.*

He inhaled smoke fiercely, blew it out fiercely. "What, they still can't find him?"

"I know," said Weiss. "It's crazy shit. They dragged the Basin all yesterday, even a couple hours this morning before the weather went south."

Bishop gave a snort of disgust.

"They figure either he was swept out to sea somehow or—" Weiss's shoulders lifted and fell.

"Or what? He hailed a cab? I shot him in the face."

"Maybe the sharks got him. I don't know."

"The cops were there in less than a minute."

"Right, that's the thing. So maybe he swam for it."

"He didn't swim for it. He was too dead to swim for it. I shot him in the fucking face, Weiss."

"What can I tell you? It's gotta be something."

"Jesus!" said Bishop. "Who's Ketchum got on this? The Blind and Stupid Division?"

"They'll find him."

"Hey, it's nothing to me. The man's dead. He's plenty dead. Just be nice if the Keystone Kops could manage to fish him out of the seaweed, that's all. I'd like to be able to move on with my life, sleep with both eyes closed for a change."

He turned away after that so Weiss couldn't see how wired he was, how uncool. Because all that stuff about moving on with his life, sleeping with both eyes closed and so on—that was bullshit, a smoke screen. It was all about the girl, really. And he didn't want Weiss to read his expression and see just how much the girl had gotten to him. Weiss could do that, too, look into people's minds like that. It was even more annoying than his universal pity.

Weiss looked out the window, meanwhile, so Bishop could suffer in private. *The girl must've really gotten to him,* he thought. Why else would he care if Tweedy's body was found? That stuff about moving on with his life, sleeping with his eyes closed, that was bullshit. He seemed sure enough that the biker was meat. Wouldn't be afraid of him if he was still alive, either.

No, it was Honey Graham who was really frightened. Philip Graham had been calling the Agency almost by the hour, asking if there was any word. He said his daughter was terrified, convinced that Tweedy was still alive, that he would come after her, kill her. The father sounded pretty nervous himself. He had the girl under heavy guard, and he was talking about getting her out of the country before long.

So unless Tweedy was found—unless the Grahams were convinced he was dead for sure—Bishop would never get anywhere near the girl again. That had to be the reason he was on edge like this.

Weiss watched the rain course down the glass in waves. It blurred the scene outside: the steel gray sky, the stretch of wet avenue. It blurred the smiling woman on the billboard advertisement for the bank so that she seemed like the hazy dream of a woman.

What the hell is she so happy about? Weiss wondered.

"Ketchum doesn't think all that highly of you, either, if the truth is known," he said aloud.

Bishop faced him, pulling hard on his cigarette again. "Well, that's not news. What's his problem this time?"

"He says you should've warned him about the blade. Says you wanted the takedown to go sour. Says you were looking for an excuse to blow Cobra away."

"That's crap."

"He's been snarling at me all morning about it."

"It's crap," Bishop said. "Why the hell would I want to do that?"

Weiss shrugged. But that wasn't good enough for Bishop. His voice grew harsher, more challenging.

"I mean it. Why does Ketchum think I'd do that? Fucking cop is on me all the time."

"It's true. He is," Weiss answered gently. "And he doesn't even know about the Graham girl yet."

Bishop felt the heat rise in his face. So Weiss already understood the whole deal, understood about the girl and everything. It made Bishop feel sour inside. If Weiss knew about that, then, being Weiss, he'd probably also figured out what the gunfight at the edge of the Basin was like. He probably even knew the thoughts that had gone through Bishop's mind and the way his finger had tightened on the trigger and maybe even about the smell of perfume and sex that had seemed to drift by him. It made Bishop sour to think that Weiss knew about all that.

Weiss rumbled to his feet now. He put a big hand on Bishop's shoulder, clutched it. "Listen. They'll find him," he said again.

Bishop felt the heat in his cheeks, the sourness all through him. "Sure."

Weiss walked to the chair where his coat lay dripping. He lifted the coat and shrugged into it.

Bishop pretended to ignore him. Pulled on his cigarette, acted as if he didn't care what Weiss did or what he thought. Because why should he? Why should he give a shit what Weiss thought about anything?

He glanced over at the big detective sidelong, watched him yank the belt tight around his trenchcoat. *Fucking Weiss*, he thought.

"It's just you he's worried about," he heard himself say.

Weiss glanced over at him. "Who? Who's worried?"

"Ketchum. That's why he's on me all the time. He's worried I'll cross the line somehow and drag you down."

Weiss just answered with a puff of air, a kind of laugh. "I'll see you, Jim."

He went to the door.

"Wait a minute," said Bishop.

Weiss pulled the door open, looked back across the room, met Bishop's eyes.

Bishop couldn't help himself. He had to ask. "What do you think?"

"About what?"

"What Ketchum said? You think he's right?"

"Right about . . . ?"

"You think I wanted the takedown to go sour? You think I wanted to blow Cobra away?"

Weiss made a face, tilted his head. "Who gives a shit what anyone wants? SWAT fucked up and Ketchum knows it." He seemed about to leave, but paused again, looked back again. "Anyway, you never would've pulled the trigger if Tweedy hadn't fired first."

Bishop almost smiled at that but stopped himself. Because what did he care? What did he care what Weiss thought? *Fucking Weiss*.

Weiss went out, and the door swung shut behind him.

THIRTY-SEVEN

And Weiss moved heavily through the rain. Hunched in his trenchcoat. Pushing through the miserable pissing downpour back to his car. Worse off than when he arrived. Heavy with guilt now and premonitions of disaster.

He could forgive Bishop his trespasses well enough, but his own plagued him. He should've taken the op off the case before the killing started. He should've taken him off before he'd gotten entangled with the girl. He should've asked if the girl had been at the Market massacre. Sure, he should've. It was just greed that stopped him. Greed and ambition. He hadn't wanted to see what was happening; he hadn't wanted to know the truth. Because he was greedy for the case to go well, ambitious to please his VIP client. Plus he had a childish hankering to relive his heyday as a cop, to have a hand in bringing Cobra and his gang to justice.

Now, if the Graham girl was at the Market, if Ketchum got wind of the way things went down, Bishop could get himself charged as an accessory to murder for helping her escape the law. Even Weiss could be guilty of it, guilty of misprision at least. And it didn't matter a damn if Ketchum thought it was all Bishop dragging Weiss into his psycho universe. It was Weiss who'd fucked up—at least, according to Weiss it was. According to Weiss, it was Weiss himself who'd let the business get out of hand.

He reached his gray Taurus. Waiting for him at the far corner, dull and dutiful as a wet hound. He huffed and grunted as he squeezed his mountainous body in behind the wheel. He got the engine going, the heater. Sat back. Watched the wipers working for a second or so.

He hadn't wanted to know, he thought. He hadn't wanted to see. And he still didn't want to. Even now, even right now. In some part of his brain, there was some nagging something . . . something he was blocking out, something he was refusing to acknowledge, and he just couldn't get at it. It was something about Honey . . . about Cobra . . . Bishop . . . something that didn't make sense, that needed to be put together. It was right in front of him. He could feel it. He could feel the looming wrongness of the whole affair.

But he couldn't see why it was wrong exactly. Because he didn't want to see. He didn't want to know.

He glanced at the dashboard clock. He sighed. Almost three. He had to get going. He still had his other pair of star-crossed lovers to deal with. He couldn't put it off anymore.

He threw the car into gear. Pulled out into the street, cruised to a stop at the traffic light on Telegraph. Sat watching the wipers, watching the rain.

What a crap day, he thought. First Bishop and now M. R. Brinks. Passion and folly everywhere. And him at the center of it, paralyzed over his own passion, his own folly. Julie Wyant; the Shadowman. Sometimes it felt like life was all salt, and he was just one big wound.

He drove east, glancing up toward the university as he went through the intersection. It was quiet now at the end of summer, nearly empty in the rain. He went on. Saw only a few students here and there. Small figures bent under backpacks, hidden under poncho hoods. Clutching books and shopping bags and purses to themselves as they trudged through the puddles toward the dorms. All the same, they were young. They were young and he was fifty, and the sight of them made him wistful, regretful, envious, yearning. Their youth underscored his dissatisfaction.

That's how he felt as he found Marianne Brinks's house in the modest streets below College Avenue. It was an old-fashioned stucco cottage on a small lot, houses close by on either side. There was a white fence on the border and white lace curtains on the windows. There was a pleasantly winding stone path dividing the grass before the front door.

To Weiss—in his sentimental mood—it looked like a picture-perfect suburban home. The kind of happy home he used to see on TV when he was a kid. The kind of home he'd figured other kids in other families had. It looked as if a decorously joyful family of towheaded Episcopalian children and their Episcopalian mom and dad and maybe an Episcopalian golden retriever or something would come pouring out onto the lawn any minute. He could remember hoping that he would one day have a home like that.

It was sad to think there was just Brinks inside. Poor little Brinks, hunkered alone with her theories and her secret and her closet full of tailored suits. Waiting for him to walk through the door and deliver the news: Her e-mail lover was a dying man whom she despised. It was sad.

He pulled to the curb out front. Shut off the engine. Sat a minute with his thoughts and his misty frame of mind. His nagging anxiety about this, that and everything. He sure as hell didn't want to get out and go in there. Break the fierce little feminist's heart. Tell her the ugly truth. He wished he could leave her fantasies intact a while longer. Give Arnold Freyberg what he wanted, too: a few more days of anonymity so he could die knowing that at least the recipient of his hate mail loved him.

But Freyberg was not his client. Brinks was. And the truth was the truth. That's what she'd hired him for.

He sat another minute, no wisdom forthcoming. And as he sat, a curtain in the house shifted. He caught the motion from the corner of his eye. He turned and saw a dim figure lurking at a downstairs window. It peeked at him, then let the curtain swing back into place.

Brinks. Waiting for word. Waiting to learn the identity of the man she loved.

Weiss groaned. *What a crap day*. He pushed the car door open.

He got out and walked slowly up the path to the house.

THIRTY-EIGHT

"How'd it go?" I asked him later.

"She wept," he said. "Like a goddamned baby. She just sat on the sofa and sobbed and carried on."

"Because it turned out to be Freyberg or because Freyberg turned out to be dying?"

"Who the fuck knows? You tell me. She just kept saying, 'I'm sorry. I'm sorry, I'm sorry.' What the hell's she so sorry about?"

"Beats me. Maybe just for crying like that."

"Maybe. She sure as hell couldn't stop. Boo-hoo-hoo. 'I'm sorry.' On and on like that. It's must've been at least half an hour."

"Jesus." I flinched at the mental image. My hostility toward feminism notwithstanding, I hated to see a lady cry. "What's she gonna do? Will she go talk to him? Call him, at least?"

He turned over one open hand: a kind of shrug. With the other hand, he swirled the whiskey in his glass. He swiveled in his high-backed chair, frowning, thoughtful.

I pretended to be thoughtful, too, but really I just didn't know what to say. I thought I ought to say something. Weiss looked like hell. The encounter with Brinks must've been harrowing. I felt I should be able to cheer him up with a sympathetic remark or two. But I couldn't think of anything, not anything I felt sure of anyway. With me being basically a kid, and him being Weiss and all, I was desperate not to make a youthful ass out of myself in front of him. So I chickened out finally. Buried my nose in my scotch. Said nothing at all.

It was one of those nights. When everyone else in the agency was gone. When Weiss would call me into his office. Pull the Macallan bottle out of his desk drawer like a private eye in those old novels I loved. Pour us each a glass. The lighted city stood vast and deep at the high arching windows: the ornate cornice of the building across the street in the foreground, the skewed geometry of the skyline rising up behind. The rush and rumble of late traffic rose to us from far below. The empty hallways and offices all around us made us feel—or made me feel, at least—as if we were two solitary creatures, floating in the darkness there, floating on the little island of lampglow around Weiss's desk.

I've never really known for sure what Weiss got out of these meetings, what was in them for him. But for me—well, that was something else again. To sit in private conversation with this tough, wise old ex-cop whom I admired and emulated. To get to soak up this character who seemed, like his whiskey bottle, to have stepped whole out of the hardboiled fiction I cut my teeth on. To get a taste, even at second hand, of what I was so hungry for: experience, worldly wisdom, life. For me, these nights were great.

The silence between us went on a long time, uncomfortably long on my end. Then finally Weiss raised his glass. Tilted the rim my way. Smelled the good malt and tasted it and went "Ah!" He studied the whiskey's amber depths. He gave a world-weary little laugh, just for himself. And he said, "Sweet mystery of love, right?"

Oh, how I wanted to respond in kind. To say something equally wry and terse and ex-coplike, man to man, as if all the big philosophical stuff were already understood between us and there was no need to spell any of it out.

"You know what it's like?" I said. "It's like computers, isn't it? Like the way computers work: binary numbers. All you have is those two kinds of numbers, ones and zeros. But out of that comes this whole unfathomable . . . everything."

I thought that was pretty clever. An elegant little metaphor with a built-in visual joke—you know: men and women, ones and zeros.

But no. Weiss screwed up his mouth. He snorted. It was too complicated, too academic, too much for him to work out this late in the day.

I was crestfallen, chagrined. What an idiot I was! What a stupid eggheaded, geeky thing to say!

But then—miraculously—Weiss got it. I could see it happen. He kind of lifted his chin and half-smiled to himself.

"Ones and zeros," he said into his glass. "That's good. I like that. Ones and zeros, definitely. They taught you something in college, anyway."

"A little," I said, in that same sardonic tone. But I was thrilled not to have screwed up the moment. I was gratified beyond telling.

"I guess a lot of times, we oughta just keep our ones in our pants, huh," said Weiss.

I laughed. "Yeah, but those zeros."

He laughed. "Right. Right. Those zeros. You gotta be careful about those zeros."

"Tell me about it."

"Hey, I will." he said. "You bet your ass I will." He made his fingers into a gun and fired it at me. "You can fall right into some of those zeros, my friend, so deep you never get out."

I laughed again—but then I stopped laughing. *Hey,* I thought, *did he mean that personally?* And *Yeah,* I decided, *he did.* Which meant he knew about me and Sissy. Well, of course he knew. The way she hung around my desk and draped herself all over me. The whole Agency probably knew by now. Which meant the whole Agency probably knew that my sex life had turned into a long, descending dance in which I and my lust and my cowardice alternated places as we waltzed ourselves into perdition.

It was perdition. That's what it was. I couldn't bring myself to break it off with her. She called me "baby-lamb." She called me "little sweetie." We'd been together just under two weeks, and she'd begun to wonder aloud if we would spend "the next fifty years" together. I wanted to kill her—but I couldn't bring myself to break it off.

Every night, I was in her bed. Most mornings, too. And I won't say it wasn't educational. For all her candied sweet talk and her mommy mannerisms, she'd lived at least ten more years than I had. She'd had time enough to acquire a mind-boggling knowledge of the human anatomy and to overcome any embarrassment about passing that knowledge on. So exotic and compelling were these informational exchanges that I would lose myself in them entirely and plumb forget my intention of telling her that I was in love with another woman. Which I was, in fact. I was in love with Emma McNair.

I had met Emma only that once. But the connection, as I've already told, verged on the mystical. Every day I made plans to call the number she had given me and every day I told myself that, no, I couldn't do that until I had honorably broken it off with Sissy. So every day I vowed to honorably break it off with Sissy and every night I found myself inserted instead into some new opening in her or linked with her in some hitherto unimagined position the very originality of which seemed to hold me in a trancelike thrall. Not to mention the orgasms, which were nitroglycerinesque. I mean, the woman was fucking my brains out.

But the truth is I would rather have stared at Emma McNair across a crowded room than have even the wildest conjugation with Sissy. No, wait a minute, that's not the truth. The truth is: The moment *after* I finished the wildest conjugation with Sissy, I continually found myself wishing that I had plunked instead for staring at Emma across a crowded room. Or doing almost anything with Emma, rather than consigning myself once again to the relentless cootchie-coo, snookie-ookum horseshit with which Sissy was mothering me nearly to death.

I don't mean to delay the main story with these laments about my youthful shenanigans, but, as things turned out, it all sort of played into what happened next.

Because, embarrassed, I mumbled, "Yeah, you can't always tell what you're getting yourself into, can you?"

And Weiss said, "Well, that's it, that's just it." He poked his finger into the desktop. "You can't tell shit. That's right. You never know what the hell is going on, who the hell you're dealing with. I mean, look at this Brinks woman. She's sitting there crying like that. Because why? What did she do? She got these letters. She fell in love with this guy in these letters. But she didn't know him. She just made him up in her head. She just fell in love with this guy she made up in her head and now she's sitting there crying boo-hoo because this Freyberg guy isn't the guy she made up." He raised his scotch glass to his lips. He looked across the rim of it, out beyond the lampglow into the office shadows. "I mean, it's all like that, isn't it?" he said softly. "I mean, that's pretty much all it is."

It seemed we were no longer talking about me and Sissy. In fact, I wasn't sure, but I suspected we were no longer talking about M. R. Brinks and Arnold Freyberg. Weiss at this point had not confided in me all that much about his personal life, but I'd already seen enough to understand some of it. I'd deduced for myself his romantic nature. And I had spied him more than once, alone in his office, staring at the ten-second video of Julie Wyant on his computer, that ten-second loop that was everything he had of her. So I wondered if that's what was on his mind. Her image, his feeling for her. Whether it was worth risking the dangers of searching for her in the flesh. Or whether he had simply "made somone up in his head," like Brinks, and would be left, like her, to cry boo-hoo.

"What do you think, Professor?" He was still gazing into the darkness. But then he drank. Then he swiveled to face me. "You're the resident genius here. That's pretty much the whole deal, right? A bunch of ones and zeros making stuff up about each other."

The question caught me completely off guard. A question that real, that deep from a man like Weiss. How could I answer him? What could I say that wouldn't make me sound like some know-nothing bookworm just out of college? Which, of course, was what I was.

My lips parted and my mind raced. And the traffic whisper from the street below, and the city at the window, and the empty halls and offices all around us, gave me that strange sense that he and I were in the dimly lit center of things and that what I said next mattered somehow more than I understood. It wasn't just that I wanted to impress him, it was that—well, the subject had been on my mind of late. It connected with other things I'd been thinking about, things that had been going through my head ever since that night at Carlo's when I had talked with the graduate students and with Emma McNair.

Looking back, I can see that the nonsense those students had spoken and Emma's practical response had begun in me the chain of thought that would develop into what you might call my outlook, the holistic philosophy that would come to guide my writing and set me in opposition to the fashionable theories of my day. The jist of it was that the inner life—the imagination or the spirit, if you will—is not some trick of culture or upbringing or even genetics, but an actual different order of reality. This imagination, I would come to believe, was a Thing Entire, as powerful a factor in the workings of the world as a bullet or a rose. Yet somehow it had become invisible to our modern intellectual elite, so enamored of scientific analysis that they were blind to what could only be experienced whole. They clung to the mere material and explained everything else away, so that when they looked at love—as when they looked at literature or prayer—they were like children baffled by one of those optical-illusion drawings: They saw the two profiled faces but couldn't make out the grail formed in between.

That's what I'd been thinking about since my night in Carlo's, and that's what I was thinking about now. But, of course, I couldn't say any of it. Not out loud. Not to Weiss. "For fuck's sake," he would've answered, or words to that effect, "what is this philosophical shit?" And I would've been ridiculed as a callow Poindexter around the Agency for weeks.

So I chose my words carefully. I said, "I guess it depends, you know. It's not just what one person's making up in his head, after all. It's what the other person's making up, too. And I guess it's what that makes up when you put the two things together."

I half expected Weiss to laugh, to snort and say, "For fuck's sake," and all the rest of it. But he didn't.

He swiveled away. He looked off beyond the lamplight again. He swirled the last of the scotch in his glass absentmindedly.

It was funny—though, of course, I didn't know it at the time—but at that moment, in a strange way, everything had just come together exactly as in a detective novel. I mean, it was the Brinks case that had led Weiss to his reflections about his feelings for Julie Wyant just as it had led me to my meeting with the grad students and Emma. And that meeting had led me to those philosophical musings, and they had given me a response to Weiss's reflections.

And it was those musings, believe it or not, those musings and that response, that eventually had their impact—their decisive and even cataclysmic impact—on the bloody and violent resolution of Jim Bishop's adventure.

THIRTY-NINE

When I left Weiss at the Agency that night, I stood a long while on the corner of Market and Third. The rain had tapered away to nearly nothing by then, a ripple in the gutter puddles, a shimmer in the sheen of the streetlights on the wet pavement. I stood while the crossing sign went from DON'T WALK to WALK. Then it went from WALK to DON'T WALK again and I was still there, still standing. I was holding my cell phone down by my side. It was off. I had turned it off while I was with Weiss. I was rolling it over and over in my hand.

I felt—well, I felt a lot of ways. But more than anything else, I felt inspired. These ideas I had—all this palaver about the full and indivisible reality of the imagination—they had never been so clear to me before, so articulate, so exciting. And I knew full well the reason for it: Emma McNair. It was because of that conversation she and I had had at Carlo's. Not just the things we said, but the way she let me rattle on without looking at me as if I were boring or insane. The way she had put her hand out to cover mine and the way she'd encouraged me in my ambitions. What would it be like, I stood there asking myself—how inspired would I be—if I could have conversations like that with her all the time? Especially if we could have them naked. What couldn't a man accomplish with a woman like her to accept him and believe in him and pretend he was making some kind of sense?

It came back to me now—I had pushed it from my mind, but now it came back—how she had written her phone number on the Carlo's coaster, how she had said so touchingly, "I'm just a girl in real life, and I'll be very hurt if you don't use this right soon." Almost two weeks had gone by since then, two weeks of nights with Sissy, and I hadn't called. What had I been thinking?

Then and there, determination flowered in me. I flipped the cell phone open. Turned it on. I had sat in my room and read the number on that coaster a hundred times. I knew it by heart. I was about to dial it. But before I could, the phone gave off a little tune. I had a message. It was from Sissy.

"Where's my little sweetie tonight?" her recorded voice whispered to me. "I've looked all over for him. Where can he be?"

I was repelled. At first. But then she went on to explain at some length exactly why she was looking for her little sweetie and what she was planning to do with him when she found him. And holding the phone to my ear with one hand, I hailed a cab with the other.

Thus, ignominiously and unworthily and a lesson to us all, my small part in this story comes to an end.

FORTY

But my spirit may be said to linger on, I guess. Because Weiss was still upstairs in his office. Still sitting in the island of lampglow. Sipping his Macallan, a fresh glass of it now. Swiveling in that enormous high-backed chair. And still thinking—or so he always claimed afterward—about what I had said to him.

It's not just what one person's making up in his head . . . It's what the other person's making up, too. And it's what that makes up when you put the two things together.

For Weiss, it had been a long, long day of love and lovers. Bishop brooding over Honey. Professor Brinks weeping over Arnold Freyberg. And me with that hunted look in my eyes, too obviously a booty slave to poor Sissy, whom he knew to be hungry for a husband, in turn.

Add all that to his own dilemma—his weird and impotent obsession over Julie Wyant—and it was no wonder that his brain felt overloaded with affairs of the heart. They were all starting to become sort of intermingled in his mind at this point. His experience of Brinks's heartbreak was becoming confused with his fear of searching for Julie Wyant, which was becoming confused with his concern—and, in truth, his jealousy—over me and Sissy, which was becoming confused with his sense, his haunted sense, that there was something, something urgent, he was missing—refusing to see—in the Bishop–Honey Graham equation.

That last—that's what he kept coming back to. That missing piece. The presence of urgency, even of danger. He could feel the danger, feel it right there, right beyond his consciousness, beyond the screen of his resistance. Its unseen presence was eating at him. At least, he thought that's what it was—because it was all eating at him, the whole long day.

He swiveled round slowly to contemplate the view through the high windows. The rain spatters on the glass, the blurred city behind them, its lighted spires woven with mist. Absently he began to raise his glass again. He thought: *It's not just what one person's making up in his head . . . It's what the other person's making up, too. Not just what one person . . .*

And his hand hung still, the whiskey halfway to his lips.

Later, he would often tease me about that moment of revelation. He would say it was my "words of wisdom" that guided him in his time of need, that lighted his way to understanding. For days, the entire Agency gave me good-natured hell about it. Even one of the lawyers from the firm upstairs began calling me the Philosopher Dick.

But, for all the hilarity, I confess to a measure of pride in the business. It really does seem to me fair to say that my words were in Weiss's mind at the turning point. It really was in that second when he recalled them that he began the process of solving two murders: one that no one even knew had taken place—and another that hadn't happened yet.

FORTY-ONE

The process led Weiss the next day to question a man named Mr. Munarolo. Mr. Munarolo, in turn, questioned Weiss.

For instance, he asked Weiss, "How about I punch you in the fucking head?"

You couldn't have made this guy up. A slab of granite with a sneer on top. A stained Grim Reaper sweatshirt with the sleeves scissored off above the shoulders. Muscles bulging on his arms under tattoos so vast and complicated Weiss couldn't tell what the hell they were—a lot of snakes and skulls, was all he could make out. Plus the guy's tree-gnarl of a face. Plus the fires of apish rage and stupidity so bright in his dead stare that it was as if his eyes were windows onto the savage past of humankind.

Weiss, standing across the desk from him, remained mild. "I don't care about your role in it, Mr. Munarolo," he said quietly. "In fact, I don't care about you at all."

Mr. Munarolo cursed in wonder—he wondered how it could be that Weiss's fucking head didn't contain enough brains to keep itself from getting punched. He was on his feet now behind his gunmetal desk, his green chair shoved back out of his way. He had his hands on his hips. He had his head down like a bull. He was all aggression, ready to charge.

They were in the office at the China Basin Storage warehouse: the same office through which Bishop had chased Cobra three nights before. The place had been pretty much put back together, but there was still the bullet hole in the wall by the door where Ketchum had fired on Cobra and missed.

There was another man here, too. He was sitting at a desk in back pretending not to watch the confrontation. The woman, the secretary, who had been here when Weiss first came in had scurried out into the bay when things started getting unfriendly.

Disgusted, Mr. Munarolo shook his head. "You fucking cops."

"I already told you," said Weiss. "I'm not a cop."

"Well, the fucking cops think they can just come in here like storm troopers and take over the place. I got bullet holes everywhere. I got blood on the floor out there. You whack some fucking dude in my loading bay. Christ. And then you come in here, you think you can push me around like I'm the bad guy?"

"I'm not a cop," Weiss repeated quietly. "That's what I'm telling you. I don't care whether you're the bad guy or not."

"A bunch of fucking extortionists, that's what you are," said Mr. Munarolo. He seemed a little confused about this cop/not-cop issue. "Now I'm not gonna say it again: I am advising you to get the fuck outta here before you get your head handed to you, you understand me?"

Still, Weiss and his head remained where they were.

The detective was not surprised by Mr. Munarolo's attitude. The warehouse manager had every reason to be upset. His warehouse had been commandeered by the police without his prior knowledge. Ketchum had arranged the raid on Cobra's gang with the owner. Mr. Munarolo had been left out of the loop. And the reason Mr. Munarolo had been left out of the loop was that both Ketchum and the owner suspected that he'd been taking kickbacks in return for allowing drug dealers to use the warehouse to make their cash exchanges.

Now, to add insult to injury, Mr. Munarolo was being questioned by the police about those kickbacks. Which put Mr. Munarolo in no small danger of losing his job, going to jail, and being killed by the drug dealers, not necessarily in that order. And that was probably why Mr. Munarolo's temper—which, let's face it, was not exactly saintly at the best of times—was particularly short just at the moment.

But the thing was—as Weiss was patiently trying to explain—Mr. Munarolo's personal fortunes did not conern him. "Look, Mr. Munarolo . . ." he began.

"What did I just say to you?" said Mr. Munarolo.

"You've got me all wrong. I know you're a scumbag who takes payoffs from drug dealers, but I don't give a rat's ass. It doesn't matter a damn to me, really. And I'm sorry you're gonna lose your job and go to jail and get killed and whatever—or, okay, if I'm not sorry, tough shit—but what I want to know is—"

Apparently Mr. Munarolo was not interested in what Weiss wanted to know. Because before Weiss could finish telling him about it, Mr. Munarolo started coming around the desk with what seemed the express intention of punching the detective in the head.

Usually Weiss's sheer size kept things like this from happening to him. That and the fact that he still carried himself with a certain cop-like authority. But Mr. Munarolo had had an aggravating couple of days and was just feeling very tense and emotional about many aspects of his life and upcoming extermination. He probably figured that by expressing these feelings to Weiss he could both release his pent-up frustration and bolster his wavering self-esteem.

This was an unfortunate mistake in judgment on the part of Mr. Munarolo. Now, on top of all his other problems, there he was, lying on the floor bleeding from the nose.

The man sitting in the back of the room leapt to his feet under the impression he had to do something. Weiss gestured at him to sit down again, and the man realized his impression had been incorrect. He sat down again.

Weiss perched himself on the edge of the gunmetal desk, flexing the elbow he had just driven into the center of Mr. Munarolo's tree-gnarl face.

"What I want to know," he said, taking up where he'd been interrupted, "is who's the drug dealer who paid you off. I'm not after him or anything—I just need to know his name."

Mr. Munarolo sat halfway up, propped on one hand. His eyes no longer looked like windows on the savage past of humankind. They just looked kind of comical, blinking very rapidly in turn, left eye, right eye, left eye, right eye, as if he were trying to catch up with the strobic flickering of the world around him. He drew his other hand across his upper lip. He examined it. He found a lot of blood and snot on it. He looked unhappy.

Breathing hard, he glanced at the man in back, maybe embarrassed, or maybe looking for help. The man in back was now sitting with his hands folded on his blotter, placidly watching Weiss and Mr. Munarolo as if they were a show on TV.

So Mr. Munarolo, finding no comfort anywhere, grimaced up at Weiss, who was waiting for an answer. He said, "Listen, you mother-fucker, I've got a lawyer—"

Weiss reached down and grabbed the front of Mr. Munarolo's Grim Reaper sweatshirt. He lifted him off the floor with one hand and with the other slapped him so hard across the mouth that Mr. Munarolo's eyes not only blinked separately but also started rolling around in separate directions. Weiss then deposited Mr. Munarolo back onto the floor with a certain amount of force.

Weiss had a temper, too, and he hated being attacked.

"I need to know the dealer's name, Mr. Munarolo," he said again.

Mr. Munarolo held his jaw in his hand. When he could talk again, he said, "I didn't tell the cops, and I'm not telling you."

"That's only half right," said Weiss. "You didn't tell the cops, but you are gonna tell me."

"What're you gonna do if I don't?" said Mr. Munarolo. He may've meant to sound defiant, but he actually sounded kind of curious.

Weiss rolled a glance toward heaven. "For fuck's sake," he muttered. "What're you, an idiot? What do you think I'm gonna do? I'm gonna kick you so hard in the ass you'll be picking shoe leather out of your teeth, how's that?"

It seemed to do the trick for Mr. Munarolo. "Santé," he said. "The drug dealer's name was Santé. He didn't come personally, but that's what they told me his name was. If he finds out I told you, he'll kill me."

"I wouldn't worry about that," said Weiss with a laugh. "He'll probably kill you anyway." He shifted his seat on the edge of the desk. "So, then, was it you brought the robbers in?"

"What do you mean?"

Weiss sighed. "I mean Cobra and his gang. They came in here with the alarm codes, the locker number, the combination. What'd you do? Sell Santé out and let them in?"

"No. Fuck no."

"Well, who was it then?"

"How the fuck should I know?"

"That's the wrong answer, Mr. Munarolo," said Weiss.

Mr. Munarolo wiped his nose again, with another part of his hand, a dry part. Now there was blood and snot on that part, too. This was really not a good time for Mr. Munarolo. "Maybe Harold," he said sullenly.

"Harold who?"

"Harold Spatz. He worked here—I don't know, maybe three months, till about six weeks ago. Little pimply-faced fuck. But did his job, y'know? Good worker; good worker—then suddenly he wasn't such a good worker anymore. He got—strange. I don't know what. Creeping around like he had some kind of big secret or something. I figured he was just getting laid or taking drugs or who knows the fuck what. But then one day he just ups and disappears. Boom. Never even came in to get his last check."

"And did Harold Spatz know that Santé was storing cash in your warehouse?"

"I don't know. He could've. I don't know."

Weiss nodded. He moved. Mr. Munarolo flinched—but the big detective was only standing up off the desk.

"Thank you for your cooperation, Mr. Munarolo," he said.

Mr. Munarolo snorted sarcastically, sending a great sarcastic gob of blood and snot down over his chin.

Weiss, hands in his pants pockets, walked from the office, shaking his head at the sad, sad folly of humankind.

Outside, the sky was gray. The clouds were foaming in a cold wind that smelled of autumn and the sea. At the corner, up near the construction site, Weiss paused for a moment on the way to his car. He stopped shaking his head at the sad, sad folly of humankind and turned it so he could look along the water.

Out by the ruined piers, the police, who had been dragging the Basin for days, were gone. For now, it seemed, they had given up the search. Cobra's body had not been found.

Weiss drew a deep breath, straightening his spine, squaring his broad shoulders. He turned away and continued walking toward his car.

He wondered how Bishop was doing.

FORTY-TWO

Bishop was running. His legs pistoned hard, his arms pistoned steadily. His gray T-shirt was dark with sweat. His sneakers went quickly, lightly over the university track. They made a short *chuck* sound every time they landed in the dirt.

The clouds boiled low in the big sky over him. The air felt heavy and wet against his face. His face was blank, his pale eyes flat, their gaze inward-turning. He hardly seemed to know that he was there.

The track was a quarter of a mile long. He'd been around it now more than twenty times. There was no one else anywhere near. The silver bleachers rising high on either side of him were empty. He was alone with the sound of his breath and the *chuck, chuck, chuck* of his sneakers.

He had been thinking things over when he started. He had been thinking about Honey. He had been thinking about how she'd wanted him to kill Cobra and how he had killed him, even though he had tried not to. Weiss had told him he wouldn't have shot the outlaw if Cobra hadn't fired first and maybe that was true. But maybe it wasn't. He remembered how his finger had tightened on the trigger, and he remembered how he had smelled Honey's perfume and had felt her as if she were a poison in him.

Now she was gone. He would probably never see her again. And he missed her, he wanted her, the way an addict misses and wants his hit, his drug. But he felt good, too. He felt better somehow. Because he remembered his finger tight on the trigger, and it would've been murder if he'd pulled it when he'd wanted to most.

He ran. Around the track again and then again. The more he ran, the more tired he got, the more his thoughts became disjointed, the more they were swept up into the *chuck, chuck* rhythm of his sneakers and the rhythm of his breath. He thought of the feel of the gun in his hand. *Chuck, chuck*. He remembered the smell of her. His harsh breath rasped. He thought how Weiss had said, "You never would've shot him." He thought: *Good old Weiss. Chuck, chuck*. He ran.

The sky darkened. The clouds tumbled over him, low. His thoughts became rhythmic fragments. What was she? Nothing. Flesh. *Chuck, chuck*. Lips, tits, cunt. Like any woman. *Chuck*. For him: a faster pulse, a stiff dick. (His mind went in time to his harsh, hoarse breaths, to his sneakers in the dirt.) And everything else was a trick of words. Words for the pulse, for the stiff dick. *Chuck, chuck*. Words like "yearning," like "passion." *Chuck, chuck*. Words to change sensation into desire, to change desire into emotion. Words to change breath. Just breath. *Chuck, chuck*. Just words. Just breath. *Chuck, chuck*.

The sound of his sneakers suddenly changed. Their soles slapped hard against the track. He came to a stop under one of the empty, silent bleachers. He bent over, his hands on his knees. He panted, waiting to catch his breath.

After a few minutes, he stood upright. He inhaled deeply through his nose. He could smell damp leaves and the coming rain. A cool smell, a lush smell. Nothing else. There was no faint scent of Honey anymore. No scent of her anywhere. She was gone. She was out of his system. He was sure of it.

He had draped a towel on the railing by the stands. He yanked it off now, hung it round his neck, wiped his face with the tail of it. He looked up over the dirt and the grass and the bleachers. The brown of the dirt and the green of the grass and the silver of the bleachers were all muted in the dull light. He felt the emptiness of the track. He felt the wind through his short hair. He nodded to himself. Yes. She was gone.

He walked home slowly. Tired. Wiping his face with the towel around his neck. He thought he would call Weiss when he got home. See if there were any new assignments for him. If nothing else, he could do some background checks for the lawyers upstairs. Weiss always had something going. When he really thought about it, Weiss was a decent guy. Probably the only real friend he'd ever had.

He walked along the edge of the university, idly running his gaze over the campus buildings: stately, stone, like red-roofed temples on the rolling grass and the winding paths. Beyond them, above them, the low, boiling clouds swallowed the backdrop of hills. The upper campus seemed to fade into the whiteness. The campanile rose against it as if the clock beneath its spire were the last signpost before a vast and ghostly nothing, the boiling clouds.

Bishop turned away. He went down Telegraph. He walked faster past the clothing shops and food shops and book shops. Vendors were hawking jewelry and crafts from stands on the sidewalk, and beggars were asking for spare change with upturned caps. Students wandered among them. Bishop wove his way through the crowd. He had no feeling for the street or the people. He would live here for a while and then move and live somewhere else. He didn't care. He never stayed anywhere long.

He reached his corner and turned. He reached his building, came into the alcove.

And there she was. Honey. She was standing right there. Leaning her shoulder against the alcove wall, tilting her head against it. Waiting, sullen. As if Bishop were late for an appointment they'd made.

She was wearing a suede parka and a pink sweater over a frilly white blouse. Brand-new jeans. Rich-girl clothes: She was her father's daughter again. Her hair was up, but silken blonde strands of it fell free as if she'd just woken from a nap or the wind had blown them. Her face looked scrubbed and fresh and beautiful, but her tousled hair looked wild and rebellious.

She stood off the wall when she saw Bishop. She broke into a bright smile. He stepped up into the alcove and came to her. She fingered his sweaty T-shirt and bit her lip and cast a mischievous glance at him. He caught the scent of her.

She was not gone. She was not out of his system. He had been wrong at the track. Now he knew better. She was not gone at all.

FORTY-THREE

So that's how Bishop was doing. Weiss, meanwhile, had left the office of Mr. Munarolo and was now approaching a dilapidated house near the freeway in Potrero Hill. The house was built in the "San Francisco stick" style: a rectangular clapboard box with a rectangular bay window jutting out of it. It was the last known address of Harold Spatz, the pimply-faced worker who had quit Munarolo's warehouse without a word.

The front door was off to one side, up a rickety flight of steps. Weiss climbed the stairs heavily, knocked heavily on the door's peeling gray paint.

The landlady's name was Mrs. Cobham. Black, heavyset, around Weiss's age, maybe fifty. She pulled the door open and saw him there and her broad face turned to granite. Weiss knew that look. She thought he was a cop.

"My name's Scott Weiss," he said. He offered her his card. "I'm a private investigator."

Her eyes went to the card, then back to him. She let the card hang there in his hand. "Yeah?"

He slipped the card back into his jacket pocket. "I'd like to talk to you about Harold Spatz," he said.

That changed things, Weiss could tell. The woman's big shoulders shifted a little. She considered him more thoroughly, her glance going head to toe. Then she nodded. "I wondered when someone would turn up."

She pulled the door back farther. Weiss stepped in.

He followed her down a bare hallway. They passed the living room. A TV was on in there. Weiss heard a man's voice, insanely elated. Laughter, applause. He got a glimpse of an unmade cot, piles of clothes, an ironing board, a picture of Jesus above a melted candle. It seemed as if the whole life of the house took place in that one room.

But Mrs. Cobham kept walking, on down the hall, on into the kitchen at the end. While she unlocked a door under the red plastic wall clock, Weiss took a look at the crayon drawings stuck to the refrigerator. One quick glance and he knew the landlady had two grandchildren, a nine-year-old boy named Howard and an eight-year-old girl named Rhea. He understood somehow that Mrs. Cobham was working hard to keep these kids out of trouble. That was why she didn't want to see any cops on her front step.

Mrs. Cobham got the door open. It led to a descending flight of narrow wooden steps. She went down first with Weiss right behind her.

He had to duck under the low ceiling as she led him across a small cellar. At the far end, there was a room, a narrow area sectioned off from the boiler with drywall.

"I rented this to Harold for about three months," she said as they stepped across the threshold. "April, May, June, part of July."

There was just space enough here for a single bed, a dresser, and a desk. The only window was a thin strip of dirt-encrusted glass half hidden by a steampipe. The only real light came from a naked bulb in a ceiling fixture.

Weiss looked the room over. He could feel Mrs. Cobham looking him over at the same time. He could tell she was still wary, the way she stood back from him, her arms crossed under her breasts.

She was a short woman—not much higher than Weiss's elbow—but she was thick and sturdy. Wherever she planted herself, it seemed she would never budge. She was wearing a man's flannel shirt and black slacks, an outfit that made her look even more blocky and formidable. And she had fierce, pugnacious features, though Weiss thought he spotted something vulnerable around the mouth. You could still get her to smile sometimes, he told himself. Or someone could.

"What happened to him after July?" he asked her.

A mangy half-breed mutt slunk in. Sniffed at Weiss's pants leg. Lay down at his feet, muzzle on paws. The dog's good opinion seemed to carry some weight with Mrs. Cobham. She lowered her crossed arms. Cocked her head at Weiss as if to say *Come here and look at this.*

She stepped to a dresser. Pulled a drawer open. Waved a hand at the briefs and T-shirts crumpled up in there. Weiss leaned over, jutting his jaw, as he peered down at them.

"Harold told me he was gonna be gone for a while," Mrs. Cobham said. "He didn't say how long. You can see he packed some things, but he left a lot, too." She tugged randomly at a pair of underpants, a T-shirt, a sock. "I got a security deposit. He's paid up to the end of this month. So I don't know. Looks like he was planning to come back. Maybe he still is. I just don't know."

Weiss noticed she averted her gaze as she said this. He understood: Her "I don't know" was pretty much of a technicality. That is, technically, she didn't know, but she knew, all right. Spatz was gone for good.

"I been having a bad feeling about it," she admitted to him after a moment.

"Ever call the police?"

She looked away again. Brushed the question off with a flip of her hand. "I can't be having the police in here every time someone runs off without telling me. I'm his landlady, not his mother."

Weiss understood this, too. She hadn't wanted to get involved with the cops, but now she wished she had. She felt bad about letting it go this long.

He asked her, "What about Spatz's family? He have anybody? Any friends?"

"Not one, not that he ever told me about, anyway. I always got the feeling he was just a lonesome child. Like a runaway or something, from a bad place somewhere. There was just something about him. The way he liked to hang around with my grandkids all the time. With me, too. Just watching TV, or playing games or drawing pictures for us or whatever. Like he wanted to have a family because he never really did."

The beginning of a smile played at one corner of Weiss's mouth. That was good, he thought. The woman was good. She was smart. She could read people. Just like he could.

"Did he say anything else before he left?" he asked her. "Anything at all about where he was going?"

She frowned. Shook her head. Pressed her lips together, keeping mum.

Weiss let the smile come now, let it bunch the saggy flesh under one deep eye. "C'mon," he said. "What d'you figure?"

That was all it took, all the encouragement she needed. "Well, a few weeks before he went away, he started acting strange," she told him eagerly.

"Strange like?"

"Just funny, that's all. Keeping down here to himself all the time. Drawing his pictures, doing whatever else he did. And he was happy all the time, too. Singing, whistling. Playing air guitar."

Weiss got it. "You think he had a girl, you mean."

She raised an eyebrow at him. "Skinny little white boy like that starts playing air guitar, honey, you know somebody's wrapping him up somewhere." She was warming to Weiss now: She sensed, as he sensed, the similarity between them.

"You sure it was a girl?" he asked her.

"Oh yes. He wasn't no gay boy. I'd clean up in here sometimes, I'd see his magazines. He wasn't no gay boy."

The detective's heavy features seemed to grow even heavier, to sag even farther as he thought it over. He was getting a feeling for the kid, this Harold Spatz. He was working through the probabilities just as Mrs. Cobham must've been doing these last six weeks.

"So what do you think? He ran off with her?" he said. "You think that's why he told you he'd be gone for a while?"

She dropped her chin decisively. "That's exactly what I think. I mean, I think that was his plan anyway. You look. He packed just enough clothes for some kind of getaway, maybe in Reno or somewhere. And look at this."

She went into the drawer. Pushed the laundry aside. Came out with a drawing pad. She handed it to Weiss and stood next to him as he lifted the cover.

There were pencil sketches on the pages inside, nine or ten of them. Not bad, either. The kid had a good eye for detail, a steady hand. You could tell what everything was, anyway.

The pictures were all more or less the same. The beach through trees. Looking down from a height through branches at the surf against the rising rocks, the ocean into the endless west, the clouds, the gulls, the sun. Postcard California.

There was a caption on one of them: "The Beach from Lost Trail."

"That was his special place he liked to go," said Mrs. Cobham. She stuck one thick finger right up against the penciled woods. "You know, he'd go out there and he'd sit and he'd draw his pictures. He was always talking about it. And one night after dinner, just before he went away, we talked together, and he went on and on about what a romantic spot it was and didn't I think it was romantic and all like that. And look. Look there."

She lifted the pages of the pad to show Weiss the last picture. She pointed to it. Weiss squinted past her fingertip.

There were two figures lightly penciled in amid the foliage. A man and a woman. Very faint, as if Spatz had hardly dared to draw them fully.

"You think he was planning to take her up there," he said. "Show her his special place."

"Yes, I do."

"What?" He gave her a shrewd glance. "You think he was planning to ask her to marry him?"

"Yes, I do. That's just what I think. Take her to his special place and pop the question. That's just what I think he was planning."

Weiss nodded slowly, getting the feel of it. Drawing the image from Mrs. Cobham's mind into his.

"So maybe that's it," he said after a while. "Maybe it all worked out for him just like that. He went out there, popped the question, she said yes. They ran off together into the sunset. Happy ever after. Maybe that's why he never came back."

Now Mrs. Cobham nodded also. She frowned down at the picture on the pad in Weiss's hand. The two sensitives stood shoulder to shoulder in the narrow space, nodding and frowning and studying the last sketch made by Harold Spatz.

"That's right," said Mrs. Cobham. "Maybe that's just what happened."

Weiss glanced over at her, read her eyes.

Nah, he thought. She didn't believe it either.

FORTY-FOUR

Bishop, now, was on the bed, watching Honey. And it was strange, he thought. He still wanted her. Even after he'd had her, he wanted her still. It was not the usual way with him. With most women, when he was done he was done. But he lay on the bed and watched her and he was ready to begin with her again.

She had pulled on a T-shirt of his. It billowed around her. It ended just at the top of her thighs. She was at the door.

"You want coffee?" she said.

"Yeah," he said. "That would be good."

She went into the living room, then into the kitchenette. She moved back and forth, coming in and out of sight in the bedroom doorway. Bishop lay on his side, on one arm, and watched.

He had had her quickly, ferociously, just as they came in. Then, right away, he had had her again. When the second time ended, he felt that there was nothing left of him. But as it turned out, there was. As it turned out, there was this desire, this low fury of desire, which the sex did nothing for. He wanted to take her and take her in every way he could think of, but he knew if he did, he still wouldn't have what he wanted.

She came back to the doorway, leaned in the doorway, his box of cigarettes in her hands. He could hear the coffeemaker working behind her, a guttural whisper.

She lit a cigarette, waved out the match. Her eyes went over Bishop's body, bare to the sheet at his waist.

"Man," she said. "You are hot, Cowboy." She gestured with the cigarette box. "Want one?"

Bishop rolled onto his back, put up his hands. She tossed the box. He caught it.

She put one arm around her middle. She propped her cigarette arm up on it. Her eyes moved over him as he lit a cigarette of his own.

"I was away from you too long," she said.

"It was only a few days," he said around the reed.

"Yeah, well, that was too long."

"I heard your father had you under guard or something."

"Just about. Daddy thinks Cobra's coming to get me. He says, as far as he's concerned, till they find Cobra's body, Cobra is definitely still alive."

"He's not," said Bishop. "I shot him in the face."

She shrugged. "I'm just telling you what Daddy says, that's all. Maybe he just wanted an excuse to surround me with all his goons, keep me safe at home."

Bishop let smoke fill his mouth, curled his tongue around it. He looked her over, toying with the cigarette box in his hands. In the other room, the coffeemaker beeped. It was done.

"So how come he let you out?" he asked her.

"Who—Daddy? Are you kidding me? He didn't. I escaped."

Bishop laughed. Looked her over. His urge to have her flared like flame.

"I did!" she said. "I asked one of the guards to get me a glass of milk? Then I stole my sister's bike and rode it down the hill. A girlfriend picked me up and drove me into the city. It's true! What's so funny?"

"I was just wondering if your father would hire me to find you again."

She whiffled at him over her shoulder as she went to pour the coffee.

Bishop drank his mug of coffee sitting up in bed with pillows behind him. Honey sat in a wooden chair, the only bedroom chair, by the window. Outside, behind her, there was half a billboard and a rooftop and the gray sky. Workmen had come that morning in the early hours and changed the picture on the billboard. They changed it every month. The smiling bank lady was gone. In her place was a sports car and the words EXPERIENCE FREEDOM.

Honey sat in the chair with her back very straight and her legs crossed at the knee. It was a prim, ladylike posture, except for the fact that Bishop's T-shirt rode up above her waist and exposed her. Sipping her coffee, she saw Bishop quietly considering her nakedness. She watched him over the rim of her mug. Then she lowered the mug slowly. She tugged the T-shirt down to cover herself.

He smiled at her expression. "What?" he said.

"Nothing." She lit a fresh Marlboro.

"No, c'mon."

"Forget it."

"No, go ahead."

She puffed her cigarette at the very corner of her mouth. She shrugged. "You're funny, that's all."

"I am, it's true. That's me all over."

"Not, like, a laugh riot. You know what I mean."

"Okay," said Bishop. "Like how?"

"Well . . . I mean, you look at me like that . . . I can tell you want me . . ."

"Shit, I give that away, do I?"

"Yeah, you've made that abundantly clear, thanks. But you never say . . ."

"What?"

"Anything."

"Like . . ."

"Li-ike . . . 'Oh, Honey, you're so bee-yootiful!' " She imitated rapture with a roll of her eyes. " 'Oh, Honey, I can't get enough of you. Mm, mm, mm, you're my sweetum sugar-pie!' Like that."

Bishop stopped smiling. He didn't answer. He knew she was joking, but it was as if she'd seen too much of him somehow. Because he'd just been thinking about that, about how he couldn't get enough of her. How he could never get enough of her to get what it was he wanted. And what the hell was that anyway? What did she have that some other piece wouldn't?

"Oh, good answer, Cowboy," she said when he'd been silent for a while.

"Is that what Cobra used to say?" Bishop asked her. It came out hard. " 'Oh, Honey, you're so beautiful?' "

"No-o. Cobra used to say—" She did a good impression of the outlaw's grinning, insinuating tone. "He used to say, 'That is pure, one hundred percent pussy you got on there, Honey girl!' "

Bishop nodded slowly. "He had a certain sophisticated charm, all right."

"Oh, now you're all pissed off, I can tell." She smiled, a surprisingly sweet smile, trying to cajole him back.

Bishop shrugged as if he didn't care.

"Stop," she said. "You don't have to be jealous of Cobra."

"I guess not," said Bishop. "Seeing he's dead and all."

"That's right. You shot him in the face, didn't you? You bad thing." Their eyes met. She was still smiling that sweet smile. "You shot him." She set her coffee mug on the windowsill as she said it this time. She took a last long drag off her Marlboro. "Right. In. The face." She dropped the butt in the mug. Bishop heard it sizzle. He saw a wisp of smoke drift up over the mug's rim.

She got up out of the chair. She came toward him. "You bad thing."

Bishop wanted her helplessly. There was no way to hide it—he was already hard under the covers. He wanted her, and he wanted to hurt her for making him helpless like that.

But he looked at her face, and what the hell. He wanted to fuck her a lot more than he wanted to hurt her.

She stepped to the edge of the bed. "What I've been wondering," she said, "these past few days—"

He looked up at her. He was still holding his coffee mug. He'd forgotten it was in his hand.

"What I've been wondering," Honey said, "is, did you do it for me? When you pulled the trigger—when you shot him in the face—did you do it so we could be together? I'd like that, y'know."

Her eyes were smoky. Bishop looked into the smoke. He swallowed. He managed to shake his head. "He threw down on me," he said hoarsely.

"Oh . . . come on."

"That's the way it was. He had a cop's machine gun. He opened fire. I wouldn't've . . ." He lost track of the rest of the sentence, forgot what he was going to say.

Honey knelt on the bed, crawled over the blankets toward him. "That's not what I think," she told him. "I think you did. Even if he did throw down on you, I think you really did it for me. I think you did it so we could be together. And I think you would've done it anyway, no matter what. So there."

She took the mug out of his hand and he let her. She reached across him to set it on the bedstand. Her face and her hair filled his vision, and he caught that scent again and was helplessly hard. It flashed through his mind that Weiss had told him . . . but he forgot what it was that Weiss had told him. And anyway, to hell with Weiss. Weiss was okay, Weiss was a decent guy and all. But basically, to hell with him.

Honey settled on top of him, gently. Her eyes went wide and her lips formed an O when she felt him under the covers. She laughed and kissed him, very gently. "Now it's just the way I wanted it, Cowboy. It is. He's gone and we'll get his money and we'll go somewhere. It's so, so perfect. Come on. It is. It's okay. Not everyone's supposed to be like everyone else. You did it and we'll get his money and we'll go somewhere and just be us. Oh, Jesus, Jesus!"

Bishop wrapped his arms around her, rolled her over onto her back. Blind and furious to have the thing in her that was her and only her and that he could never have, he went into her hard, as hard as he could.

That was the way she liked it.

FORTY-FIVE

Weiss was driving north out of the city. Passing the Sausalito bluffs just then. Watching the lowering sky, catching glimpses of the water.

It was late afternoon. The clouds were gathering dark and burly on the tops of the headlands. The bay was choppy with whitecapped waves, and its depths looked thick as blood.

Weiss followed the curl of the highway west toward the edge of the open ocean. He knew what he was looking for now. He also knew that he would probably never find it. But what else could he do? He had nothing else—nothing but a feeling, his instinctive sense of other people's lives. That wasn't enough for him; he didn't trust it. Down-to-earth cop type that he was, he wanted more logic, more proof. Whatever there was to see, he wanted to see it for himself.

It's not just what one person's making up in his head, after all. It's what the other person's making up, too. It's what that makes up when you put the two things together.

Those were the words that had brought him here in the first place: the words of wisdom I'd delivered in my conversation with him the night before. They had started him thinking. Thinking about Brinks and Arnold Freyberg and how they'd imagined each other. Thinking about himself and how he'd imagined Julie Wyant and the whores he hired to act his imagination out. And thinking about Bishop—mostly he started thinking about Bishop. Because it was then he finally saw what was bothering him, worrying him, nagging him with so much urgency.

Bishop had fallen for Honey Graham—and no one knew what it was that she imagined. No one knew what she dreamed or what she wanted. No one, when you came right down to it, knew who she was at all. Her father had spent his money to find her. Weiss had turned a blind eye to keep Bishop on her trail. And Bishop—Weiss could see how he wanted her, how she'd reached him. But who was she? How did she really feel about him? What was she after? No one had even bothered to ask.

Weiss knew her history. He had Bishop's report. He'd heard how the rich girl had crawled naked through mud to collect a drug dealer's hundred-dollar bills. Then she'd ridden backseat to a killer—and then she'd switched to Bishop when the law closed in. There was a logic to it, Weiss could feel that, but he couldn't quite put it together. He couldn't quite figure her out.

And then he could.

Or he thought he could. He thought maybe he was beginning to get a sense of the pattern of her actions. But it was just another of his inspirations. He couldn't be sure of it. So here he was, driving off the highway now, headed up a rising road, stopping at a rustic pinewood toll booth.

There was a ranger in the booth, a short, big-breasted young lady with a homely face as round as a pie plate. Weiss reached out his car window to show her his photographs.

"You seen either of these two?" he asked.

The ranger studied them, first the newspaper photo of Beverly Graham, then Mrs. Cobham's snapshot of Harold Spatz. She shook her head, handed them back. It was what Weiss expected. If they'd been here, it would've been more than a month ago now.

He waved in thanks. Drove on.

He chugged up the side of the mountain. The big trees closed over him. The big clouds tumbled low. He parked near the gift shop and visitor's center, a slanting rhombus of pine and glass. There was another ranger there, inside—a strapping man. And there was an older woman with frosted hair working the cash register. Weiss showed them the pictures, too. They shook their heads, too, just like the ranger in the toll booth. Then he showed them a page of Harold Spatz's sketchbook. "The Beach from Lost Trail." The ranger pointed to the spot on a big green map taped to the wall.

"You might want to be careful going up there now," he said. "Weather looks like it's deteriorating pretty fast."

Weiss returned to his Taurus. Drove on.

He maneuvered as close to the peak as he could, but the paved roads only reached so far. In the end, he found himself trudging up the mountain on foot. Under redwoods that skyrocketed to the very belly of the gathering storm.

It was hard climbing. The ground was spongy and damp. The ascent was steady, sometimes steep. Weiss's wind was good and his legs were strong from walking the hills of San Francisco, but he was way out of his element here. He followed the trail, head down, breath heavy. It was a big chore for him. A big, probably useless chore.

But he couldn't help it. He had to keep going. He had to see whatever there was to see.

After a while, he lifted his eyes to gauge the distance left. And even he—days later, in his office, in his chair, with his feet up—had to admit the sight was magnificent. The rough-jacketed trees rose up so straight and swiftly into heaven they were like so many prayers, so many prayers solidified into spires, spires that broke startling out of the mossy tangle of branches in the underbrush as if they were the remnants of a lost city, a lost city of the spirit and its prayers. And the clouds above them. The black, black clouds. Churning and muttering at the tower tops. They were so low it seemed he might walk right into them. It seemed he might discover giant gears in there, and pulleys and presses, and sweat-streaked musclemen in their midst: a whole great skyborne factory of making and destruction—

"Uy," Weiss muttered. Well, he was no outdoorsman. And he still had a ways to go.

He toiled on. He met no one going up or coming down. Not in this weather. Even the birds had stopped singing. Even the insects made no sound. The air itself had grown weirdly silent, weirdly green. A faint irritation of electricity was everywhere.

Finally he saw it. A break in the tree line ahead and above. An opening vista of dark sky. The top board of a railing visible. And a descending side trail off to the right that the ranger had told him about.

He followed that smaller path. It corkscrewed down steeply. For a moment, the forest grew clammy and shadowy and close. And still, unnervingly silent.

Then, very suddenly, the land ended. One more step and he was on a promontory of earth and stone. It jutted out, dizzying, into the wind over the Pacific.

Below, far below, there were rocks rising out of the water. One enormous formation, cleft in two jagged halves, seemed to reach up nearly to his shoe soles. Others had lower peaks and looked like distant mountains. Some just barely showed their domes above the whitecaps. The waves smacked against them all, hurling spray, then retrieving the falling mist as they snaked back foaming through the crevices and sank again into the body of the sea.

Weiss fought off vertigo. He felt as if he were standing on the farthest effort of the continent. With his feet planted wide and his arms lifted slightly from his thighs for balance, with his tie and jacket whipping and fluttering in the strong air, he had to force himself to look down.

He did look down. He saw the living image of Harold Spatz's sketches. He recognized the curl of the cliffs around him, the reach of branches into his eyeshot, the rocks—more than anything, the shape of the rocks below. They were all in the pictures.

He stood there a long time. A long time, in spite of the first rumble of thunder. After coming all this way, he didn't even turn to search the surrounding ground. What was he going to find there? A pair of moss-covered tickets to Reno? A cheap engagement ring discarded in the dirt? An uncorked bottle of sparkling wine?

All right, he'd look—eventually. Before he left, he'd take a good long look around. He had to do that, too. But right now, just standing there, just squinting through the wind, he thought he saw enough. He thought he saw everything.

He saw Harold Spatz. He pictured the pimply-faced boy as he'd barely dared to sketch himself, walking in his special place with the special woman who had unaccountably come into his life. Standing with her out here at the edge of everything. And she coming toward him, her face uplifted to his, her hands pressing lightly against his chest.

The whole scene was clear in Weiss's imagination. The girl with her fingers on the boy's shirtfront, the boy working up the courage to propose. He saw the swift and unexpected motion of her slender arms. He saw Spatz stumbling backward. Poor, spotty Harold Spatz, with the taste of the best kiss he'd ever had still on his mouth—hardly able to relinquish his hopes so he could understand that he was falling—hardly willing to reshape his lips so he could scream before he hit the rocks and died.

PART FIVE The Cobra's Treasure

FORTY-SIX

The storm followed Weiss down the mountain. He heard it growling at his back. He looked over his shoulder to see it whipping the high treetops. He heard the first gouts of rain hit the trail like footsteps behind him. He went down quickly, bracing against the slope.

He was breathless by the time he reached his Taurus. He yanked the door open. Slid behind the wheel as fast as he could squeeze his big body in. Just as he shut the door, the downpour came. The rain spattered against his windshield on great, heaving gusts. Then, the first outbreak over, it hammered down steadily.

"Woof," Weiss said.

He switched on the ignition, switched on the heat. But he left the wipers off and for a while he just sat there. He watched the patterns the water made running over the glass. He watched the storm behind the patterns, driven by the driven wind.

She was like that, he thought. Honey Graham. The patterns, the storm . . . He couldn't have put her into words exactly, but he felt he knew her now.

She probably hadn't planned her long-term progress, not at first. The pattern had simply emerged as she was driven forward by the laws of her character, the laws of her desires. She had two desires: tough guys and money. She learned to use one to get to the other.

She craved her ice-hearted, ice-eyed men. Santé, Cobra—Bishop, too. She got her thrills from their offhanded domination of her. But she also saw how her submission ensnared them. And she saw how that could be useful to her.

It was strange stuff. They treated her rough and she manipulated them and it was all somehow of a piece, all one interaction. With Santé, she crawled naked in the mud—and, at the same time, she teased the location of the dropoff locker out of him, the place where millions in cash were waiting to be picked up. Maybe he'd dumped her like her father said. But Weiss suspected she'd walked away on her own. To go home for a while. Home where it was safe, where she could think, where she could plan her next step.

She needed to get the warehouse alarm codes first. She found an easy stooge in Harold Spatz. She coaxed the codes out of poor Harold, but she had no use for him aside from that. He wasn't cruel or daring enough for her. So she shoved him off his special cliff into that ocean view he loved—it was the only way to make sure he'd keep his mouth shut after he found out he'd been used. Then she was ready to move on.

Weiss didn't know how she'd found Cobra, but it probably wasn't all that hard. She must've hung out around the bars and the bikers and the thugs until she settled on her perfect thief. Weiss could imagine how she'd climbed, adoring and obedient, onto the back of the outlaw's bike, how she'd sat nodding at his feet while he spewed out his dipstick philosophy, how she'd fawned over him in front of his gang—and how she drew him into a raid on the warehouse.

It almost worked. He almost brought home Santé's millions to her. Weiss wondered if Cobra would've survived long after that or if he would've gone to bed with Honey one night and woken up the next morning dead. He'd never know. Before the outlaw could pull off the job, his time ran out. Bishop showed up. He had tracked her down and was sure to bring the police in his wake—and if he didn't, the next detective would. She could see that Cobra was finished, and she had to improvise. As much as she must've hated to abandon all that money—the money she didn't have, the money her father refused to give her, the money that meant freedom for her—she knew she needed to get out, to avoid the closing dragnet. So she gave herself to Bishop . . .

Weiss gazed through the rain on the windshield.

She gave herself to Bishop, he thought. He thought: *Why? Why Bishop? Why not just go home to Daddy like she did before? What could Bishop do for her?*

The answer came to him quickly. She needed Bishop to get rid of Cobra—Cobra, who would hunt her down as long as he was alive.

Weiss's hand moved to his stomach. It was turning sour in there. He told himself Bishop could not have planned Cobra's escape from the warehouse raid. He told himself again that Bishop would not have killed Cobra unless Cobra had fired first. Still, he could feel what it was like for Bishop, standing there with the gun, standing there with his rival on his hands and knees in the water . . .

Weiss sighed. What a mess. What a fucked-up case.

He fished his cell phone out of his pocket. Held down the number two. He heard the machine-gun rapid tones of the speed dialer. Then he heard a nasty, rasping, angry growl.

"This is Ketchum."

"It's Weiss."

The cop snorted. "Shit, I was just gonna call you." This happened to them a lot.

"Anyone found any bodies at Stinson Beach lately?"

"Not that I know of. Why? You boys drop another corpse in the ocean? Damn it, this has gone beyond homicide now, this is illegal dumping. Who was it this time?"

"Guy named Harold Spatz."

"Uh huh. Pimply boy from the warehouse, right? Lemme guess. He was in a sausage-and-doughnut situation with a girl named Beverly Graham."

Weiss closed his eyes, drew his breath in, held it. Ketchum was not supposed to know about the Graham girl. He listened to the wind and rain outside his car for a long second. "So Cobra's boys are talking," he said.

"Oh yeah. Oh yeah. They are chattering like mechanical teeth." Ketchum's angry snarl grew even angrier, snarlier. "And guess what? It seems Miss Graham was the one who brought Cobra the warehouse codes. In fact, it seems she was the getaway driver at the Bayshore Market. And yet, where oh where was she, Weiss, when the raid went down?

I know Bishop didn't help her slip out of the net so he could—oh, I don't know—fuck her. I know he didn't do that, Weiss, because that would be accessory to murder."

Weiss opened his eyes. The rain streamed down the windshield. The treetops bowed and rattled in the swirling air. This conversation was not helping his stomach any. And even worse than his curdling gut was the cold line of premonition beginning to creep its slow, slow way up the back of his neck.

"You have her in custody?" he asked Ketchum.

"Well, you know, that's a funny thing," Ketchum said. "Because that's exactly what I was planning to call you about. Right this minute, I am driving back from Marin County, where I went to pay a call on the little lady. And do you know what I found when I got there? Lo and behold, she seems to've run away."

The walls of the car, the storm on the windshield, seemed to spread away from Weiss on every side—spread away and then suddenly snap back tight around him.

"She's gone?" he said. His voice was distant, hoarse.

"Slipped right out from under her daddy's guards."

"Have you found Cobra? Have you found his body?"

"Cobra? Shit, no. Don't you think I'd've told you if I did? What's he got—"

"She's gone and you haven't found Cobra's body?"

"Yeah. Why?"

Weiss blinked hard. Lifted his eyes to the ceiling. Stared at it, unseeing, clutching the cell phone in his sweaty hand.

"Is there somewhere where Cobra would've hidden, you know, his stash, his money?" he asked softly.

A hesitation on the other end. Then Ketchum said, "Yeah. His boys were just explaining to us about their clubhouse. Pine Lane in Oakland. We're getting a warrant to search it now."

"Shit, shit, shit," said Weiss. "Fuck the warrant. Get a car over there. Tell Oakland to get a car there now."

"What—"

"Do it. I'll meet you. Do it."

Weiss hung up. He switched the wipers on with a quick, hard gesture. He stuck his phone in the car's speaker device. His hands were slick, unsteady. He had to shove the phone into place a couple of times before he got it right. Then he jammed the car into reverse. Backed up, swung around. Put the car in drive and headed down the winding road. Through the slanting rain, under the thunder.

As he went, he held down the number one on his phone and speed-dialed Jim Bishop.

FORTY-SEVEN

Bishop's palmtop rang, but he couldn't hear it over the roar of the Harley. The bike wound over the long road uphill, and its roar engulfed him. His attention was on the twisting pavement. The pavement rose and switchbacked along the edge of the forest canyon. The pine trees screened the dropoff, but glimpses of it flashed out between the trunks and branches. This was the place where Mad Dog had fallen. Bishop roared past it, his eyes on the road.

Heading for Cobra's clubhouse. Heading for Cobra's treasure.

Honey was on the pad behind him. He felt her leaning against his leather though she was light as air. He felt her arms around his waist, her head between his shoulder blades. He liked the feel of her against him and the bike underneath.

His palmtop went on ringing. It was in his jacket, zipped into a side pocket. Bishop didn't hear it at all. After a while, the ringing stopped. The Harley went on, winding up the hill.

The rain hadn't reached the East Bay yet. The clouds were swirling, dark and low. The day was edging toward evening, and as the light died the thunderheads seemed to press down toward the mountain. At the same time, the Harley climbed closer and closer to the churning gray mass. It felt to Bishop as if he were riding right into the thing, as if he were going to punch through the cloud cover and motor through lightning and rain and break out finally above the storm to coast along in the brilliant blue sky. But it never happened. The clouds kept whirlpooling continually closer and closer. The night kept coming on, kept pressing down. The wind grew wet and cold as if they really were nearing the heart of the downpour. But the Harley just went on growling and stuttering as it followed the rising road higher and higher still.

The palmtop began to ring again. The Harley's engine drowned it
out. The palmtop rang and rang and then, again, it stopped.

A little ways on, Bishop felt Honey tap his shoulder. He glanced
down and saw her slender hand extended. He followed the gesture.
There was a small lane to his left, curving away through the trees. He
guided the bike onto it.

They came into an enclave of houses overlooking a cliff. They were
small houses, run-down. They looked as if they'd been planted here
years ago and forgotten, left to decay. Honey tapped him again,
pointed again. He guided the Harley down a dirt drive.

They reached the clubhouse. Bishop hardly remembered the place.
The last time he'd been here he'd been too jazzed from killing Mad
Dog. Then later he was drunk and even later he was hungover. At this
point, the whole experience was foggy to him, like a dream. He could
never have found the place again on his own.

The house was still visible in the last light from the west. It was a
two-story cabin made of raw pine. There was a porch out front with a
rocker and a swing. There was a dusty yard beneath the porch. There
was a dead Chevy in the dusty yard and a junked armchair stacked on
top of an old sofa.

It might've been any weekend cabin on the edge of any hill. But
there was a wood fence out front with razor wire coiled along the top
of it. And there was razor wire on the roof gutter, too. The windows
were black and empty and gave the house a hunkering, aggressive look
somehow. And there was a plaque with a death's head nailed roughly
into the center of the door.

Bishop brought the Harley to a stop. He sat before the front gate, the
bike idling. Honey dismounted, walked to the fence. She had the key.

She swung the gate open and held it for him. Bishop motored past
her to where the driveway ended under an old oak. He killed the engine. Swung his leg over. Walked to her in the rising dust.

She put her hands against his chest, tilted her head up. He held her
shoulders and kissed her. He looked over her to where the lights were
beginning to appear in the city below. The lights twinkled on as the

night grew deeper and then winked out as the storm moved over them. The bay was already completely hidden. The clouds flickered above it, lightning in their bellies.

"Big storm coming, it looks like," Bishop said.

"Let's do this," Honey whispered, pressing her cheek against his chest. "If we're gonna do it, let's do it and go."

He hesitated there another second, his hands on her soft shoulders. It was a pretty crappy thing to do, he reckoned. Stealing the money, disappearing with the client's daughter. A pretty crappy thing to do to Weiss. Maybe he wouldn't, after all. Maybe he'd just go in with her, help her get the cash and let her go. Or maybe he'd get the cash himself and turn it in to the Agency. Or what the hell? Maybe he'd get the cash and ride Honey down to Mexico and fuck her till Jesus came again. It was hard for him to say exactly what he was planning at the moment. But he figured he was about to find out.

She felt his hesitation. "Do you still want to?" she asked him.

He stood there another second. He stood there, thinking: *What the hell*. He knew he was pussy-blind. Sure he did. But so what? There were worse ways to stumble to perdition.

"Come on," he said.

He followed her to the house.

FORTY-EIGHT

Weiss raced the darkness across the San Rafael Bridge. Pushing the Taurus to seventy-five, sluicing left and right through the gaps in the swift, steady traffic, he broke out of the rain and glimpsed the last light of sunset over the hills ahead. But the clouds came after him, pressed down from above, pressed in on the water at either side of him. The storm was following fast and night was coming.

Weiss drove faster. His thoughts were fragmented, jumbled. Bishop . . . Cobra . . . The girl . . . Ideas flashed into his mind, disjointed. She wouldn't have left the safety of home if she were still afraid of Cobra . . . She wouldn't have left if there were not still money to be had . . . Cobra must've had a stash . . . Cobra . . . He couldn't quite string it all together.

But it didn't matter. He pressed the gas pedal down harder. Rushed into the red taillights crowded ahead of him as the white headlights, glaring in his rearview, crowded behind. Because he felt as if that cold line of premonition on his neck had turned to ice. He felt as if it had seeped into him through his pores and spread in his blood through his whole body. Maybe it was pure intuition—his sense, his feeling for the character of Honey Graham. Or maybe he'd actually reasoned out her motives and just wasn't conscious of it yet. Either way, he knew that if Honey had left home, she would head for the clubhouse, for the money. He knew that she would bring Bishop with her.

And he knew that Bishop was a dead man—that he'd be murdered, as soon as darkness fell.

He sped west, the lightning on his heels. He pressed the speed-dial button on his phone again.

FORTY-NINE

Honey was quick and agile up the porch steps. Bishop watched her. She was slender and shapely in her suede parka and jeans. Her long blonde hair moved with her motion. Bishop felt that motion inside him. It changed the way he breathed.

I'm a fucking idiot, he thought. But he didn't care. *What the hell.*

He let her lead the way to the door.

She had her key in the keyhole when his palmtop rang again. She turned back the bolt and paused, looked over her shoulder at him. Bishop was working the phone from his jacket.

"Come on," she said nervously. "Aren't you coming?" He could see the spark of panic in her eyes.

The phone glowed bright in the thickening dusk. He read the incoming number: Weiss—but he already knew that. There was no one else it could be. The readout said this was the third time he'd called. Must've been during the ride. Must've been urgent. He rarely called at all. For him to call three times like that so close together—

"Cowboy!" Honey whispered. "Come on."

The palmtop rang.

Bishop held it in his hand, looked down at it. Maybe they'd found Cobra's body, he thought. Maybe that's why Weiss was calling. But he knew it wasn't true. The cops had already stopped the search; they wouldn't've started it up again in weather like this.

No. It was Honey. Weiss had heard she was gone. Weiss knew—because Weiss always knew these things—that she would come to him.

The palmtop went on ringing, ringing. He held it in his hand, looked at it. A sense of misgiving tightened his chest, like a screw turning.

And Honey said, "Come on," again quickly.

It annoyed Bishop: Weiss meddling and the phone ringing and

Honey urging him on. He knew what he was doing. He didn't need anyone to tell him.

He slipped the palmtop back into his jacket. "All right," he said.

The palmtop stopped ringing. But the misgiving lingered in Bishop's mind. *To hell with Weiss*, he thought. But still—the misgiving lingered.

Honey pushed the door open. She stepped across the threshold. He went after her, into the house, into the living room. Honey shut the door.

It was dark. The air was stale. The smell of the stale air brought the place alive in Bishop's memory. He remembered the night the gang had come here after he'd killed Mad Dog and how everyone was howling and celebrating and how they drank beer and tequila and he woke up with the coarse-featured part-Mexican girl. Somehow even the smell of the girl came back to him in the smell of the room. He smiled a little to himself.

A line of light cut through the shadows. Honey had a flash—one of those keychain Maglites. That stirred something else in Bishop's memory but only for a moment and he couldn't place it. He watched as the strong, narrow beam picked out portions of the room. The leather recliner, the TV. Empty tequila bottles, empty bottles of beer. He remembered seeing Shorty sprawled in the chair, asleep, clutching his Xbox controller on the morning after the party. He remembered how Shorty's head exploded into a fine spray of blood when the police sniper took him out in the warehouse.

He felt Honey's hand slip into his. A small, cool hand. His own hand closed around it. She began to shuffle forward carefully, panning the light back and forth in front of her. Bishop felt the gentle squeeze of her hand as he moved along beside her.

They followed the beam of light down a hall. A long, low growl came at them from somewhere. Honey pulled up short at the sound. She swung the flashlight nervously this way and that. Bishop saw her eyes gleam as she looked at him. He heard her give a little laugh, starting to breathe again.

"Thunder," she said softly. "Like a fucking horror movie."

She went on again, her hand in his.

They came to a doorway, a room. Honey stood on the threshold a moment. She let the flashlight explore the space wall to wall. Bishop remembered this, too. The stacked boxes. TVs, computers, stereos. All the electronic stuff the gang had hijacked. It was all still here.

"Good," she said softly. "The cops haven't found this place yet."

"They will," said Bishop.

"I guess. I don't know. There's a gang code. You're not supposed to tell about the clubhouse no matter what."

Bishop snorted. She glanced at him. He shrugged. "They'll tell. The cops'll offer to take fifteen minutes off their sentences, they'll tell everything. I'm surprised it took them this long."

"Right," she said. "Right." He made out her smile in the light of the beam. "Everybody's so full of shit, I swear."

"Yes, they are," said Bishop.

She tilted her head. "C'mon, help me move some of these."

They went into the room. She set the flashlight on the floor. They worked in the dim outglow, carrying boxes from one corner to the opposite wall. There was only darkness at the windows now. Their big panes rattled with the rising wind. Night had fallen, and the storm was blowing in fast. Another grumble of thunder sounded, then the first washing patter of rain on the leaves and grass.

"Now what?" said Bishop.

They had cleared a place in the corner. Honey took the Maglite again and knelt down.

"There's supposed to be a place . . ." she murmured. She ran her fingers over the rough floorboards. "Here," she said.

Bishop stood over her, watching.

"Hold the light for me," she whispered.

She handed the flash up to him. He trained it on her hands. He watched as her fingers sought out a space between the boards. They found it, half a knothole. She reached into the opening.

"You need me to lift it up?" he asked her.

"No, it's just—there's a lock . . . There," she whispered.

Bishop heard the mechanism shift. He trained the light on her while she pulled the floorboard away easily. She pulled away another. The wind rose, and the window rattled again. Bishop glanced up, glanced out at the darkness. His own reflection looked back at him from the window. His image was faint, stained with the night, half his face obliterated by the stains of night. A gout of rain pasted itself against the glass and erased the image completely.

"Okay," Honey said.

Bishop leaned forward, looked down again. She'd lifted two more boards out. There was a space underneath. He shone the flash into it, but all he could make out were some rotting joists and some more old boards.

Crouching now, Honey shifted. She worked knowingly. One of the joists separated and twisted around in her hand. It was another secret lock.

"That's it," she said.

Bishop's heart beat faster. He fidgeted with the Maglite, rolling its grainy grip in his fingers. His mind raced, and for a moment the memory about the light came back to him. Cobra had had a Maglite just like this one when they had raised the warehouse at China Basin.

And he thought: Weiss was calling because he knew Honey had run away. He was calling because he knew Honey would come to him. He was calling because—

But now Honey pulled up on one of the joists. A long section of the underfloor lifted up on a hidden hinge. It was a trapdoor. There was a hole underneath it, a deep hole at least four feet across with maybe more of it hidden under the boards.

There was a suitcase in there, at the bottom, a small, black overnight bag.

"There it is," said Honey breathlessly. Her face turned up to him, white as white in the light. "I can't reach. Can you get it, Cowboy?"

Bishop nodded—but for a second, he didn't move. There was that tight sense of misgiving in his chest and he just stood there, looking down at the bag, looking down into the hole and thinking how deep it was, deep as a grave.

"C'mon," said Honey. "Just reach down there, would you? Come on. Reach down and get it."

Bishop began to lower himself—and then the palmtop in his pocket started ringing again.

He heard the sound. It caught him, froze him. Thoughts crashed in on him all together. *Weiss . . . Urgent . . . Honey . . .*

He straightened quickly, tightened, every muscle suddenly ready.

In the same instant, a clap of thunder shook the place. Lightning exploded blindingly white at the window. Bishop's eyes went to it. Blackness followed fast, and for an instant he saw the reflection in the glass again, the face half stained with night.

Only it wasn't his reflection this time.

It was Cobra's. It was Cobra, standing right in back of him, his face half blown away.

With the other half, he was grinning like a madman.

FIFTY

Bishop turned and Cobra struck.

The outlaw had the bayonet in his hand. He brought it up from down low to drive it into Bishop's guts. Bishop, still coming around to face the killer, pulled his belly out of the way. The blade slashed past him, just past him, catching a hunk of his jacket, carving a deep gash in the leather.

Bishop was nearly on tiptoe, off balance. Still, he managed to drive his elbow into Cobra's mutilated cheek. The blow didn't have much force behind it, but the outlaw's wounds were still raw. Cobra let out a quick shriek. He staggered back, clutching the place where his left eye had been.

But Bishop lost his footing. He stumbled. His legs tangled over one of the boxes on the floor. He fell, crashing down on top of the box, rolling off it, smacking shoulder first into the wooden boards.

A manic rattle of thunder wiped away every other sound. Bishop—his movements hemmed in by the stacks of boxes, his heart all fear and rage, all panic and a vicious fury—twisted onto his back as fast as he could, trying desperately to see the next attack.

He saw—he got one good look.

He saw Honey. She was pressed against the wall. She had one hand up as if for protection. The other was still holding the flashlight, letting it droop, forgotten, in her fingers. Bishop could see her elegant, chiseled, ivory features shiny with sweat. Her lips were parted, her breath came quick, her eyes were blurry with excitement. All her attention was inward, alert to her own sensations, the thrill of it all.

Cobra was in front of her. He had just recovered from the blow to his face, was just steadying himself to locate Bishop on the floor. The light from the flash came up from under him and cast him in a weird play of clarity and shadow. For that one moment, in that dancing glare,

Bishop saw his face, what was left of his face. The right side was as it had been, all intact. The remains of his thin lips were twisted upward there, and the angular crags rose from the sharp point of his smile to the sharp point of his widow's peak. His hair was in disarray and spilled down over his brow, and through it stared one piercing emerald eye.

The other side of his face was raw flesh, ripped asunder, gouged out and only half-repaired by whatever renegade sawbones had kept him alive. Black stitches wove through the red underskin, and something that had once been his other eye was now a red-black hole. His grin, his whole expression, his outward self, appeared to fade here into gory nothingness—and yet even that nothingness crawled with living hatred as he brought the bayonet to bear.

The rattling thunder rose and crashed. Cobra rushed at the fallen Bishop. Honey let out a sweet, sharp cry. The Maglite slipped from her fingers, hit the floor, went out. For a single instant, Bishop saw Cobra driving the bayonet down toward him. Then nothing, there was nothing, no light at all, pitch darkness.

Blind, frantic, Bishop scuttled back wildly. His head struck the wall behind him. His hand went out and found a stack of boxes. With a fierce heave, he toppled the stack over, sent the boxes flying in the direction he'd seen Cobra last. He heard them hit the oncoming body. He heard Cobra grunt. By then he was already twisting his body away, pulling his legs up, fighting to get his knees under him, pushing off the floor with his hands to get to his feet.

He staggered upright. Cobra grabbed him. The outlaw's groping hand found his shoulder and clutched leather. Bishop knew the blade was coming at him but he couldn't see it, couldn't see anything. He spun in the outlaw's grasp and drove his shoulder into black space. He felt himself connect with Cobra, hard. He felt Cobra go down and he went down with him, grappling with the invisible adversary, waiting for the driving point of the bayonet to come for him out of the black nowhere.

Cobra and Bishop crashed into the boxes, then crashed to the floor.

Cobra was still clutching Bishop's jacket. Bishop pulled away with all his might, desperate to get clear. He rolled free. He jumped up. But Cobra was up, too.

The outlaw must've slashed out blind. This time, he managed to bring the blade slicing across Bishop's front, so close that Bishop felt the whisper of it on his naked throat. Then the edge of the thing sliced through his right shoulder and the coal-blackness went blood-red with pain.

Bishop let out a growling scream. His rage flared and his panic flared and he wanted to bust up everything. He felt the point of the bayonet snagged in his jacket. He found Cobra's wrist with his left hand, clamped it fast. The pressure dug the bayonet edge back into Bishop's gashed shoulder, and the detective screamed again as his whole body became one shattered nerve.

Then, with the force of his agony and anger, he pistoned his stiffened hand into the darkness, knowing where Cobra's face should be. The blow struck home. He felt a ferocity just like joy as his fingertips buried themselves in the mutilated flesh.

Cobra let out a wild, high howl. His body twisted violently. At the same time, the pain became too much for Bishop and he lost his grip. Cobra spun away from him and vanished again in the pitch-black.

Bishop crouched low, peered hard into blind space. His shoulder throbbed and burned and he could feel the blood coursing out of it. He tried to keep from sobbing with the searing pain, tried to keep his breath as quiet as he could so Cobra wouldn't hear him. And he listened, listened with his whole furious self, trying to place Cobra by the sound of his ragged, agonized panting.

But he was lost now, disoriented. He had no idea where he was standing in the room. A swirling vertigo was making a slow whirlpool in his head. He wavered where he stood. He knew if he could just stay alive another second, maybe two, his eyes would adjust. He'd see the window, the door, maybe even make out the shadowy shape of his adversary.

But Cobra also crouched in the dark, clutching the bayonet, waiting for the same moment. And as Bishop scanned the nothingness, searching for him, he realized it was Cobra who had the upper hand.

Bishop was crouching there, listening, peering. He heard Cobra breathing, moving. He heard his own heart pound. He heard the rain lashing at the window. He heard the wind lashing at the rain. By those sounds, bit by bit, he became aware that the window was just behind him, just off his left shoulder. He realized that if Cobra got into the right position, he—Bishop—would be visible: a silhouette against the window, against the slightly lighter dark of the night outside.

At the same instant the thought occurred to him, he knew it had happened: Cobra had found him. He heard the outlaw's breath catch on a grunt of effort. He heard the scrape of Cobra's boots as he rushed forward. For one terrible instant, he knew Cobra was charging at him, invisible, hurtling out of the blackness, impossible to see.

Then lighting struck again. The room flickered with a long, stark silver flash. In the momentary strobic glare, Bishop saw the monstrous face, maimed on one side, twisted on the other like the mirror of his own rage and hatred. It went white and black and white and black in the lightning and it was almost on top of him—then it was gone in the darkness.

Cobra roared and drove the bayonet at Bishop's body. Bishop, having seen him, was able to pivot out of the way. He caught hold of the outlaw's neck as he flew past. He hurled him headlong into the window.

The glass exploded into the night as Cobra crashed into it. The furious storm exploded into the room, washing Bishop's face with rain. Bishop, still turning, was alongside the outlaw now, clutching his neck, bracing his forearm against his back. Before Cobra could even start to struggle, Bishop used all his weight to drive him downward.

The outlaw's face smashed full force into the bottom half of the broken window. Over the rising wail of the wind, Bishop heard the thick, wet, unmistakable noise of sharp points driven into flesh.

Cobra never screamed. He just gagged, just thrashed and spasmed under Bishop's weight. Bishop heard the bayonet drop heavily to the floor. Cobra's body twitched and then went still.

The wind blew the rain in. The rain pattered against Bishop's leather, ran down. Bishop let go of Cobra's body. It slid off the windowsill and collapsed at his feet.

Bishop stood up, breathing hard. That was the end of it.

FIFTY-ONE

Bishop stumbled to the doorway. He clutched his wounded shoulder. He felt the blood running out between his fingers, making them slippery. As he neared the door, he banged his leg on the edge of a box. He grunted with pain. He rested against the wall.

As he leaned there, he saw the light switch. He reached out weakly, flipped it up. He squinted against the sudden brightness. Then he turned to look at the room.

It was pretty much what he expected. Cobra was dead. No question about it this time. He was one hell of a mess.

And as for Honey—what else?—she was gone. She had done Cobra's bidding—she had set him up for the kill. But the second it turned into a fight, an uncertain thing, she was in the wind. She was gone.

With another grunt, Bishop peeled off the wall. He staggered forward again. Out into the hall, then into the living room. Lightning flickered at the big windows here, and he saw the lie of the furniture, the path to the front door. The lightning flickered out with a long, sharp crackle of thunder. But Bishop could still see the room in the glow of the flashing red-and-blue lights outside.

The cops. And Weiss. He knew at once it would be Weiss out there. Magical Weiss, who always somehow figured out what everyone would do. Bishop thought about that, and he thought about what had brought him here. How he was about to steal Cobra's money and run off somewhere with Honey. Weiss had probably figured that out, too. *Well, to hell with Weiss,* he thought. But he felt pretty rotten about it.

He kept shuffling to the door, clutching his wounded arm.

Sure enough, he reached the front door, yanked it open, and there they all were, the whole party, parked in the front yard. Three Oakland PD black-and-whites and that dull-as-shit Taurus Weiss drove. And here came Ketchum, too, just pulling up in his crap Impala. The lights whirling round on the cop-car racks turned the slanting silver rain red, then blue.

Bishop stepped out onto the porch. The sound of the rain grew louder. He heard it hit the grass and the roofs of the cars. Thunder rumbled. It was louder, too, out here.

Bishop let his right arm hang down limp. He clung to the balcony railing with his left hand. The blood was drying now on his palm and fingers, and they felt sticky on the splintery wood.

He made his way slowly to the stairs. Stepping out from under the porch, he felt the rain pelt him. His hair was soaking by the time he came off the last riser. His boots sank half an inch in the puddling mud.

Weiss was standing by his Taurus, massive in his trenchcoat, his hands shoved deep in the pockets, his shoulders hunched. He had a Giants baseball cap on, the brim pulled low over his big, sagging features. From under the brim, he gazed at Bishop with that droopy deadpan look of his. Bishop approached him and met the gaze defiantly. Then after a moment, he couldn't hold it. He looked away.

"Cobra in there?" Weiss asked him. There was nothing in his voice to tell Bishop what he was thinking.

Bishop nodded, staring down about two feet in front of him, staring at where a muddy pool hopped and spat as the rain hit it. "What's left of him," he said.

Weiss answered nothing. He gestured with his head, and a young cop came over to take Bishop by his good arm. The young cop helped Bishop to one of the patrol cars. It was the second cop car to Bishop's right. As they walked past the first cop car, Bishop saw Honey sitting in its backseat.

They'd caught her. Bishop was surprised. He'd figured she'd outsmart everyone, slip away, go home to Daddy. Weiss again. Weiss was too quick for her.

He could tell by the way she was leaning forward that she had her hands cuffed behind her. She strained forward in her seat, pressing her face to the window, peering out at him. Their eyes met through the slanting rain that was silver and red and blue.

Honey shrugged. Bishop shrugged. What the hell.

The young cop led Bishop away and helped him into the car.

EPILOGUE

It was a bad day, the start of September. Everyone in the Agency walked on eggshells, wore long faces, traded glances, rolled their eyes. Every time the phone rang at the front desk, voices fell silent in corridors and alcoves. Every time the door opened, anyone nearby faltered in his tracks.

Weiss had come in early, rumbled down the hall like some great brooding beast. Shut himself into his office, and stayed there, quiet as a stone. No one went near him for a long time. Everyone who passed looked at his door as if he might come raging out of it, or as if he could be seen through it mulling his troubles, fist to chin.

We imagined Bishop was the worst of it for him. The personal betrayal and so on. Jaffe & Jaffe, the lawyers upstairs, were telling anyone who'd listen that Bishop had done nothing wrong. That he hadn't known about Honey's involvement in the market killings. That he was just trying to do his job. He had gone to the clubhouse to recover the money for the police, they said, unaware that Cobra, patched up and morphined and powered by an almost supernatural thirst for revenge, was lying in wait for him.

The arguments had kept Bishop out of jail so far, had even kept any criminal charges at bay. But prosecutors in three counties were making ugly noises—murder, accessory to murder, conspiracy to commit burglary, grand theft, the works. And Ketchum was raging—raging—swearing in that guttural rasp of his that he would take Bishop down, so help him, that he would save Weiss from whatever mental defect it was that had caused him to hitch his wagon to such a psychopathic star.

As for Weiss, no one was sure what he believed or how he felt about it. But we all knew that Bishop was his personal reclamation project, his prodigal, proxy son. He was so sharp about these things that he must have at least suspected that the man had simply gone after the money for himself—gone after the money and the girl, and Weiss and his Agency be damned. So there was that on his mind, in his heart.

Then there was Beverly Graham—Honey. Behind bars in San Mateo, charged with murder, conspiracy to commit murder, felony murder, accessory to murder, and a whole bunch of other things, most of which ended in "murder." Her father's lawyers were laboring feverishly to get her sprung, but they were a hardworking crew and still found time to harrass the Agency with all sorts of threats and accusations. Apparently Philip Graham was not too happy about the fact that Weiss had set the police on the trail of his runaway baby. Plus his political career was over before it started, and that seemed to make him irritable, too. He was not, in short, the satisfied customer Weiss had been hoping for. Instead of the Agency thriving on his future business and the business of his wealthy friends, it had become a question of whether Weiss Investigations would survive his furious campaign to destroy it.

So it was a bad day.

Sometime around eleven, I finished sorting the mail and made my deliveries office to office. I left Weiss for last, but there was no way to avoid him forever. I knocked at his door meekly. Heard him grumble something. Opened the door a crack and peeked through.

He was in his chair, the phone to his ear. He was listening with sorrowful eyes. He gestured at me brusquely. I went in.

As I dropped the mail off on his desk, I caught a glimpse of a yellow legal pad on his blotter. One corner of the pad's top page was covered with doodles. At the center of the doodles there was one word: *Paradise.* That was the name of the town that Julie Wyant's phone call had come from. The last place he knew she'd been.

I turned to go—and as I did, I saw her image. It was that video he had of her—that ten-second loop—it was playing on his computer screen, over and over. I caught a sidelong glimpse of that angelic face of hers, that red-gold hair, that otherworldly expression as if she were beckoning you out of reality into a dream. Then I put my head down and hurried out.

———

A few moments after I left, Weiss set the phone down. He turned off the video of Julie Wyant. He sighed. It was Professor M. R. Brinks who had just called him. She had asked if she could hire him to do one more service for her. He'd agreed.

So, after lunch, he drove his Taurus out across the Bay Bridge again. It was a fine, bright afternoon, crisp and clear. The professor was waiting for him in front of her stucco cottage. She was standing very straight at the end of the flagstone path. Holding a little purse down in front of her, a small, ladylike purse, not her usual briefcase monstrosity. Other than that, she was in one of those mannish getups she favored. Another angular jacket, tweed this time, and jet-black slacks with dagger-sharp creases.

But as she slid into the front seat next to Weiss, the detective caught the scent of perfume on her. She'd never worn that before, not so he'd noticed, anyway.

Brinks smiled at him briefly, thinly, then quickly looked away, then just as quickly bowed her head so that her black hair fell forward, screening her reddening cheeks.

Weiss faced the windshield, made himself busy maneuvering the car from the curb into the street.

As they drove along, she stared out the window. "I feel like an idiot asking you to do this," she said bitterly.

Weiss made a noise, a little puff of air. "Nah. Forget it."

"I just somehow can't bring myself to go alone," she said. "And there's no one else who knows. It's nice of you to come out on such short notice."

"Forget it. I'm telling you: It's no problem."

"You're—" She seemed about to say more, but must've decided against it. They drove the rest of the way in silence.

The hospital wasn't far, a gleaming box of white stone and shining glass near the border of Oakland. Weiss tried to take Brinks's arm as they walked together across the parking lot. She stiffened, so he let her go, lumbered along beside her instead, his hands in his pants pockets. Dwarfed by his giant frame, she clopped over the asphalt in her thick heels, staring forward, clutching her purse in front of her like a squirrel with a nut. Her narrow, attractive features were set fast, lined. She looked nervous. She looked grim.

They found Arnold Freyberg alone in a room on the third floor. By now, he had shriveled nearly away. He was lying very still in bed, breathing on his own, but breathing hard. The sagging flesh seemed to have melted off him, and only a patina of translucent skin was left to cover his skeletal frame. His hands were lifted up to his chest as if to clutch the edge of his bedsheet, but the strength to clutch the sheet was gone; the hands lay limp. The eyes alone still lived—they were staring, motionless, but the fear in them made them live.

Weiss walked M. R. Brinks to the door. She signaled him with a touch of his elbow and he stayed there in the hall, on the threshold. She went into the room alone.

Weiss watched her move to Freyberg's bed. There was a plastic chair nearby. She pulled it up to the bedside and sat down. She sat primly, her back straight, her knees clamped together, her purse held upright on her thighs. Her lips pressed to a thin line as she gazed down at the fading figure where he lay fighting for breath.

I will remake you into your body, he had written to her, Weiss remembered. *Lips and nipples and clefts. You will have no hopes, no anxieties. No thoughts, no philosophy. Only flesh, only sensation.*

"Arnold," she said. Her voice was steady. "Arnold, it's me, I'm here."

Freyberg's big eyes blinked in slow motion. Painfully, he drew in a rattling gasp. "Marianne?" he whispered.

He couldn't turn to look at her, but with a tremulous effort he lifted his hand.

Professor Brinks swallowed hard. Carefully she set her purse down on the floor by her chair. Then she took Freyberg's hand in both her own. She brought it to her lips. She bowed her head over it. She closed her eyes.

Weiss turned from the door and walked away.

He drove back alone. Down University Avenue, toward the bridge.

Nearing the water, he stopped at a red light. He sat waiting there, thinking nothing, tapping his finger on the steering wheel. He gazed absently through the windshield. There was the sign for Interstate 80 just ahead.

The freeway ran in two directions, west over the bridge, back into the city, and up toward Richmond and San Rafael, where it met the 101 heading north. It was the 101 that went eventually to the town called Paradise.

Weiss gazed at the sign. Once again, he felt that chill of premonition on the back of his neck. He thought of the Shadowman, the killer who had sworn he would hunt Julie Wyant forever. His eyes went nervously to the rearview mirror.

He'll be watching you now all the time, every second, she had told him. *If you come to find me, he'll follow you and he'll find me first.*

Weiss looked back at the freeway sign. West across the bridge. East and north to the 101, to Paradise.

The light turned green. Weiss started driving.

ACKNOWLEDGMENTS My deep thanks to Oakland Police Sergeant Fred Mestas, motorcycle maven Larry Mousouris, newswoman *extraordinaire* Sherry Hu, Private Detective Lynn McLaren, Santa Barbara Senior Deputy District Attorney Ron Zonen, computer expert Chris Soriano, and my excellent assistants Wendy Miller and Sarah Pariso.

My further and likewise deep thanks to my agent, Robert Gottlieb at Trident Media; Tom Doherty and Robert Gleason at Forge; West Coast agents Chris Donnelly and Brian Lipson at Endeavor; publicist Kim Dower of Kim-From-LA; and my beloved wife, Ellen.